Praise for *"In Plain Sight"*

"In Plain Sight" weaves a believable high-tech thriller from a remarkable combination of up-to-the-minute elements: Chinese economic espionage, ISIS global warfare, terrorist recruitment from the Minneapolis Somali community, cyber security and strained relations between, local, federal and military law enforcement.

Greg Gardner's first novel fits sleekly into the niche created by authors like Tom Clancy and Vince Flynn. He has created a main character in Jon Wells who is familiar with both the skyways and underground tunnels of Minneapolis, and the bureaucracy and procedures of cops and federal agents. Gardner uses many recognizable Twin Cities location to bring a gritty sense of reality to his story.

He also taps into his experience as a naval officer and computer expert to explain in elaborate detail how foreign governments and terror organizations can, and do, attack the United States in both brutal and sophisticated ways.

The novel launches Jon Wells as a continuing character for a projected series of novels that will be welcome additions to the techno-thriller genre.

– Rick Shefchik - author of the Sam Skarda thrillers

IN PLAIN SIGHT

A Jon Wells Novel

Greg Gardner

To Hammond Library

Enjoy the read!

Greg Gardner

Copyright

Acknowledgments

This is my first novel. Growing up and into my first several professions, I was always told by the powers that be that I was not a good writer. My personality is such that if you tell me "you can't do that" you know exactly what I'm going to do. It just fuels the fire. So, I guess, thanks to everyone who stoked that fire over the past thirty some years.

I need to thank a group of people that encouraged me, challenged me, and allowed me to finish this book. First, my wife. She let me write, cash in our retirement, and chase this dream. I can't ever say thank you enough. I love you. Second, my parents. They read every version of book and gave me their input, provided heartfelt and honest feedback, and encouraged me. You made me feel like I really could do this. I love you both and thoroughly enjoyed working with you on the book. Third, to my editor, Amber – my sister-in-law. I asked you to not let me look stupid with my grammar skills. To the Western Suburbs Writers Group who made me re-think how I addressed certain issues. I didn't want to make those changes initially, but I must say, the result of those changes is a much better story. My brother created the book cover and always lent his ear to listen to me yap away about the book. My youngest son, Trevor, who read the first 3,000 words I wrote and told me, "Yeah, I'd read more of this." My brother-in-law, John, who made some initial edits and was the first person, not actually related to me, to tell me he liked to story. Also to Katherine, Amber's mother, who gave up vacation hours from her work to give it a final edit. Finally, to all the people who created and nurtured the websites I used to gather information to make things as realistic as I could.

Abbreviations

C-Suite – Executives of the rank CEO, CIO, CFO, COO
DDS – Dynamic Denial of Service
DMM – Digital Multi-meter
EPD – Edina, MN Police Department
DOJ – Department of Justice
FDA – U.S. Food and Drug Administration
FBI – Federal Bureau of Investigation
HR – Human Resources
IDS – Investors Diversified Services, Inc.
ISIS – Islamic States of Iraq and Syria
ISIL – Islamic States of Iraq and Levant
IT – Information Technology
MBA – Masters in Business Administration
MIT –Massachusetts Institute of Technology
MKL-U-MD – a take-off of the word macluumaad which means
        information in Somali.
MnMedDev – Minnesota Medical Devices
MO – Modis Operandi
MPD – Minneapolis, MN Police Department
NCIJTF – National Cyber Investigative Joint Task Force
NFC – Near Field Communication
NGO – Non Government Organization
NSA – National Security Agency
PII – Personally Identifiable Information
PR – Public Relations
QA – Quality Assurance
QC – Quality Control
RAT – Random Access Trojan
RFID -Radio Frequency Identification
SETI – Search for Extra-Terrestrial Intelligence
SLA -Service Level Agreement
SUV – Sport Utility Vehicle
TA – Teacher's Assistant
USB – Universal Serial Bus
VA – Veteran's Administration

Characters

Federal Bureau of Investigation
Jonathan "Jon" Anderson Wells
Richard "Rick" Cunningham
Gloria Ransik (NCIJTF)
Antonio "Tony" Suarez
Dr. Jasmine Gomez (NCIJTF)
Shannyn (NCIJTF)

Minneapolis Police Department
Detective Tyler Bancroft
Sergeant Robert Mitchell
Reginald "Reggie" or "Reg" George Benkins
Roger – in gang unit
Judge Singer

Somalis
Adnan Ali – has several sons and daughters
Abdi Ali – Adnan's son
"The Man" – recruiter for al-Shabaab
Yusef Waberi
Hodon Waberi – married to Yusef
Omar Waberi – Yusef's son
Jamal Kusow

Saudi
Ahmed Al Khadi Nihal

China
Zhang Xe
Chen Li – Zhang Xe's alter ego
Bei "Sam" Liping

Data Center
Dominic "Dom" Seragosa
Donna Seragosa – Dom's wife
Mike Seragosa – Dom's son, entering 10th grade
Laura Seragosa – age 13
Kylie Seragosa – age 11
Abdi Ali – son of Adnan
Amber – software technician
Celeste Van Dorn – VP of Operations
Marty – security guard
Avril – security guard

MnMedDev
Matt Scoggins – VP of QA/QC
Dr. Nancy Pillery – VP of Manufacturing
Dr. Ranju Chatray – Lead Engineer
Allissa – Nancy's administrative assistant

MKL-U-MD
Malick
Fatima

Others
Security guard 1 in skyway
Jasper – security guard 2
Coroner - Dr. Horatio Blevins
Somali Gang – Riverside Thugs
Guled – everyday leader of Riverside Thugs
Frank – homeless veteran in North Loop neighborhood
Alice – coffee shop owner in North Loop neighborhood
Nicole "Nicky" – diabetic
Zander – Nicky's boyfriend
General Carter Jensen – Homeland Security
Andreas Braun – German engineer
Katja Braun – Andreas' wife

Chapter 1

Present Day

Jon bolted up from his sleep. Sweat dripped off his eyebrow. Another bad dream. He reached over to his night stand, pulled out a memorandum book, and opened it to the next blank section. God, it has been over 20 years. Why is this still happening? He never had bad dreams when he was still in the military, only after he got out. The doctors at the VA told him to write it all down. So he wrote.

Mogadishu, Somalia - Fall 1993 during the Somali Civil War

"Hang on tight boys," grunted the Master Sergeant as the MH-60L "Black Hawk" helicopter spun. A rocket-propelled grenade or RPG just hit it. The collision of the warhead at speeds in excess of 250 meters per second at a height of 200 feet damaged the tail rotor. With no remaining ability to counteract the gyroscopic force of the main rotor, the aircraft began its descent at a blistering speed. Smoke spewed from the helicopter as it spun unevenly, seemingly out of control. The pilot and co-pilot, both uninjured in the blast, frantically attempted to slow the descent to a more manageable crash landing in hopes of keeping their cargo of six U.S. Army Rangers as safe as possible.

No such luck.

The chopper hit with a sickening thud, the residual spin of the main rotor causing it to roll on its side. Soldiers spilled out onto the dusty streets of

Mogadishu just as another RPG rammed into its underbelly. The explosion left no survivors.

I was only a First Lieutenant but those men who were just blown to smithereens were my men. My responsibility. I remember the intel briefing specifically said no combatants in the patrol area. In fact, this area had been clean for the past week. It was supposed to be a quick in and out, meet and greet, show some force — but smile and be nice type of patrol.

Now this.

I'd only been on a few patrols and now I lost an entire squad. I found out later I was the first in my commissioning class to lose that number of troops. I wasn't the last though. Some consolation. I spent an entire evening writing letters to the parents and spouses of my men. I was just starting to get to know them. I remember an anger swelling inside me that I never experienced before. It was overwhelming. I was a Ranger — albeit a rookie, but still a U.S. Army Ranger."

Special Agent Jonathan "Jon" Anderson Wells finished his writing and replaced the memo book on the nightstand. He filled twenty of these with what he remembered of his dreams when he awoke like this over the past several years. Mostly the same dream — not always. He dutifully dated the entry along with the time. It was three o'clock in the morning. What he would give for a good night's sleep again. Instead, he got up, went to the bathroom and wiped himself down. He checked the thermostat. It read 65 degrees. "You'd think that should be cold enough to sleep," he mumbled and trudged back to his bed. Maybe sleep would embrace him now.

Data Center in suburbs

"Hi Marty. Hi Avril," said Dominic Seragosa. He had just entered the data center to start his ten-hour shift. "How is everything going? Did you miss me while I was gone?" He winked at Marty who immediately looked somewhat out of sorts. "My eyes twitch when I walk through that contraption and you zap me like that." Dom hated the scanner everyone had to go through. It made him feel like he was at the airport, not work.

"You're clear. Now get out of here and into the pen," Avril ordered and hurried Dom along. She shushed Marty with a stare she normally reserved for bad children.

It was the beginning of six days on after four straight days off. He was relaxed and ready for a slow evening. Dom was the shift supervisor for the operations center. For years he longed for the responsibility this job demanded and it had been his for the past several months. It was his dream job, especially now that the data center was out in a corn field, in the "exurbs" only several miles from the home he shared with his wife and three children. He and his wife, Donna, purchased the house ten years ago when they had only two children. They planned on having one more so he suffered the long commutes to and from work knowing his children were in a good place. But he commuted no more. He could even ride his bike to work now. Not that he did, although it would help take off the belly fat that had accumulated over the years of sitting behind a desk. Donna routinely encouraged him to improve his health, lose some weight, and get some exercise. Dominic liked the idea of riding his bike to work more than the reality.

Prior to his four-day reprieve from work, he thought he noticed a slight slowness on some servers in responding to requests from the client networks. It had been a long six days on and the time off was refreshing. He came back with a new vigor to explore some ideas that popped into his head while mowing and getting Donna's honey-do list done. He needed to gather more information and cross-check some other reports. He wanted to impress his boss, but knew he had to have his "i's" dotted and "t's" crossed. Within the past year, two shift supervisors had been fired for raising issues. He replaced one of them. He was not privy to what those issues were, but he knew the company was a profit machine. During "All Hands" meetings the upper management would come in and show charts displaying how profits and share prices kept increasing over time. Then they spent the next hour hammering the team on improving service revenue, internal margins, profit per client, profits, and revenue split out by Service Level Agreements. The number one recommendation was to keep the clients happy at all costs – but those costs had better be low. Anything that went against the SLA was considered bad. Dom knew one of the fired shift supervisors wasn't happy with how the SLA's were being re-worked. Maybe that's what got her canned, he wondered.

Years ago

Zhang Xe was identified early in his life as an exceptional mathematician. The state removed him from his family, placing him in a state run school located in Kanming, China. There, he was raised by the state and did not see his parents again for nearly ten years. Families who "gave" their children to the state in this manner were held in high regard. This was an honor for his parents and they were allowed an exception to the one child rule. Zhang's excellence continued even in this new environment. Many students did not make it and were sent away. The superintendent of this school was a general in the Chinese military. Seeing the potential Zhang possessed, the general moved him into computer science training, where he prospered under the tutelage of some of the brightest math and computer science minds in China. Zhang mastered English and showed an aptitude for finances and the communication skills associated with negotiations. Representatives of the Chinese Security Services interviewed Zhang and others at the school, looking for candidates for their clandestine services. Once again, Zhang made the cut. He selected a name for the alter ego his new sponsors were creating for him – Chen Li. It was as Chen Li that he first published a paper on computer networks. A professor at Stanford University, in Palo Alto, California, read the paper and convinced the school to offer him a scholarship, as a visiting student, even at the age of 15 years. The advisors at his school requested a two-year deferral, citing Zhang's lack of social skills. Stanford agreed and held his scholarship. Over the next twenty months, he was tutored in the "finer skills of social grace," a finishing school so to speak. It was at this time Chen Li blossomed and Zhang Xe was inducted into the military as a member of the Chinese Security Services – Cyber Division.

Chen Li's academic prowess meant he could have graduated from Stanford in only two and a half years; however, he was there to do more than study. He needed to meet people, a lot of people. Zhang's handlers wanted him to have a large collegiate network. Chen took the number on the high end of the range he was given and broke down how many people he needed to maintain contact with every week in order to meet the end goal. He gave himself a quota of new people to meet, knowing many would never become part of his network. In essence, he ran a sales networking scheme. One sale meant one long term contact. To get one long term contact he postulated he needed to meet fifty people. Four years would be required to meet his numbers. This was approved. He joined a fraternity of international students studying computers, partied hard, and made sure people would never forget him. The social aspect he projected was important, as it aided in recognition. His schoolwork, however, cemented his reputation as one of the finest minds around. He completed studies as a double major in Applied Computer Science and Business. Members of Chen Li's network included people who would go on to work at most of the major companies in Silicon Valley and throughout the world. After the standard four years at Palo Alto, he graduated with honors with the classmates he met as a freshman. During his junior year, he was introduced to a professor from Massachusetts Institute of Technology who taught Cyber Security. This was not a "chance" meeting by any means. His handlers in China spent years mentioning Chen Li's name in all the right circles. It worked.

After Stanford, Chen Li travelled across the country to spend the next four years in Cambridge, Massachusetts. Chen and a classmate drove through all the states in the lower contiguous United States. They camped and hiked through national parks when they could. At other times, they stayed with friends as they inched their way to the Northeast. Often, several more Stanford classmates would join them for several days at a time. A few of these people would stay life-long friends. Just prior to arriving in the Boston area they made one last stop to rock climb in the Green Mountains of Vermont. There, Chen broke both bones in his lower left leg just above his ankle. He had just completed a climb, stepped out of his gear, and started down a steep rocky path on his way back to the car. He paid more attention to the backside of a young co-ed coming down another route and tripped. He tried catching himself but that just twisted his body. His left foot stepped out, rolled grotesquely, and the rest of his body crumpled forward in a heap. Chen spent the first three months at MIT in and out of hospitals and clinics. First in surgery and then rehabbing. He never fully recovered and now walked with a limp.

One of the best things about studying at MIT was the camaraderie and rivalries between students in the Boston area. Not only MIT, but Harvard, Boston University, Boston College, and Northeastern University students co-existed. And if that got boring, Yale, Brown, and other Ivy League schools were close. Chen continued to make friends, expanding his network into students in the medical field while earning both his Masters and Doctoral degrees in Cyber Security.

1994
Somewhere over the Atlantic Ocean

Adnan Ali and his family were homeless, penniless, and now nationless. Even so, all eight of them – his wife, two daughters, and four sons, were in the coach class of a Northwest Airlines 747 flying into Minneapolis, Minnesota. A doctor in Somalia, he knew those days were over.

He could not understand why the President of the United States of America had opened up his country to people no one knew and probably didn't even care about. No one in Adnan's family knew where Minnesota was or if their spartan English would allow them to communicate when they got there.

"The people in Minnesota know refugees. In the 70's and 80's they took in tens of thousands from Vietnam and Cambodia and helped them successfully transition into American life. You need to understand how successful they were. Where you are going, the metropolitan area of Minneapolis – St. Paul has the largest density and population of Hmong refugees from Cambodia anywhere in the world. Refugees move there from elsewhere in the U.S. Trust us, they will welcome you, they will integrate you – they want you there," said an aid representative at the refugee camp who was attempting to assure him Minnesota was a welcoming place.

Adnan was not sure. Religious freedom or not, he did not believe the American people would accept conservative Muslims. He felt they will not understand them because they were outsiders. His fears were mirrored in the faces of his sons. If he could have seen his wife's and daughters' faces, they were asleep and underneath the blankets provided by the attendants, he would have seen the same. He stared out the window of the plane down to the white snow-covered landscape of the Northern Minnesota tundra.

"It looks cold," he thought. *"I pray to Allah the people are not as cold as the land."*

Chapter 2

Present Day
FBI Headquarters, Downtown Minneapolis

"I need the report on the last case you two worked on," barked Antonio "Tony" Suarez. Tony was the Assistant Chief of the Minneapolis office. Jon Wells and his partner Rick Cunningham looked at one another and suppressed groans. They didn't have time for this. They had just come off a long investigation into money laundering and were eager to return to their primary objective – Somali immigrants in the Twin Cities and their ties to al-Shabaab and The Islamic States of Iraq and Syria (ISIS). Those violent fundamentalist terrorist organizations had interesting ties to Minneapolis. Jon didn't care for Tony's bureaucratic, administrative bullshit. Nor did he care for Tony's leadership style, or was that his lack of leadership? Tony wanted "his" numbers to outshine his peers so he could continue making loud noises about being promoted. He didn't show much regard for the people he was charged with leading.

"I can pull those up," Jon said before Rick could blurt anything out. "My files are in better shape than yours anyway," he grinned and smirked at Rick.

"I'm continually surprised that an old geezer like yourself knows how to use a computer. Must be all that Army training you have," snorted Rick back at this partner.

"Better training for this than the self-righteous, East Coast, prep boy education you received. Just because you Cunningham's are and always have sucked at the teat of the government troughs doesn't mean you know everything."

"Not my fault generation after generation of fine upstanding men of character in my household served the greater good," retorted Rick.

Six generations of Rick's family had served the U.S. government in various forms. The military had been the home of the earliest generations upon immigrating to America. Later generations expanded into other branches. His great-grandfather had been a diplomat, his grandfather a federal judge, and his father in the Senior Executive Service or SES within the Department of Labor.

"I know I'm from the D.C. area and attended damn good prep schools in Northern Virginia. I even earned a lacrosse scholarship to Loyola in Maryland. What can I say? Just good luck I guess."

Rick attended the FBI Academy within weeks of finishing college. While not top of his class by any stretch, he expected a posting to D.C. or New York. No such luck – the plains of Des Moines, Iowa, called him. What a shock. There were no strings that could be pulled – even with his pedigree. Turns out, though, Rick loved the Midwest. When he was eligible for a transfer, it wasn't back east. No, he chose to amble up I-35 north to the Minneapolis office. Why? Because of 9-11, he was personally focused solely on anti-terrorism. He saw first-hand the horrors inflicted at the Pentagon while he was in college. He didn't believe he could benefit the FBI in New York City, even though the counter-terrorism effort was heaviest there. He felt the real danger would come from the interior of the country – where least expected.

As Jon brought over the files to Rick's desk, Rick needled him more. "You know, Mr. Gung-Ho, the grunt train you rode here just makes you older, slower, my way or the highway inflexible, and most importantly, less attractive to the fairer sex than I." Jon responded by flinging the report through the air and barely missing Rick's coffee.

With the morning ritual of partner bashing now complete, Rick verified the report would satisfy the boss's demands. Jon shook his head at his younger partner's never-ending need for self-promotion and grimaced as he recognized so much of his younger self in Rick.

He turned to the window and surveyed the skyline of Minneapolis looking southeast over the girders of the billion-dollar temple being built to house the city's professional football team. Jon enjoyed football, but never understood the amount of money people threw at it. Banks in this town spent millions to put their names on both the collegiate stadium across the river and now this behemoth. Jon had dubbed this one, "The Vault."

Over the top of "The Vault," the 39-story McKnight Building was the largest of a series of towers within the Cedar-Riverside Complex. It was slowly vanishing from Jon's view as "The Vault" grew in size. With its mosaic tiles of late 1960 pale blues, yellows, and reds, the Cedar-Riverside Complex seemed like a golf flag marking of the center of the area known as Little Somalia. That area held the focus of his work and he and Rick needed to get back to it.

Jon Wells was a singularly focused individual. His connection with the convictions of his partner ran deep. After the fiasco in Mogadishu over twenty years ago, he transferred from combat to intelligence. The next decade had been spent identifying and removing threats around the world. His team knew something was up prior to 9-11. There was just too much chatter. Unfortunately, at that time, he was part of just one of many competing intelligence arms who fought as much with one another as with the enemy. Quality, confirmed, and timely intel never seemed to get far enough up the chain.

At age 42, he retired as a Lieutenant Colonel after tours in hot spots the world over. As a veteran, he was granted an age waiver to attend the FBI Academy. The FBI needed people like him with intelligence experience encompassing all phases of Islamic terrorist organizations. After 9-11 the newly formed Department of Homeland Security sought to bring the intelligence and federal law enforcement services under one roof — or at least fewer roofs. Numerous joint task forces with local law enforcement agencies were created, especially in areas flush with Muslim immigrants. This is how Jon ended up in Minneapolis. The Somali immigrant community here was the largest in the nation. Other units, similar to the one Jon joined here, were set up in metropolitan areas such as Detroit and San Diego. Whereas his boss had visions of one day becoming the FBI Director, Jon didn't want that. Being on the frontline, attacking the terrorist organizations where it hurt them the most was all he wanted.

Little Somalia – an area rife with disaffected youth – was the frontline for Jon.

Just to the southeast of downtown Minneapolis across I-35W, is the area known historically as the first stop for generations of immigrants in the largest city in the Upper Midwest. First large influx was the Norwegians and Swedes. Eastern Europeans followed later. After World War II many upwardly mobile black families supplanted those who left for the suburbs. Now, this neighborhood was the domain of the Somali. The city holds the nation's highest number of Somali immigrants – around 14,000 in total. With the influx of Somali refugees, this neighborhood quickly picked up the moniker "Little Somalia."

Jon and Rick drove through the main business district of Cedar-Riverside on Cedar Avenue South. They saw men in khameez, macawiis, and koofiyads, or "koofis," gathered around some of the buildings closest to the complex. Jon rolled his window down and breathed deeply to inhale the scent of curry, cinnamon, and cumin which were heavy in the air. It no longer felt and certainly did not smell like the city predominantly settled by immigrants of Northern European descent. His mind often drifted back to his short time in Mogadishu when he drove this street. He embraced the memories of the different, yet wonderful food the smells brought him. His other memories of that time were not as kind. Jon understood these people unlike the many suburbanites driving through on their way to the West Bank Campus of the University of Minnesota. They viewed this area only as one that should be avoided. If you needed to drive through, do so rapidly. They routinely rolled up their windows and locked their doors out of fear. This lack of understanding was disrespectful and spoke volumes of the welcome the Somali community received in the land of "Minnesota Nice."

Jon pulled his vehicle to a stop in the parking lot. He and Rick alighted from the vehicle while he loosened his tie. Jon hated ties. Every time he came here he would spend a moment gazing upon the complex. The military had taken him all over the world. He saw many places, mostly in Eastern Europe down through Turkey and into the Middle East. This complex seemed to transport him to many of those places.

"Hey Rick, what do you see when you look at these towers?" Jon asked as he reflected.

"Well, it isn't D.C. That's for sure. I think it's an eye-sore. I've seen pictures of buildings like this, but not here in the states. What about you?" Rick replied.

When Jon looked up and viewed the architecture he felt he was no longer in Minneapolis.

"Did you know this Cedar-Riverside neighborhood is home to one the most unique housing projects built in the United States? It was originally designed to cover four entire neighborhoods, holding up to 30,000 people living in a utopian environment containing mixed racial, economic and social classes, schools, entertainment centers, and green spaces. All funded by the U.S. federal government. They called it the New Town-In Town program from the late 1960's."

"The 60's huh, well that explains a lot." Rick was still looking up at the towers, shielding the sunlight with his hand. "You know, you sound like some travel guide when you explain this type of stuff. But, please go on."

"Why, thank you. As you can probably imagine, a federally funded program designed around a Utopian vision does not generally work out as planned. Well, Cedar-Riverside was no different. One person put it this way, 'poor people don't mind living with middle and upper class people, but the upper class don't want to live with middle and lower class people.' So much for Utopia. Do this. Close your eyes, put your hand down, and take a deep breath." The men breathed in and paused to reflect. Jon continued with his eyes closed. "To me the smell is wonderful. It reminds me of Mogadishu. Too bad the freeway is right here though. The noise ruins the effect. So onto the next sense – sight. Open your eyes now. The architecture itself looks like when I was in Odessa, Warsaw, or one of the many horribly planned communities the Soviets forced upon their satellite nations. I think they call the style 'Brutalist.' I've seen a lot of awful architecture in the name of community. But this mess takes the cake. There, was that less touristy?"

"Well, maybe less touristy but certainly still professorial," replied Rick who was still looking up at the towers.

Jon swung good-naturedly at his protégé and started toward the building. They walked through the complex stopping to say hi to several children. Most adults either shied away or said hello at most. They feared the government in Somalia. Twenty years in Minnesota did little to change this. But that was why they were here – to put a human face to government and law enforcement. Jon brought this idea up to his boss, Tony, who grudgingly approved of the time, but only if it didn't interfere with "actual" work. Every week one or both of them came down, walked around, and pressed the flesh. Jon didn't set out to do anything specific, so there would be no blowback of any kind towards anyone. Nonetheless, positive movement had been made and today they would meet with a group in the community center. Jon spent a lot of time talking about the U.S. in general and how the government was set up to work. He told everyone he could that the U.S. was, and probably always would be, a work in progress.

Chapter 3

Several years ago
Peavey Park, Minneapolis, MN

A mixture of athletic looking young men gathered around the sidelines watching the three-on-three pickup game of basketball. The backboards were wobbly, the rims bent but usable, and the net was made of chain. You could see the weld spots and additional steel strips and bolts meant to reinforce the otherwise shoddy construction of the backboards.

The man wearing the knee length grey khameez trimmed in gold and silver stitching, with an embroidered koofiyad on his head, appeared to be in charge of the activities. Yes, this was more than a simple game of hoops.

Once a team was ousted they would jog to the sideline area while another set of three took their place. They would gather around a cooler filled with cold bottles of water and engage "The Man" in conversation. It was an animated and heartfelt denouncement of the position these men felt in the American society. "Yes, you are Muslim. It is good to be a Muslim. We must look out for other Muslims, for the so-called Christian love espoused by the peoples of this land certainly will not. Who among you has not been ridiculed at his school? Who has or knows others that have been made to feel lower than cattle due to how they dressed or how they smelled? What did it matter what one looked or smelled like?" asked "The Man." "Does not your heart, soul, and body belong to Allah? Only Allah can judge."

"I have been sent from the heart of Islam to look out for you. Your parents don't, your classmates don't, and certainly the people of Minneapolis and the United States don't. They don't care for their native peoples. They don't care for their black, brown, or yellow people. If you are not white and Christian, they don't care. They only care for themselves. You see evidence of this each day. They only want us here to drive taxis, work in their turkey factories, and the other low-end positions they would never themselves stoop to. When you are home, look out your windows across the freeway to the new football stadium. How many of us are allowed to work the high paying union jobs there?"

Outings to the movie theaters often followed. "The Man" paid, for the young men did not have enough money of their own. A new father figure was emerging for many of the young men. One of these was Omar Waberi, son of Yusef.

Omar had been an active student involved in many extra-curricular activities at his high school. There was even a time that he enjoyed academics; however, there was a growing discontent welling up within him. He was born in Minneapolis at the medical center in his neighborhood. As such, he was of the new generation of U.S. citizens of Somali descent. This should be his homeland. He lived in the towers of Little Somalia and attended kindergarten through third grade in the elementary school spread across the pavilion level of one of the three towers in the Cedar-Riverside complex. Omar never ventured more than several blocks from his home until he entered the 4th grade at a school ten blocks away. There, he saw for the first time non-Muslim children. *"Were these the children of the people who worked in the tall skyscrapers across the freeway?"* he thought. Omar thought of the clothes those children wore, purchased undoubtedly at the Mall of America. They were so different from the oversized, worn, and thread-bare clothing on his body. Those children smelled immensely different to Omar and he to them. By the time his middle school years were over his white classmates no longer even turned up their noses at him and called him "stinky." They just ignored him.

As with many of other Eastern Africans, Omar could run. He could run far and fast. He was on the cross-country team in middle school and progressed well enough that he participated in several high school meets during his 8th grade year. This was the only time he was not ignored. Even though he normally felt excluded from the non-Muslim children, he was pleased to be accepted on the athletic field.

Walking back from school to the apartment complex his junior year of high school, Omar saw the activity around the basketball court. It was different in Peavey Park than at most ball courts. There was no graffiti. There was no trash strewn all over – it was in the provided trash receptacles. No swearing was heard, nor were punches being thrown. The men looked like him. He understood bits and pieces of the language being spoken. He was drawn to them. Especially to "The Man." Over the next year "The Man" taught Omar and others their native Somali tongue and explained the Quran in a manner they could understand. It made sense to Omar.

He felt loved. He felt like he finally belonged.

By the next year, Omar quit the cross-county team. He disavowed his friends, especially the few non-Muslim ones who had ventured from their school-aged cliques to befriend him. To some, he appeared to become seriously withdrawn. Never a devout Muslim, he began spending time at the mosque with his new friends – but almost never with his parents.

One night he left the apartment never to return.

Present Day
Youth Awareness Center, Cedar-Riverside

Jamal leaned over the table to correct the spelling of the young man seated across the table.

Jamal Kusow came to America in the mid-90's. He excelled in school, gaining a scholarship to the small liberal arts university right down the road. There he was a member of the newly created Diversity Connection program that reached out to people of non-

Caucasian descent in order to offer opportunity to immigrants. This program would eventually be recognized as one of the premier diversity programs in inner city colleges and universities. Upon graduation, with honors, he matriculated to the classrooms on the "West Bank" where the business school of the University of Minnesota was located. Once again he stayed within blocks of "Little Somalia." There he attained his MBA with specialization in entrepreneurship. In the twenty years he lived in Minneapolis, he never had to move away from "Little Somalia." Everything he needed was there. As a young, successful businessman with several restaurants serving Somali food, he now gave back to the community.

Jamal's flagship restaurant was located in a trendy part of town close to the famous Greenway bike trail. His clientele was often clad in only biker spandex, especially on summer weekends. He employed mostly Somalis through a program with a local community high school and vocational college. He didn't discriminate against non-Somalis, but he focused his energies on providing positive ways to influence his community. It was hit and miss though. He was able to cultivate a few store managers for his other restaurants over the years but his overall employee turnover was much higher than fellow restauranteurs. It was a source of never ending frustration for him.

Jamal's thoughts were interrupted by the shouts of a mother walking briskly towards the young man he was helping. "Why you get in trouble? School is good for you. Why you not be good boy? Is it so hard? You bring dishonor. You turning into criminal. You should just leave. Maybe I throw you out, see what good that will do." She grabbed the boy by the cuff of his shirt, pulled him up, and shoved him towards the door.

Jamal was no longer shocked by this. It happened too often. The communication style of many of his countrymen was, more often than not, vivaciously intense. Children emulate their parents in many things. The style of communication is one of these. Unfortunately, the interpersonal intensity and passionate style of the Somali is often misinterpreted by teachers and peers as overly assertive and emotionally charged, especially when compared to what many Minnesotans feel is acceptable. Also, Nomadic cultures such as the Somali have a hard time with the American concept of being on time. Trouble brews when a young Somali male comes to class late, doesn't look the teacher in the eye, and seemingly is aggressive when finally pushed to answer why they can't ever be on time. For the Somali child, looking at an adult or other authority figure was a sign of disrespect. The boy Jamal was tutoring had simply refused to look at his teacher when she addressed him. Jamal was helping him catch up on work he missed while in the principal's office that day.

Somalis pride themselves on independence and on an unwillingness to submit to unrecognized authority. Prior to the Somali Civil War, the authorities, led by General Barre, were the problem. Here in the U.S., anything that could potentially lead to a confrontation with an authority – even if just at school – would lead to the type of parental overblown reaction just witnessed. The child, already disappointed with themselves for either getting in trouble at school, getting poor grades, or something else, was further frustrated. *"Don't they understand me when I tell them they cannot embarrass their children like this?"* More often than not, the trouble was simply a misunderstanding of the cultural differences the child was attempting to navigate. *"We must teach our children how to successfully navigate these issues and not disown them when they inevitably make a mistake,"* thought Jamal. These were the precepts of his philosophy. He spoke these words so often it became a sort of mantra for him. This was why he came every afternoon to preach his epistle of how to be an American of Somali descent rather than a Somali living in America. It was not always being heard. In fact, he had been the target of much ridicule, taunting, and even threats over the past several years by his own community.

He knew the distant look in the eyes of some of the young kids who gathered here was cause for concern. Especially the impressionable teen males who harbored great resentment towards almost everything and everyone.

Chapter 4

Years ago

It can be said that each new "economy" in the U.S. was built on the backs of immigrants and foreign workers. The "dot-com" economy of the 1990's and into the early millennium was no different. There were simply too many jobs available to be filled completely by citizens of the United States. Visas for education often turned into employment visas as companies eagerly sponsored students from universities across the country. Zhang Xe, aka Chen Li, was one of these.

After two years as a security officer at several dot coms in the Washington, D.C. area, Zhang returned to his homeland. In truth, he never really left. He spent those years in the United States with a two-pronged plan – create an extensive network of cyber experts around the world and build up his resume.

Hi-tech employees during the dot-com craze were a highly transitory community. Companies routinely poached from each other, often with no other reason than to deprive one another of employees and their skills – real or perceived. Money and bonuses for 'jumping ship' flowed like rivers flooded with monsoon rains.

This culture provided Chen access to an expansive potential network. Due to the training he received from his mentors in China, he had uncanny social skills. He honed those skills at Stanford and MIT. At the dot-coms he learned how to manipulate almost anyone without a smidgen of suspicion. He sought out only the best technicians, especially among the foreign students and workers ostracized by the Americans. With and even without their explicit knowledge, many of them ended up working for Chen or more directly for Zhang Xe.

The resume Zhang was building was not to get that next great job. No, it was to help create the bona fides of his alter ego – Chen Li. As a tool of the Chinese Army, this identity would be used when he returned – to his real purpose in life. Zhang lived a split life in China. His public persona, Chen Li, was that of an entrepreneur. He hired many of the people from his collegiate and dot-com careers. His first public venture was in internet security services. Like many start-ups in the states, he locked up an enormous amount of money with early funding from Chinese venture capitalists. With the millions in profit from his initial government contracts, Chen's company had the resume to convince American and European venture capitalists to provide additional rounds of funding. He used this funding to purchase other technology firms. These new firms expanded his corporate reach from its foundation in internet security services to software, electronics, and medical devices. His network grew in new and rewarding measures.

Zhang's real title and job was as a Major in the Chinese Army's Security Services. Work "created" by Zhang was mostly funneled to Chen Li's companies. Additionally, Zhang also provided the manpower that made up the remainder of Chen's personnel. Zhang was given the assignment of building a cyberespionage organization that could speed up Chinese economic development. He was given an almost unlimited budget. The initial venture capitalists that funded Chen Li were actually bankrolled by Zhang Xe's organization.

Zhang succeeded beyond all expectations. He was a demanding task-master beyond reproach. He recruited only the best and was a zealot in pursuing the goals placed before him. Those who did not achieve his standards were ruthlessly removed from his group. There were reports of summary executions for failure. There simply was not enough time to catch the West and allow people in his command the luxury of failure. To fail was unacceptable. His team, highly motivated, became fanatical as their success grew. With each new success, power and prestige for each team member also grew. He lavished them with the spoils of their exploits. Zhang no longer needed to actively recruit. Recruits came to him.

One of the most spectacular achievements Zhang's cyberespionage team accomplished came when they helped undermine the terms several European manufacturers negotiated when entering the Chinese market. The Europeans simply wanted to export finished products made in Europe to China. Zhang's team gathered timely information and passed it on to the Chinese negotiators. They, in turn, were able to coerce the Europeans to sell their designs and send "experts" to help build and run factories. Factories owned by the Chinese government and leased to Chinese companies.

With success came more prominence, money, resources, and demands. The leadership within the Chinese government was not one to let individuals rest on their laurels. Promoted now to a Colonel, Zhang's old schoolboy network, gathered together as Chen Li, would be put to the test.

Chapter 5

Present Day
HyDek Data Center Complex, outskirts of the Twin Cities
metro area

"Abdi, I need to bounce something off you." Dominic toiled for several days pouring over reports that simply did not add up. Abdi Ali was the data center's security threat analyst. Abdi and Dom had worked together at various companies the past ten years. Abdi received a $2,000 employee referral bonus when the company hired Dom. He and Dom often joked who made more over the years on referral bonuses from one another's employment.

"How can I be of assistance my liege?" said Abdi, with emphasized drama, as he looked up from the ten monitors scattered throughout his double-sized cubicle in the corner of the operations floor.

"You know how there was a huge theft of PII from the headquarters of that retailer several years ago?"

"Yeah, so. Loss of personally identifiable information happens. What does that have to do with us?"

"Come on. We both worked at that data center. Even though it was a hack from the outside, remember all the additional security concerns we found, documented, and recommended changing?"

"Yes. Glad we didn't get fired. Lots of people did," responded the now alerted security expert.

"It's just, well…," Dom poked his head up from the cubicle and looked around. No one else was within earshot so he continued. "How would I know if we had a breach? I'm more than competent at my job but some of this goes into areas I simply haven't been able to spend enough time to learn well. I've done my job extremely well for years but always left the cyber security side for you. I think I need to know more. The better I understand this, the better I'll be at my job overseeing everything. That way maybe we can identify a problem before it gets too big. I figured you'd be the best person to talk with."

Abdi placed his hands over his heart as if appearing to be in shock. "God, you had me going there for a moment. I thought you were going to tell me you found out I wasn't doing my job. You sure you aren't trying to get my job?" Abdi continued to mock Dom. Seeing his friend was not taking the good-natured joshing in stride he sighed, straightened up, and said, "You're serious aren't you? In that case, let me point you in the right direction."

Chapter 6

FBI Headquarters
Downtown Minneapolis

Returning to his desk, Jon sought out his "to do" list for the day. One email caught his eye. Jon only needed to scan it to know what it contained.

During the big sting of al-Shabaab involvement in Minneapolis, Jon had enlisted the assistance of a local Somali businessman. Jon respected what Jamal Kusow stood for. Jamal embraced his new American citizenship and yet did not turn his back on his heritage. He took the best of what America had, turning perceived immigrant difficulties into strengths. He created a strong business and still found time to give back to his community.

As a businessman, Jamal knew his local police. Some of Jamal's restaurants were not in the best of neighborhoods. Several had been broken into or vandalized. He even suffered several thefts from his own employees. He could have blamed the police for his problems like many did but he chose an alternative path. Jamal forged good relationships with the police. He introduced the police to his employees and fellow businessmen. He even sponsored several meet and greet sessions for locals and the police. He attended city meetings to educate himself on how the system worked. The Lieutenant at the local police precinct became aware of Jamal and his efforts in community building, not only where his businesses were located but for his Somali community as well. Because of this, Jamal often represented the Somali community when a grievance with the police was raised. More often than not, a peaceful and acceptable resolution to the grievance was negotiated – due in large part to Jamal's skill as a moderator. In the same manner, when the police needed a person of influence within the Somali community, Jamal was called. He was sought, rather than the Imam at the mosque, because the police department felt not involving the Imam would be more respectful of his position in the community.

Due to this arrangement, Jamal was also invited to consult with the Minneapolis Joint Terrorism Task Force. The task force was an amalgamation of officers from area metro police departments, the FBI, and expert consultants. It was here he met Jon Wells.

Jamal had asked Jon for a favor a while back. A young man Jamal had tutored years ago had gone missing. Jamal feared the worst. He knew the relationship the boy had with his father was more than strained. His father had never wanted to come to the U.S. He never learned more than a limited amount of English, gained his citizenship, nor managed to find more than spotty manual labor. As a result, his family lived off the social generosity of the state. He could not effectively feed or clothe his family of his own accord. The community had struggled to help the children out. The father, already a bitter man, took umbrage to this and every other offer of assistance. He took it out on his son Omar.

Jamal had lost track of Omar. There were too many like him to effectively keep track of. Sometimes, Jamal felt the successes he had achieved were a barrier to helping some of the children. Too many young members of this community fled to Syria to fight with ISIS at the behest of al-Shabaab. The FBI probe and ensuing imprisonment of some of these men shook the Somali community to the core. Trust within the community needed to be re-built.

Jon called Jamal. They arranged to meet at a downtown restaurant. After making the call he felt sick to his stomach. Another Minnesota born and bred terrorist. How did it get to this?

The restaurant Jamal chose overlooked the atrium of the IDS Center. The IDS Center was the first modern skyscraper in Minneapolis. The blue tinted exterior walls of glass topped by a seven-story rim of black made it the signature building of Minneapolis since the mid 1970's. The atrium was seven stories high with a series of skylights at multiple levels mimicking the step back façade of the IDS Center itself. The skylights allowed sunlight to cascade into the atrium. With reflections bouncing off the interior windows and the skylights themselves, the atrium had the appearance of being on the inside of a crystal – hence the name Crystal Court.

Jamal chose this restaurant because few Somalis ventured here during the day. Nighttime would have been different – that was when the cleaning crews ruled the skyscrapers. Jon saw Jamal already seated at a table tucked near a corner. The wall next to the table was high enough to keep utensils and glasses from falling three floors to the bottom of the atrium filled with tourists and employees of the surrounding buildings. Too high for people to recognize anyone and yet providing an expansive view of the restaurant layout and area. *"Jamal could easily be a spy,"* Jon thought. A smile began to cross his face until he remembered the reason for the meet.

Jamal, dressed in a dark blue business suit, white shirt, and a solid red pique tie, had ordered for both of them. His hair was cut short, over his ears, and he was clean-shaven. They looked like two bankers meeting for lunch. Jamal cut his hair years ago and vacillated between having beard or not, like many other men his age. They ate and after going through some routine chit-chat Jon pulled a sheet from his suit pocket.

"Jamal, thanks for seeing me so soon." Jon slid a sheet of paper across the table. It contained the context of the email he had received. "The news is bad, I'm afraid. Omar Waberi is dead. He was killed in a suicide bombing in Syria. There is not enough of his body left to be returned."

"How many people did he kill?" asked Jamal.

"That's what is so weird about this. Only Omar died."

Jamal's head shot up from the paper. "What?"

"I know. It doesn't make sense. I doubled checked after I called you to make sure I knew the particulars."

"Why would someone leave here to train with terrorists, conduct a suicide bombing attack, and not kill anyone? Did he not get to his target?"

"It wasn't that sort of suicide bombing. The target appears to be a telecommunications building of some sort. In fact, he went into the building and away from the populated bazaar area. The only thing that was damaged was the interior of the building. It was empty except for Omar. Nonetheless, ISIS took credit for it. Homeland Security, CIA, FBI, and the State Department all consider it a terrorist act."

Jamal teared up. It took several moments for him to regain his composure. "Jon, thank you for telling me this. I know you do not need to provide me with all the details and those that you did are more than enough. I will inform his family. His father is a vile man and I don't look forward to it. I will only tell him his son died a traitor to his country. The country where he grew up. The country best suited to provide him with a positive future. I am ashamed. Tell me, Jon, do the news channels know about this yet? I don't know how much more the community can take. I need some time to figure this out."

After a short period of silent prayer Jamal looked at Jon and said, "Peace be with you." He then slowly rose from the table and left. He, too, had failed yet one more of his own. He needed to be alone.

Jon hadn't slept well again. Another flashback, this time somewhere in one of the mountainous regions of Afghanistan, or was it Pakistan. This particular dream was not clear at all, except something bad happened. Again. Finally, at 4:40 a.m., after waking up for the fourth time, he showered, clothed himself, and began the trek to the office. He exited his condominium and took a quick elevator ride down six floors to street level. The coffee shop around the corner should be open. It was.

"Morning Alice."

"Hi Jon. You're up early today. Bad dreams again?" Alice owned the small shop. It was a local venue. Jon tried to always support local

27

shops whenever he could. They needed the support. It was shops like this that made the neighborhood a great place to live after all. Owners of these establishments were generally in the store and always available to talk. He was comfortable here.

"Yep. Sleep, dream, wake up in a sweat, and write it all down. I'm getting better at going back to sleep, but not last night."

"That's too bad Jon. Keep at it. My dad suffered through a lot coming out of Vietnam. He made it, but it wasn't a walk in the park if you know what I mean. Hey, you smell those scones I'm baking? Want one? I have a pan that just came out of the oven." Alice leaned mischievously towards Jon and waited for his answer.

She didn't have to wait long as Jon replied, "Tell you what. Why don't you give me enough for the office? I feel the need to feed the masses today. Oh, and don't forget the coffee."

"You picking one up for Frank today? I heard he's back in the neighborhood." Frank was a veteran who lived on the streets. He did three tours in Iraq and Afghanistan. He was doing fine finding his way back into society and his family until a drunk driver ran a red light and slammed his F-350 Super Duty into the car Frank's wife and two small children occupied. They all died, except, that is, the drunk. He walked away without a scratch. Jon never crossed paths with Frank while in the service. He often wished he had. Maybe then he could connect more with him.

"If you say he's here, absolutely. Thanks." Jon was the only person in the shop at this hour of the morning. He sat down at one of the three small tables and looked out the window while waiting for his order. The lacey curtains that covered the bottom half of the window were hand-stitched by Alice's mother. The interior was painted a light blue with Scandinavian Rosemaling edging on the door and window frames. It was this attention to detail he enjoyed. Alice brought everything to him.

"I made a bag special for Frank, on me. Just give it to him for me will you?"

Jon pushed himself back from the table and walked with her back to the counter so he could grab a few other items and pay for everything. "You're a dear. You know that Alice, right?"

"Oh gosh no. Now take your stuff and git. Go!" She whisked him gone with a smile. Jon smiled back. A smile – the day was getting better.

He continued on his walk through the old warehouse district where he resided. Once a forgotten part of the city, it was becoming more and more trendy. It even had its own neighbor moniker - the North Loop. Over the railroad lines to the southwest lay the heart of the downtown office district.

The sidewalks in his neighborhood undulated up and down following the loading dock ramps of the old warehouse buildings. The city removed, or simply neglected to replace, the asphalt on many of the roads in this neighborhood. This revealed the original cobblestones, which added to the ambiance. At the base of one of these ramps he found Frank.

"Hey there. Morning." Jon nudged the leg sticking out from under the remains of a cardboard box repurposed with duct tape as a small collapsible shelter.

"Go away."

"That's not nice Frank. It's me, Jon. I have treats from Alice. You know she worries about you."

Jon squatted down and gave Frank the coffee and bag full of breakfast.

"Where you been?" asked Jon.

"Oh you know how it goes. Here and there. Staying one step ahead of the cops."

"See anything interesting? Anything this cop should know about?"

"Cop hell, Jon. You're a Fed, a G-Man, the real deal." Frank woke up enough from his sleep to carry on the banter he and Jon had developed. "You sleeping OK?" he asked Jon.

"Oh you know how it goes. Here and there. Staying one step ahead of the dreams," Jon replied with the second smile of the morning.

They both drank Alice's coffee and watched as the sun began its daily ritual of rising over the tops of the surrounding buildings. The shadows slowly lost their battle and receded past both men, showering them in warmth.

"Gonna be a warm one today." Jon grabbed a bottle of water from his suit pocket and handed it to Frank. "Use this today."

"Jon, you're a good man. Don't let the dreams get you like they got me. OK?"

"You got it. I better get to work. You be OK?"

"I be fine." Frank smiled and waved Jon on his way. Frank wanted nothing from anyone and turned away most offers of help from Jon. He did, however, always take the coffee and food Alice sent. Jon never saw Frank in the winter, but every April through November, he was around.

He looked down from the bridge he crossed every day at the train tracks. Soon the trains from up north would arrive and begin disgorging themselves of the thousands of commuters using them every day. What would it be like to live like that? He was up because he couldn't sleep. They had to be up just to get to work. How much of their day did they miss traveling 45 miles each way, every day, just to try and make ends meet? *I suppose if I'd have met someone willing to put up with me and my career I could have had kids and…*Well, that boat had sailed years ago. Once over the rail lines he could either continue at street level or enter the skyway system, which was warmer during the winter months. It gerrymandered around so many buildings that Jon rarely took it in the summer and fall. Here in Minneapolis, you had to take advantage of nice weather during those seasons because winter was – well cold just wasn't sufficient enough to describe it.

Jon continued on foot crossing First Avenue and worked his way toward 5th Street and the tracks of the light rail system. This was the entertainment district of the downtown area, an eclectic mix of sports venues, hipster pubs, gangster style late-night clubs, restaurants, an occasional strip club, and off-Broadway style theaters. After several blocks he entered his building. Normally he eschewed the elevator, choosing to run up the far stairway to the sixth floor. Today though, he brought goodies, so the elevator would suffice.

As he approached his desk, the phone rang. Placing the bags of food down, he lifted the handset off its cradle and hit the speaker button. These phones were ancient. "FBI Minneapolis, Special Agent Wells speaking."

"Hey Jon, Gloria here. How the hell are you? Been thinking of you a lot lately. Glad you're in early today."

"Agent Ransik, cyber geek of the year, greetings and salutations back-atcha," replied Jon. Computers were not his thing. Anyone who spent twenty hours a day staring at monitors that appeared to look like those in the movie "The Matrix" and could interpret them were way out of his league. Special Agent Ransik had been the lead analyst in the computer hacking case that came close to shuttering one of the largest retailers in America. Their corporate headquarters happened to be in the suburbs of St. Paul. Gloria was skilled in identifying cyber threats and beating them. She was a rising star in the FBI, not just because of her computer skills, but also because she was superb at dealing with people. Jon had recommended her to an old Army buddy in D.C. soon after wrapping up that case. His friend headed up the FBI's Cyber Division in Washington, D.C. Based in no small part of Jon's recommendation, she was promoted and whisked away from Minneapolis to be a member of the National Cyber Investigative Joint Task Force (NCIJTF). Jon's immediate supervisor, Tony, hated it that Jon knew so many people and that his recommendations meant so much.

"What can I do you for?" Jon said as he was taking scones out of the package Alice prepared for him.

"I need some help."

Chapter 7

Cedar-Riverside Complex

Jamal got out of his car and headed towards the complex. He took a deep breath and looked up, shielding his eyes from the sun. How many years had he spent here in his youth? Several small children were playing throughout the patios, running around in and out of the passageway that connected one of the interior courtyards. Was it some new form of "keep away?" Moving through the passageway and around the playground in the courtyard, Jamal walked up the concrete stairs to the pavilion level. The stairs were 150 feet wide beveling to one third that at the top of the 15 steps. A beat up soccer ball bounced towards him. He moved quickly to his right, catching the ball with his left foot before it bounced down the stairs. He dribbled it searching for the source. Seeing four young boys looking at him he waved and called out, "Is this yours?" The boys looked as if they were in trouble. "It's OK. Who should I pass it to?"

The short boy in the red shirt quickly shot his hand up and yelled, "Me! Me!" Jamal passed the ball on one bounce directly to the boy. The others quickly converged on the ball and the game began anew. Jamal smiled. This is how I want to be when I am here.

Turning to his right, he continued underneath one of the six towers. A cloud passed in front of the sun, casting a dark pall over him. All of a sudden it felt as if he was downtown in an office complex, and yet, young girls dressed in jeans and hijabs played, shouts from mothers in a mixture of Somali and English echoed through the concrete buildings while the wonderful smells of his favorite foods told him he was home.

But he was not headed towards his family's apartment. Not right away. No. Tonight he had to call upon a family friend and deliver bad news. Another young Somali man was dead. Not here in Minneapolis, but far away. He had fallen victim to al-Shabaab.

"Yusef, Assalamu Alaykum Wa Rahmatullaahi wa barakato. May I come in?" Jamal spoke the formal Muslim greeting "peace and mercy and blessings of God be upon" you to signal the formality of his arrival.

"Wa alaykum assalam," gruffly replied Yusef, offering peace upon Jamal also and offering his home to him. He extended the welcome only because it was expected.

Jamal followed Yusef into the living room. Yusef's wife, Hodan, ushered the children and women to the second story. Upon taking care of this, she assembled a tray of Somali Tea – black tea steeped with cardamom – along with sugar and steamed milk. She placed it on the table and served a cup to each. She politely asked if either needed anything else.

"No thank you. You are most kind. Please sit and stay with us as we talk," offered Jamal.

"No. This is my house and I am in charge. Not you. She will go and mind the children." Yusef glared at Jamal as Hodan excused herself, leaving the men alone.

Both men were silent as they drank their tea. Once he finished Jamal looked into Yusef's eyes. "Yusef, you are not a kind man, but you asked me to find out about your son."

Yusef Waberi knew that Jamal had contacts with both government agencies and non-government organizations, in addition to being well connected throughout the Somali and Muslim neighborhoods. Because of this he had asked Jamal to help find his son, Omar, who had gone missing eight months ago. Omar should have been celebrating his high school graduation. Instead he had dropped out and disappeared. Omar's relationship with his father had never been good. Yusef constantly berated Omar for not living up to his ideals. Nevertheless, Yusef was concerned. Reluctantly, he went to the police after no one in the community could figure out where Omar had gone. Unfortunately, this was only after several months had passed. The police took down his information and politely told Yusef that there really was not much they could do since so much time had expired. Secretly, Yusef felt the police never cared anyway, but as the man in the house he had to explore all avenues. Well, most of them anyway.

"I have bad news, I'm afraid. I've been notified that your son, Omar is no longer with us. The police received word from the embassy in Syria confirming the worst yesterday. I am sorry to be bringing such bad news."

"No, you are wrong. It cannot be."

Jamal knew he had to be honest and forthright or Yusef would not hear his words. He could not mince them with any ambiguity.

"Yusef, al-Shabaab recruited him from the playgrounds of our own community. You know that happens. They became his family because you wouldn't fill that role for him. Why is it that no one who embraces our new country is Somali enough for you? You did not let your son succeed here. Is it any wonder he found someone else to show him love and respect and to be his mentor? All the things a father should be doing. Then they filled his head full of Jihad and virgins. They filled him with hate. When they had him in their grasp, they sent him to Syria to be a terrorist – and now he is dead. You know this in your heart as I tell you."

Yusef rose from his chair shouting, "Omar would never do such a thing!" Tears were welling in his eyes. He struggled to hold them back. "I do not believe you. None of you are good Somalis, Jamal." He grabbed Jamal by the arms and shook him while pushing him towards the door. "You all have to be so American. You and boys like Omar turned your backs on your heritage. Shame on you. Now leave."

Jamal heard Hodan's wails of grief as he was pushed out the door. He hated the man Yusef had turned into. Omar never had a chance.

Chapter 8

FBI Headquarters
Washington, D.C.

"Thanks for coming so quickly," Gloria said as she hugged Jon. "You must have caught the direct flight."

"You know I don't like running through airports catching that last minute flight, but anything for you. Tony is pissed I took off. Screw him. Rick says hi though." Jon looked her over. Gloria's dress code reminded him of a cross between a hipster librarian, an English Literature professor, and Diane Keaton's character in Annie Hall. He knew she loved her brightly colored scarves and glass bead eyeglass chains that somehow always complemented her otherwise drably colored outfits. That must be where the hipster vibe came in. Either that or she was a reformed hippie. Her milky gray hair was cut in a wavy bob; the soft bangs, rumpled texture, and imperfect ends gave her an aura of pure class. It had been a long time and it felt great to see a familiar face. Jon knew a lot of people in Washington, D.C., so finding a familiar face here was not that difficult; however, finding that familiar face and knowing it would never stab you in the back was uncommon. So it felt great to see her.

Gloria stepped back. He noticed the lines on her face had grown more pronounced and her face did not have the rosy glow he remembered. "Gloria, I hope you don't mind me saying this but you look like you've seen a ghost."

"Not a ghost per se, but close enough. That's why you are here. Let me explain." Gloria walked Jon back to her desk and opened up a series of files, photographs, and charts to show Jon. "Remember how we caught those hackers back in the Twin Cities? That was one tough nut to crack."

"If I remember correctly, you said it was so hard because there was no defined signature to the code," replied Jon.

"Look at that. You remember. I'm impressed." Gloria quietly chuckled while suppressing a smile. "It wasn't so much that there was no defined signature, rather the signature seemed to float all over the place. I couldn't put my finger on it until I realized the floating itself was the signature. It was a sort of algorithm that randomized itself."

Gloria stopped for a moment before she continued. "We've seen a lot of that from the Chinese lately."

"The Chinese?"

"Exactly. You may not realize this, but the Chinese Security Services have ramped up their cyber espionage divisions tremendously over the last decade or so. We view them as the number one government backed threat to the United States today."

"I'm not sure I'm following you."

"Look at it this way. Say someone wants to break into a computer system. You need people that can spend a lot of time doing brute force hacks like Denial of Service." Jon was confused and interrupted her, asking, "What's that?" Gloria was taken aback, but only momentarily. "Sorry, Jon. I guess this is a lot. Denial of Service is when someone sends thousands or even millions of requests during a short period of time directed to one website or other network connected resource. The server or servers hosting the website can't handle it and no one can access the site. The hackers have denied others the service the website or resource provides. You can also write malware and other malicious things to negatively affect those systems. That takes time. We are not talking about 'script kiddies' here Jon. Time and people. That means money. With the 'do more with less' mentality businesses have these days, no 'for profit' organization has the amount of overhead available to expend on this. In fact, most criminal organizations have dropped out of this altogether. There are some still out there, but there just isn't the volume of business per se to fund all the resources."

"Are you saying that foreign governments and most specifically the Chinese, are funding cyber 'attacks' on businesses here in the U.S.?"

"Now you're beginning to understand."

"But to what end? Don't the Chinese have enough money in their pseudo-capitalist companies over there to just buy out companies here? Seems to me that would be the most straight-forward way to have a controlling interest in the U.S. economy."

"True, but what if it isn't just a 'controlling interest' as you say, that they are after. What if we are talking about a new type of warfare? I'm not talking the type of economic warfare that we engaged in during the Cold War. Outspend the enemy to make them keep up with the Jones' thereby crippling their domestic economy. I'm taking about real destruction here. The work we are doing here is designed to not let that happen."

"Gloria, you have my undivided attention. Believe me, you do. I just don't understand why you need my help. This doesn't sound like terrorism and it doesn't sound like something that is taking place lakeside in Minnesota."

"That's where I believe you are 100% wrong Jon. And that's what scares me the most."

Years ago

Minnesota has long had economic ties with China – the world's most populous nation. China is the state's second-biggest trading partner with Minnesota firms exporting over $2 billion worth of goods and services. Those ties trace back to James J. Hill, the 19th-century railroad magnate from St. Paul who built the Great Northern Railway to the West Coast as a way to spark trade opportunities with China. China's business culture is one that values relationships. The longer the relationship, the better. Minnesota's long history there gives the state an edge. As China's 17th biggest trading partner, trade missions from state government agencies or corporate firms are received with fanfare and high expectations on both sides. The last five Minnesota governors led trade missions to China in hopes of cementing connections between current and prospective business partners.

Many of the Minnesota connections with Chinese businessmen began as student exchanges. The University of Minnesota, the state's premier university, has an estimated 8,000 Chinese alumni, dating over 100 years. Zhang Xe, who studied in the United States at Stanford and MIT, took advantage of this. During one trade mission, he – as Chen Li, a Chinese businessman looking for business with Minnesota firms – sponsored numerous Chinese students. Many of these were accepted into the University of Minnesota. One student was Bei "Sam" Liping. Sam was a member of Zhang Xe's spy network. He would go to Minnesota to study computer science. Sam's directives were two fold. Create a large network of people, who would be successful in the U.S. or abroad, and cultivate contacts or spies who could broaden Zhang Xe's reach. How he did this was up to him. It simply needed to work.

Chen Li's attendance at these trade missions gave him insight into how to work with state governments and Non-Government Agencies or NGOs. He used this to set up several small businesses as a trial balloon. Several failed miserably; however, their failures provided the framework for what would become his most successful operation in Minnesota. Success was defined in many ways; profit was not always one of these.

Present Day

Jon walked out of Tony's office and over to Rick's desk. He sat on the edge of Rick's desk and waited for him to acknowledge his presence. He waited for a couple of minutes while Rick's face never left his monitor. Jon knew Rick wasn't aware of his presence so he thought he'd open with something guaranteed to get his attention.

"Gloria says hi. She wanted to know if you've managed to sway any girl into marrying you yet."

Rick never even looked up from his monitor. "Like she should be questioning me? Does she even date yet?" Rick's eyes looked like saucers as he made a face during his retort. "Gotta love her. She can be little Miss Works all the time. But us guys? No, we're supposed to find us a missus, get all settled down, and start pumping out kiddies. Enough of that. I thought you were going to spend a couple of days chasing bad guys down from her computer like Call of Duty. Why are you back anyway?"

"Had to. The news Gloria provided was for action – here."

"What?" Rick's head snapped up and looked directly at Jon.

"She found a connection between Chinese cyber-espionage and the anti-terrorism work we are doing here."

"You don't say. Read me in."

"I just finished getting the boss up to speed so now it's your turn. Gloria's team has been hearing a lot of chatter in the geek world about something called a DoomsDay RAT. RAT standing for Remote Access Trojan. RATs have been around for a while and the cyber guys and gals are generally on top of them but this one is different."

"How's that?"

"Evidently, it's isn't so much the RAT itself but the end game. What happens if a company or industry was so large that failure of that company or industry would cripple the economy of a country?"

"Like the automotive, banking, and mortgage industries? The government had to spend billions to bail them out and we still had a major recession."

"Close. Those were in essence self-inflicted problems. What if someone purposefully caused the next super failure to occur?"

"OK, now I see where you are going with that. But why would they want to do that?"

"Nearest the NCIJTF can figure out is that a foreign government has found a new way to wage war."

"Whew." Rick let out a long breath. "That is not good. That is definitely not good. So cyber espionage has moved into cyber-terrorism/cyber-war? Is that our connection? I'm not seeing where we fit in?"

"Gloria says everything points here. The question is what is it we have here in Minnesota that could affect the nation's economy?"

Chapter 9

Jon lay back on his teak wood chaise lounge and looked over the skyline of downtown Minneapolis. His loft condominium in the North Loop neighborhood offered a fantastic view. This was the one indulgence he allowed himself. After his parents passed, he and his siblings inherited the mineral rights from the family land holdings. Oil companies drilled years ago and the money seemingly never stopped flowing. Approximately three times larger than the nicest quarters the Army provided him, his residence was nonetheless the smallest on the penthouse level. For Jon, the loft itself was more than adequately sized. The real selling feature was the rooftop cabana. That's where he was now. One of four cabanas on the rooftop, his corner unit could be enclosed with glass siding and heated in the winter. It offered views of Target Field, home of the Minnesota Twins, as well as the high rises on both sides of the Mississippi River. He often took the spiral black iron staircase from his living room to this perch to relax after a hard day's work. Luckily for him, the fellow penthouse neighbors generally sought their refuge elsewhere providing him with the solitude he desired.

His trip to Washington D.C. and back had thoroughly exhausted him. Originally, he thought he would spend several days there and be able to unwind walking through the monuments of the National

Mall during the late evening hours. Gazing upon the fountains of the WWII Memorial, with the reflecting pool and the Lincoln Memorial providing the backdrop, was an exquisite way to relax and unwind; however, after hearing what Gloria had to say, he knew he needed to return quicker.

The ice cubes in his drink clinked softly against the crystal glass. His drink of choice was a bourbon Manhattan. This was a new choice of alcohol for him starting three years ago. Prior to that he was strictly a beer guy. Grain alcohol had bothered him a great deal in college and besides, he wanted to enjoy the taste of his drink. Spirits were too strong, a bottle was too expensive to experiment with, and no one had taught him the finer points of mixology. Beer on the other hand was easy. A six-pack of quality beer was at most $12.00.

The craft beer craze had taken the Twin Cities of Minneapolis and St. Paul by storm. Home to some of the major micro-breweries in America, the metro area was also the location for 50 additional breweries, tap rooms, and micro-breweries. He could see several of them from his perch. Not satisfied to brew the best pilsners, lagers, and ales, these new brew masters made beer out of just about anything. For Jon, this was the heart of the problem with beer today. Just because you could use chocolate and pumpkin to make beer did not necessarily mean you should. Also the push for highly bitter beers confounded him. He always associated bitter beer with bad or "skunky" beer. He even remembered commercials from the 80's that touted a respite from "bitter beer face." Hence, bitter was bad.

Bourbon though, for the most part, had remained unchanged. True, there were many more distilleries these days and they were starting to add flavors such as honey and cinnamon. But that made it a bourbon infused flavored whiskey. Jon didn't bother with any of those though. He stayed mostly with Maker's Mark out of Kentucky. He was not one of those puritanical bourbon drinkers though and also enjoyed a whiskey from Tennessee called Jack Daniel's. The charcoal mellowing through sugar maple charcoal changed it from a bourbon into a Tennessee Whiskey. It was smooth and close enough for Jon.

During one business trip, Jon found himself at the hotel bar ordering food. Tired of having the same basic fare he asked the bar patron next to him what drink he was having. It was in a martini glass but was an amber colored liquid. Certainly not a martini. The gentlemen responded it was a Manhattan. Something clicked in Jon's mind. Wasn't that the drink his father enjoyed? Jon ordered one. Finding out it was made with Maker's Mark, he was determined to discuss this with his father the next time they were together.

Several months later, Jon was at his parent's retirement home at the base of the Appalachians in Northern Alabama. He asked his father about the Manhattan, telling him about his experience at the hotel. Grinning, his father sauntered to the pantry, pulled out the ingredients, and said, "About time you drank a man's drink son."

"Thanks, I guess," responded Jon. "How do you make them?"

"Two ice cubes, two Maraschino cherries, a dash of bitters, one shot vermouth, sweet not dry, and two shots of bourbon. Eat one of the cherries to cleanse your palate, sip for an hour or so, and then eat the second to finish the drink off."

Henry Wells died three months later of cancer. Jon now rarely drank anything else.

As he sipped his drink his mind shifted from his father back to what Gloria had shared with him.

What do we have in Minnesota that could affect the nation's economy if it were crippled? Mining? Not anymore. Back in the day the iron ore mines up north provided all the iron for the steel mills in the rust belt, but not anymore. They were shells of their former selves. Banking? I know we have a lot of those here. Regional center, even a few headquarters. That could be it. What else? Food? Minneapolis used to be the flour milling capital but once again, not so much anymore. We do, however, have several corporate headquarters for food and agri-business companies. Those can go on this list for now too. Not far removed from banking is the insurance industry. We have a couple headquarters for those as well. In fact, one of them is the largest medical re-insurer in the country, I think. Anything else? We have a lot of hospitals, medical type companies, and of course the university and all its research. What about the airport? It is a major hub.

Jon placed his snifter on the end table and opened the book resting on his lap. He often went to the new city library downtown. It was a beautiful building, designed by award winning Cesar Pelli. The archivist provided him with numerous volumes of drawings and maps detailing how the city was built over the past 160 years. Jon was a historian and cartographer by nature. His major in college was American History with a minor in geographic information science.

This hobby proved beneficial over the years by giving him an in depth knowledge of municipalities not even known by most inhabitants. This particular tome followed journalist Walter W. Liggett's career and still unsolved murder after exposing corruption in the Minneapolis City government during the 1920's and 30's.

Three pages in, his eyelids drooped. Surprisingly, he fell asleep. The nightmares mercifully left him alone.

Athletic practice fields

"Dom. How are you? I haven't seen you around for a while. Been burning the midnight oil so to speak? Your boy is really getting a feel for face-offs. With all the new rules, the face-off in lacrosse is more important than ever. If they don't change the rules, the face-off man will be the most important person on the team. Remember how Notre Dame kept Duke from ever touching the ball for almost an entire game last year. Personally, I thought it was awful. But hey, the powers that be are the powers that be." It had been a long time since Jon had slept so well. He felt invigorated. His motor ran full-throttle all morning.

Dom didn't respond. He just stared seemingly into space.

"Earth to Dom. Hey, everything ok?" Jon had never seen Dom act like this.

Dominic Seragosa was the father of one of the lacrosse players for the high school team Jon helped. Jon couldn't count on his schedule to let him be available on a consistent basis so he assisted when he could. Jon played in college at Cornell after being cajoled by his fraternity brothers to try out. He had won letters in three sports in high school but had never even seen lacrosse before. He brought pure athletic energy to the field, mastered sticks skills, and played on the varsity squad his last three years. His knowledge and experience playing at a high level were more than the coaches had so they welcomed any help he could provide. Besides, it was good to have a law enforcement type around for the kids to emulate.

Young Mike Seragosa started playing lacrosse last year after his friends finally convinced him it was more exciting than baseball and still allowed physical play like his favorite sport – football.

Unfortunately for Mike, he was not big enough to play football coming in at only 5' 3". With his dad standing a mere 5'5" and no one on his mom's side within several inches of six feet, Mike figured he would never be big enough to not spend more time healing than playing. After years of trying to enjoy baseball, he realized it was boring. Mike had lighting quick reflexes, was strong as an ox, and could out run most lacrosse players – perfect for a face-off specialist. Jon had been working with him during lacrosse camps like this one and expected him to play in every varsity game as a sophomore.

Mike and his dad had one of those great relationships. The last few weeks though, his dad's work seemed to engulf him. While he was physically here for most practices and every scrimmage during summer camps, his face was more often than not stuck looking into his mobile devices. Gone were the shouts of encouragement. As a result, Mike's play on the field was beginning to reflect his father's lack of attention off the field.

"What – oh. Yeah, I guess," Dom finally replied. "How is work going yourself? You're with the FBI right?

"Special Agent with counter terrorism downtown. Why? Is there something I need to know about?"

Chapter 10

2005
Berlin, Germany

Prior to any summit, the Chinese Security Services carried out exhaustive background checks on all scheduled attendees. The purpose of this was to find any weakness they could potentially exploit in order to achieve better results during negotiations. This conference was no different. Several potential targets had been identified. The most promising was a mid-level engineer on the German Trade Board as an expert consultant. Andreas Braun, from Stuttgart, Germany, was a troubled man. He was no longer rising through the ranks of civil service as fast as he had during his early years. Several peers had passed him by, which exasperated his status-seeking wife. Looking at it from the outside, this was to be expected. Katja hailed from the Ore Mountain Mining Region of Freiberg, in old East Germany. An "Ostie," referring to those Germans who grew up in the old East Germany, she harbored deep-seated insecurities and required her husband to lavish her with only the finest of everything. Andreas simply could not keep up with it any longer.

Andreas, from the Ruhr Valley, met his wife at university. She was one of the first "Ostie" to matriculate in the Ruhr Universitat. She was failing as a second year student. Soon to be sent home she opted instead for a time honored plan B – marry an aspiring upper-classman. All went according to plan. She met Andreas and within a year they married and moved to Koln. Parties and a flourishing art scene; a renewal on life for her. Andreas was not home much. He worked long hours and was remunerated for his efforts with promotions and raises. Andreas, who was older than Katja by five years, due to his service in the Bundeswehr, wanted children. Katja was too busy to be bothered with additional responsibilities outside of her parties and the work she found volunteering at the many museums in the area. Children ultimately arrived, but only after another woman commented on how the firm Andreas worked with valued the commitment of family. The old guard in charge evidently felt workers with families to support were more loyal to their employer. Those were the people they promoted to higher levels. Within three years, Andreas and Katja welcomed two young children. But Andreas was not promoted as Katja had counted on.

She berated him unceasingly for his lack of value to the family. Why hadn't he been promoted and sent to Berlin? After all, that is where all the important people were now. Instead, he was transferred to Stuttgart. She almost didn't move with him. Once again, he begged for her to at least follow and put forth a proper public face so he could attempt to turn things around. She came. While they shared a bedroom still, they shared no affection, emotional or physical. She hired a nanny to look after the children, put them in expensive schools, and spent even more lavishly, sending their finances into a deep tailspin Andreas could not pull out of. During a meeting one day at work, one of Andreas' friends mentioned the government was looking for a consultant with Andreas' skills to be an advisor in an upcoming economic summit with the Chinese. He could pull some strings and get Andreas assigned. It could lead to a better job. A transfer to China was not completely out of the question. That should help financially and who knows, maybe even in the bedroom. Andreas agreed without a second thought.

Soon he found himself in Berlin preparing for the summit. Spouses were brought only for a weekend. They were sent home after a large bash at the Grand Hyatt in Potsdamer Platz near the delegation's pre-summit headquarters. Katja was in heaven – mingling, positioning herself within the government jet-set, and partying. Katja made it abundantly clear there would be no sex during her stay. Each of the three nights she spent in Berlin she passed out from alcohol and exhaustion, sleeping till noon. Before she left, she informed Andreas he had better not screw this opportunity up. She already knew where she wanted to live when they moved here. Then she and the rest of the spouses boarded buses and went back to their respective homes. It was time to work. It was expected that the work would take everyone's time. No interruptions were allowed. For the next eight weeks Andreas felt better than he had in years. Great work, great colleagues, and much to his surprise, great sex with the prostitutes who made Berlin famous for its excesses. Two months later, the German delegation moved to the Hotel Adlon in central or Mitte Berlin.

Hotel Adlon was the epitome of luxury and the site of numerous royal visits during the twenties and thirties. The hotel is located on Unter Den Linden on the south-eastern corner of Pariser Platz by the Brandenberg Gate. The Mitte district, situated in old East Berlin, houses much of what present day tourists flock to see when visiting Berlin. Seen as a den of capitalist and then Nazi extravagance, the East German government, with the consent of their Soviet overlords, left this area to rot, post WWII. They preferred to spend their money on the Soviet styled "wedding cake buildings" lining Karl-Marx Alle further to the east, across the River Spree, and beginning at Alexanderplatz. The hotel, which had almost completely been destroyed in the final days of WWII, operated only a small wing through 1984.

When the wall came down, money flowed from the coffers of the new German government for reconstruction – especially in Mitte Berlin. It was said, not so jokingly, that the city bird in the 1990's and early 2000's was the crane – given all the cranes used to rebuild the city core. Hotel Adlon was the beneficiary of the largesse of monies as it received funding to completely rebuild in the style of the original.

Still viewed as one of the most luxurious hotels in Europe, it hosts a wide variety of government, research, and corporate meetings. The Sino-Germanic Economic Summit exemplified these gatherings. Designed to increase German presence in Chinese automobile, aerospace, and heavy manufacturing, numerous executives and government leaders were in attendance. Chen Li was one of the attendees. He was the CEO of China's premier computer security firm. He was well connected globally in the IT industry. His network stemmed from schooling in the U.S. and working at dot-coms. Chen was not a vocal player in the negotiation room, leaving that to the politicians. Instead, he worked the hallways, bars, and restaurants in between and after sessions with the real decision makers – the advisors.

When powerful men gathered for intense negotiations, the built-up stress needed a release. Berlin was living up to its old reputation as a place where anything could be obtained. All you needed were connections and money. It was truly remarkable what liquor, drugs, and women would do to otherwise stable men. The job the "advisors" had was to do all the research and ferret out information "behind the scenes." They felt they did all the work but received none of the glory. They were easy pickings. Working women were available at any time. Several of these were operatives of the Chinese Security Service and they were directed to "assist" those identified by Chen. Andreas was one of these.

Each evening after negotiations a mixer was thrown. It was here Andreas first saw her. She approached. The slit of her dress rose almost to the bottom of her inner thigh. The sequins on the red dress accentuated her dark skin and hair. Not overly voluptuous, she nonetheless more than adequately filled out what constituted the top half of the dress. Open to the navel, the two front oblique triangles of fabric tapered to simple black straps which joined together behind her neck with only a clasp. When she turned, her back was uncovered to the mid-portion of her behind. Her body and dress exuded sensuality. But it was her eyes, slightly almond shaped, dark and yearning, and her mouth that sent Andreas over the top. He had to have her. She looked at him while placing a cherry from her drink between her partially opened lips. Walking up to him, she deftly grabbed his tie, turned, and allowed the tie to slip between her hands as she sashayed down the hallway. He followed her like a puppy dog would its owner.

He woke up with a headache. He couldn't move his arms or legs. His eyes, when he finally was able to open them, had difficulty focusing. He thrashed in a vain attempt to free himself from the binds that held him. He felt someone approaching. Then a sharp pain in his arm, followed by the most soothing sensation he ever knew. Warmth fully enveloped his entire being and then he passed out. Suddenly his eyes burned from the intense light. His head felt as if it would explode. He was grabbed by several strong hands while his binds were removed. The effect of the lights faded and he was soon able to open his eyes and focus on the assembled people in the room.

"Hello. You've been a bad boy," said the man's voice. "Please, watch the monitor and see just how bad you've been." The television monitor was on and he saw a video of several men and women in S&M gear on a bed. The man on the bed was engaged in sexual relations with one man and several women. It appeared all of them were spent. Several moved, revealing the man in the binds... *"Oh my God, that's me!"* realized Andreas.

"You will tell us what we need to know and provide your delegation what we want you to tell them or this will be released. Your career will be over. Your family, well you know what will happen there. You may never get another job again. This was, after all, your last chance anyway wasn't it?" continued the man. Andreas could not see him, but he certainly felt the icy stare emanating from the direction of the voice. "You will be paid, of course. We can't have you lose your job because your debts get in the way after all. You will work for us, and we'll see you get your promotions. We got you this far after all, didn't we? Do you now understand the reach we have?" All Andreas could do was shake his head. He understood the situation. It was the classic honey pot scenario the Bundeswehr was so afraid of and warned all its personnel about during the Cold War.

He remembered his training from all those years ago. Escape if you can and report it. If you can't, play it through and then report. Once reported, the opportunity existed to potentially turn the situation around. But it must be reported.

He was allowed to dress. The man limped out from behind the shadows, handed him 10,000 Euros, and made him sign paperwork acknowledging receipt of the funds. "Don't worry about your debts, they will be taken care of in time. Who knows, your wife might even sleep with you again. You will receive instructions this evening on what we need. You will provide it or…why don't we not bother having to go down that road?" Andreas nodded his agreement, put the wad of Euros in the breast pocket of his blazer, and waited to be released. It appeared they were going to release him after all.

The door opened and the light of the setting sun filled the hallway. He recognized where he was, back in the Grand Hyatt. He and the Chinese man with a limp were the only ones left in the room. The other people in the room left earlier to attend to "others." He assumed he was not the only mark they had. Now was his chance. He needed only to disable the man, grab the tape, and slip away.

The man followed as he entered the hallway. Suddenly, Andreas planted his right foot, rotating 180 degrees on the ball of his foot, and thrust forward with his left leg. His hips moved forward as the heel of his right hand arced forward. The thrust generated by this movement was directed completely on the man's chin knocking him out. Andreas, jumped over the body to the video recorder. He fumbled with the buttons, knocking the tripod it was still attached to over. Shit. He dropped down yanking the device off the floor. Finally, it opened and presented the 8mm video tape. He grabbed the tape and felt the man stirring behind him. Andreas, a footballer in his youth, connected with the man's head again. This time with his dominant leg. There was not enough room to get a full kick in but nonetheless the man didn't move again.

Andreas ran out the door, turned right, and ran. Another Chinese man opened a door and stepped into the hallway after hearing the commotion in the next room. Andreas dropped his shoulder, ran though the man, and continued down the hall. Seeing the stairway, he leapt down stairs three at a time until he exited at street level. Before the door closed he heard footfalls hurriedly following him.

The last vestiges of the sun's rays were now obscured by the tall buildings. He turned to the north heading across Potsdamer Strasse and into the crowds under the 48 individual white membrane panels of the oval roof covering the Sony Center. The dinner crowd was not out yet, too early for that, but the tourist crowd was returning in full force from a day of sightseeing. He could lose them here. Just then, a hand grabbed his jacket and pulled. Andreas felt his left arm free itself and fall from his blazer. He twisted violently to the left. Suddenly he was free again – blazer and all. He side-stepped several empty tables sending chairs flying as he skirted the fountain and headed for the north exit between several of the buildings which made up the center.

Traffic on Bellevuestrasse was surprisingly light and he made it to the small but open area known as Henriette-Herz Park. The Tiergarten was just across the Lennestrasse to the north. The Hotel Adlon was on the eastern edge just past the Brandenburg Gate. If he could just get into the Tiergarten and run the paths he could make it. He could report this mess he was in. He caught movement to the right and slightly behind him. Men running in suits. Not good. Shit. They would block his path to the east. Traffic on Lennestrasse was jammed with tour buses. He danced in front of one and kept running without looking, praying no vehicles would suddenly appear in the next lane. None did and the tree canopy of the Tiergarten soon enveloped him. He heard horns blaring and shouts of people upset with the men jumping on their cars in an effort to reduce the distance Andreas had on them. It was working. The gap was closing.

Andreas saw a bike next to a tree up ahead. Someone was lying on the grass close by. He altered course and without slowing much grabbed the handlebars. Pray God the bike was not locked. It wasn't and he swiftly jumped on. No other bikes were close by. He had done it. Minutes later his legs burned from the muscle fatigue. He was in great shape for a man his age, he just didn't ride bikes much. That and he was currently riding, not on a path, but on the grass heading due north. If he could get to the main east west road quickly he might be able to turn and head directly to the hotel. They might be too close though. An option would be to ride all the way to the new Hauptbahnhof and catch a train – any train. He didn't know if there were any other U- or S-Bahn stations closer.

Andreas found himself back on a bike path near the Goldfish pond. Unfortunately, the park was now filling with evening strollers, so the path actually slowed him down and back on the grass he went. Nonetheless, he still found himself swerving at the last second to avoid people lying on the ground doing God knew what in the cover of the darkness that was this part of the Tiergarten. There, up ahead, the cars on Strasse des 17 Juni. Finally, almost there. A tree branch suddenly exploded to his left. "Sffft!" the sounds of a projectile whizzed past his head. *"Shit, they're shooting at me now."* Another path intersected up ahead next to the road. Andreas shifted his weight and made a high-speed right hand turn. Five more pedals and then he shifted his weight to make a hard left-hand turn. He shot out between two buses, braked hard, just missing a sedan. He continued across the remainder of the road, barely missed several more cars before hitting the back fender of one. He recovered, increasing speed to jump the curb, and propelled himself across the sidewalk. He passed the tanks flanking the west entrance to the Soviet War Memorial. *"I can lose them here,"* he thought. Swerving left into the memorial grounds he neglected to see the granite steps until it was almost too late. Andreas attempted to jump up the four granite steps. Instead, as he pulled hard on the handlebars and raised his body off the seat, he felt an excruciating pain in his right shoulder. He lost grip with his right hand causing the wheel to turn perpendicular to the steps. The result was Andreas flying up and forward. His left arm extended to protect his head. Years ago he would have tucked in his head and somersaulted onto his feet and continued running. But he was no longer a teenager and all he managed to do was dislocate two fingers on the uneven granite pavers of the memorial. He had to get up. The pain was all absorbing. He heard footsteps and shouting. Someone grabbed him. He let it happen. When he heard the question in German coming from the would be rescuer, he opened his eyes. No Chinese. He turned around. There they were. Kept at bay on the other side of the road by the now busy and fast moving traffic.

"Thank you. I'm fine," he managed to say before stumbling off through the columns and out the back side of the memorial. He could not fix his dislocated fingers since his right hand was immobile due to the gunshot wound. His head hurt and was bleeding somewhat from the hard landing. He stumbled across a less trafficked road and into the open space in front of the Reichstag Building. The plaza was filled with tourists queued for entry to the glass dome of the building. It was the number one tourist destination in Berlin. Andreas was up there just last week. The view was incredible, especially at night. Without that excursion he would not have known where to run. This was his first visit to Berlin. *"Would it be his last?"* He made it through the queues of people and into the colored water fountains in between the Chancellery building and the Parliament offices. Too many Federal police here. *"Certainly they won't shoot me here."* Andreas looked but didn't see any police to talk to though. *"Shit. Probably watching on cameras. Probably think I'm just drunk. No help coming."*

Ahead, the large glass encased facade of the Berlin Hauptbahnhof appeared. Andreas knew the River Spree was now his only barrier to freedom. *"That's funny,"* he thought. *"People died swimming across with that same thought only sixteen short years ago."* The pedestrian walkway across the river made his journey safer. The nightly summer fireworks started over the river and the masses assembled here oohed and ahhed. He was half-way across the river when he felt a sharp pain in his lower back and then another from his stomach. He looked down. The flickering multi-colored lights dancing above provided only enough light to see something was not right. That and the dizziness coming over him. His stumble turned into a forced shuffle. Andreas made it to the edge, tottering before finally plummeting into the river below. All eyes around him were looking up except those chasing him. No one saw him fall. His body turned up the next day downstream next to one of the many riverside cafes.

Chen Li's head still hurt from the attack when his team reported the events of the evening. He just shook his head. All Andreas had to do was comply. He would actually have been better off working for Chen. He was not the only target and the gluttony they caught on tape in all forms paid great dividends. All the others he revealed the tapes to grabbed at the offer. They provided new advice more favorable to the Chinese and information for the price of silence.

While slanted to favor the Chinese, the negotiations brought many financial benefits to both countries. The Germans made money by being allowed to participate in the largest automobile market in the world. They also were placed in a "preferred status" for contracts in aerospace and heavy industry. A "concession" the Germans agreed to was the creation of a Sino-German joint venture rather than simply exporting or being able to set up German subsidiary companies. The Chinese, then, were able to bypass a large part of the manufacturing learning curve as they now had complete access to manufacturing designs and other data. Most of the information flow stemmed from the structure of the joint venture and was viewed as "above the board" growth. However, the Chinese learned even more from other methods. Additionally, the Chinese had also "negotiated" handling all IT security for the joint venture.

Chapter 11

Present Day
HyDek Data Center Complex

Dominic's mind was racing. On his desk were reams of printouts. He had spent the better part of the past week trying to determine why no security alarms had gone off. There had been an intrusion. Of that he was sure. But why no alarm?

The intrusion was so infinitesimal that he was actually surprised he caught it. He was never the smartest of technicians, but he read journals copiously and learned much on his own. The information Abdi shared certainly was worth the time spent digging in. His strength lay in putting all the pieces together and seeing the bigger picture. That, more than anything, accounted for his rise within the company.

He left his cubicle looking out over the operations center section of the data center and began making his rounds. He did this at least one time every shift, preferably at the beginning. While he was "connected" via computers and video screens to everything, he nonetheless felt more comfortable walking around. He did some of his best thinking and troubleshooting during these 'walkabouts' as he called them.

The ops center looked somewhat like the Johnson Space Center – only significantly cooler. Thirty 150 inch screens were assembled in a 50-degree arc and towered over the four rows of operators. The monitors gave off a lot of heat meaning the air conditioning was for them – not the humans. Each operator had an additional set of four monitors and were connected to each other through a series of headsets, cameras, and locator devices. The floor descended in a 15-degree slope providing everyone with an unobstructed view of the large monitors and floor. Dom checked on several operators asking how the shift was going. Satisfied that all was well, he continued his rounds.

Offices used by client representatives, with individual heat and cooling controls, were located behind him. Only a few of these were occupied. Dom knocked on the door of one of these.

"Hey, how is it going?"

"Not bad. No issues today," replied the woman who looked up from her laptop.

She was relatively new here and Dom wanted to make sure she felt welcome. Too often these client representatives felt like outsiders even though their servers were the sole purpose of the complex. Posturing and finger pointing could lead to high turnover within his staff. Dom felt his communication skills with the client reps had an impact on reducing client complaints. Unfortunately, he still had to work on the overall staff turnover rate which was still too high. And Abdi's recent anal attitude on security didn't help.

The main entryway, a breakroom, restrooms with lockers and showers, and a guard station with two security personnel completed the public facing section of the data center complex. A series of large windows allowed visitors to view the expanse of the operations center. The cool factor was high and management used it to their advantage. What no regular visitor was ever allowed to see was the actual server room. That one area occupied the majority of the remaining seventy percent of the building.

The server room was brightly lit. It was also extremely cold. You didn't work in this space without a coat, a hat that covered your ears, and gloves. There were over ten thousand servers, routers, and switches located in the space. All of which generated heat. Each server itself could burn the tissue off your hand if left uncooled. Ten thousand of them required a cooling system like no other. This was the reason the data center was located in the exurbs. The local city owned its own electrical power company, meaning the municipality controlled the charges. As an enticement to locate the 100 jobs in their city, the price charged to power the data center was basically negligible. Dom knew of studies where data centers saved $250,000 annually by raising the temperature of the server room by only two degrees. He brought that concept to the management team – once. *"Why could he improve the relationships between the client representatives and his staff and yet have nothing but failures when approaching the management team with suggestions for improving the technology aspects of his job?"* he thought.

Dom entered by opening the door with his key card and retinal scan of an eye randomly chosen by the security system. He then took several stairs to reach the raised server floor. The server floor was made of large tiles placed upon a network of girders that raised the height of the floor several feet. The space created by the raised floor housed all network and power cabling, provided tracks for conduits, and chilled water piping, while also being the principal passageway for conditioned cold air. With the infrastructure below him, the rest of the server farm was stark. A vision of white on the walls, floors, and ceiling broken only by the fifty longitudinal rows of black metal cases containing the actual servers.

Dom walked through the rows and used the cross-channel walkways that broke up the rows of servers providing easier access to individual cases. Seeing one of the software technicians working on the slide-out keyboard and monitor strategically located within a cluster of server racks, he made his way over to her. Bundled in an oversized hoodie, gloves with the finger tips cut off, green army type pants, probably purchased at the Army Navy Surplus store, and boots, she almost looked like a homeless person attempting to jack an ATM.

"Amber, what are you working on?"

Amber jumped and exclaimed "God Dom, you scared the shit out of me. You really have to be a bit louder. You can't just creep up on me like that!"

"Sorry. Jus doin' me walkabout." He tried on an awful Australian accent. "With your hoodie on I'm not surprised you didn't notice me. So what are you working on?"

"Just a security update that got called in for an immediate rollout. Everything is always 'needed ASAP.' Just for once I'd like to see a nice long, well-planned out release plan for this stuff. You know, when we just put out fires and jump from one hot button issue to the next we miss stuff. I've been telling Abdi for months about this. I'm getting tired of it."

"You have a point. But on the other hand, with all the black hats out there with nothing better to do than make our lives miserable, I suppose you should be happy that lovely people like you are highly coveted and therefore employed and cashing a paycheck – and a good one at that – every two weeks." Dom smiled until Amber reluctantly grunted and returned to her work. *"One more highly strung staff member placated for the moment,"* Dom thought.

HyDek sold its services to numerous companies, not all of whom were as ethical or as trusting as the others. Its clients included retail, financial, and manufacturing companies in the Twin Cities metro area. Periodically, a chain link fence almost reaching the ceiling with locking doors would surround a subset of servers. It didn't add much more security but the clients demanded it. The chain link fence disfigured the otherwise clean lines and sleekness of the space. It was the cheapest solution for additional security – and money saved was money earned.

Dom heard nothing except the quiet hum of the equipment and the occasional keying from Amber's keyboard. To an outsider it would be hard to think anything was wrong.

Passing through the main server area Dom proceeded to the chilled water and air conditioning plant. The plenums for the forced air could each hold a mid-sized Winnebago. The operators who watched over these systems were highly-specialized professionals and had their own control room. Dom waved at them through the window and chuckled as he saw them dutifully note the time he entered and left the area. *"Man,"* he thought, *"they are even more paranoid than I am."* True, failure of these systems would incapacitate the entire data center. Often, he thought the weak link would be something he had little or no control over.

His inspection of the interior of his realm now completed, Dom exited through one of the back doors. The process needed to exit these doors was the same routine of key card followed by retinal scan needed to enter the server room. Computerized logs noted the opening and closing of the door down to the second along with the identity of the person going through the access.

The backside of the data center was lit extremely well and security cameras were strategically placed and timed so that all areas were in view at all times in triplicate. A fence surrounded by fifty feet of sand, inspected every day, made up the interior security zone. A small tractor and disc turned over the sand every week to ensure that it was never compacted by footsteps. A grass covered berm kept prying eyes from seeing anything of the building from the area surrounding the site. A final fence, with signs warning of prison sentences for trespassing, formed the outer ring of security. There was no coiled razor wire on top of the fences thankfully; otherwise it would have appeared to be a prison.

Prison. That was indeed what most people working at the HyDek Data Center felt it was. But the clients loved it. Just looking at it made them feel their data was invulnerable. Sighing, Dom figured anything that kept him employed was fine with him. He continued his excursion around the rest of the building, returning to the ops floor after chatting with the security guards, with the knowledge that all was well.

Unknown to him, the logs never recorded his return.

Years ago
China

Chen Li's firms received a monopolistic share of the contracts to "harden" IT systems within the joint ventures. This allowed his team to steal secured intellectual property from the Germans. The successful syphoning emboldened Zhang's teams to broaden their efforts. One team, in particular, learned how to control computerized equipment in the Chinese factories without the knowledge of the manufacturing leadership.

The team showed how far it had come by effectively slowing the output of several lines. During the effort to control the computerized manufacturing devices, numerous machines seemingly "went wild" causing accidents and casualties. One plant, in fact, was rendered almost useless for a week by a fire caused by a series of machines that overheated. Zhang's team had remotely shut off its hydraulic cooling while sending feedback output to the control center signifying to the engineering staff that all was well. A simultaneous intrusion into the fire retardation system reduced its output by 75% which enabled the fire to grow almost out of control when finally, manually started. The team learned how to cover its tracks so successfully, the accident was blamed on the plant's lead engineer who was relieved of his duties, stripped of all personal finances and possessions, and then shot.

These intrusions had other effects that Zhang's team did not control nor expect. An "accident" in a manufacturing plant that slowed production was immediately reflected on the trading floors on the Shanghai Stock Exchange. The devaluation of the stock in the company affected by Zhang's cyber intrusion, in turn, often affected other stocks. Zhang's team had learned how to manipulate their own manufacturing and economic systems. It was now time to take that to the next level.

Present Day

Abdi's security updates were mostly legitimate. They followed security protocols and closed loopholes hackers used to gain access. He was good at his job. Embedded within some of the updates, however, were sub-routines that most hackers would be proud to call their own. The sub-routines were small snippets of code, generally written in Python, that were harmless on their own; however, Abdi wrote and installed hundreds of these over the previous two years. In doing so, he created an entire set of programs that, as a whole, became the nucleus of the hack of a lifetime.

The key to not being detected was in employee turnover – it was high. It was high because Abdi wanted it that way. He did this through a series of seemingly unrelated events that he controlled. As the data center's lead security officer, he identified security threats. He preached that people were the biggest threat to the data center's security. To back up these claims he often falsified security logs, placed malware on unsuspecting employee's laptops, and then found it with a "random" security sweep. His first targets were temporary employees from contracting agencies. He then went after key permanent employees. Each was called before a review board and swiftly fired.

Abdi argued that temporary employees should be on short-term contracts. Human Resources bought into this on the basis that a temporary employee would never feel as if they were actually full-time employees and could therefore never sue for benefits. Abdi also interfered with the new hiring process, by requiring lengthy background checks. The time it took to replace an employee mushroomed. This placed an enormous stress on the remaining employees. Many of these left for less stressful jobs – even those that paid less.

Retention was low, stress was high. Word got out. Not many technicians wanted to work there. Even when the pay rates went sky high, the pool of candidates willing to fill the outstanding positions was low. Those that made it through the gauntlet often left as soon as they could find alternate employment. The turnover rate forced changes within HR and with the recruiters. As a result, only a few people had an ongoing "corporate, historical knowledge" of how the data center worked. Abdi had created the perfect environment – all in the name of high security.

Chapter 12

Years ago
China

"Colonel Zhang, please take a seat." The voice came from across the table. Zhang recognized none of the men assembled here. It felt like he was on trial. He knew, in China, one could often be tried for something even without the knowledge that you had been accused. It was an unsettling part of his society. But one that he had used for his advantage in the past.

There was a "Central Committee" for almost everything in China. Every group that wielded any power had a "Central Committee" or other functionary decision-making body. *"Which 'Central Committee' was this?"* he thought.

"We have been watching your career for many years now, Colonel Zhang. Impressive. Your team's performance has been beneficial to many. The automotive industry thanks you. The workers and industries who supported the construction of the Three Gorges Dam thank you. The information your team has extracted from companies the world over has produced an unblemished string of unbelievable accomplishments."

Zhang's mind was racing. He had not been showered with such accolades in such a public setting as this – ever. Not that this meeting was particularly public. Zhang had been whisked from his work several days ago. He was blindfolded and placed in the back of a vehicle. He was not physically manhandled or anything like that. It was just "suggested to him" that he allow whatever was happening to happen. A series of train rides and transits via small-engine planes and another ride in a vehicle along what appeared to be a twisting road brought him to this location. For all he knew, he was in the same place he left. His internal bearings were so completely messed up.

Brought indoors, his blindfold was removed – as were his clothes. He was cavity searched, electronically swept, and examined via x-rays. Once those personal violations were completed, he was given a new set of clothes and led down a corridor. Reaching the end, the door automatically opened. Inside, he saw a large room, similar to a sound stage, with a frosted glass enclosed structure placed upon what appeared to Zhang to be dampers or springs. He knew what this was. It was an acoustically soundproofed room built to stop eavesdropping from electronics, satellite, thermographic, or any other electronic or human intelligence measures – aka ELINT and HUMINT. The discussion that followed, whatever it was, would be private to only those who were allowed into the room.

"Thank you for your words. They are not necessary. All that I do is for the people and country I serve."

"But, of course, they are Colonel. Or should I say – General. You have been promoted and will now report directly to this committee. Do you have questions?"

"Do I have any questions? Only a thousand," thought Zhang.

"Thank you. I am honored to serve at your pleasure as a General." Never one to shy away from a conflict Zhang added. "May I ask though, to whom am I reporting?"

Another voice responded, "We are the top economic and security advisors to the Premier, General Xe. That is why you now report directly to us. You have been given carte blanche over the past decade to do as you wish. Your actions will now, however, be driven directly by this group. We receive our instructions from the Premier, who as you know, receives guidance from "The Central

Committee." Your work is integral to the continued success of the Chinese economy.

"I see."

"But do you? We have brought the dragon out of its cave and its strength is recognized the world over, so to speak. In the past, the next viable step after years of strengthening our position would be the total destruction of our enemies. This was always done to ensure the continued success of our country. Many would choose to continue this path; however, the world is no longer made up of individual countries. Can't you see? The economies of the largest countries in the world are completely intertwined with other large countries. Our most recent growth was due to providing services for the rest of the world. We are dependent on their wants, needs, and desires. Our economy grew with money flowing in from the rest of the world. We must proceed carefully. Our goals of dominance can be achieved, but the timing is one that must be chosen carefully. It will be at a time we choose. You will not execute the endgame without our authorization. To do so now, would break us – along with the United States. This cannot be allowed to happen. You are to initiate Program Golden Peacock but nothing else."

Zhang was stunned. *"How did they know of Golden Peacock?"*

"Of course. You are correct. I shall continue to serve as directed, and only as directed." Zhang bowed slightly to each, showing his deference to their authority. He felt a hood placed over his head and a sharp pinch on the left side of his neck. Then nothing.

Chapter 13

Present Day

Abdi sat in his home office. Saturday mornings were always relaxing. He reached for the cappuccino he just brewed using his new automated espresso maker. He paid $2,500 for it and it was worth every penny. He raised his cup to the window and saluted the sludge he endured at work every day. His laptop finished its security sweep, beeping completion. He opened a browser and navigated to Pinterest. He did not have an account but was still able to view everything. He did not want to risk being tracked via the registration demand that popped up on every page. So he wrote a script and installed it in his browser. The script made the browser skip all the overlays and pain-in-the-ass popups that ask for your registration. He searched on flower gardens in Minnesota and then searched for user UbaxHua, which are the words for flower in Somali and Chinese. To most, it simply looked like a weird username – and those were all too normal.

UbaxHua's interest was photos of corporate landscaping. If you looked at the profile close enough, the image was a stock photo, cropped and edited to look like a selfie. UbaxHua posted hundreds of examples of landscaping. UbaxHua and others in the community graded each poor, so-so, good, and great. The most recent post was the entryway to MnMedDev in St. Paul, Minnesota. Graded good by UbaxHua, the community weighed in with their thoughts. Posted only yesterday, 500 had already pinned it.

MnMedDev was the target.

Now Abdi could get to work.

Chapter 14

Several years ago

Chen Li and his entourage landed on runway 32L at Minneapolis-St. Paul International Airport after a week-long trip from China. The airport occupied the high ground to the north and west of the confluence of the Minnesota and Mississippi Rivers. Originally called Speedway Field, the airport was renamed Wold-Chamberlain Field, in honor of two local aviators lost in combat during World War I. In 1948 its current, more generic but geographically accurate name, replaced the Wold-Chamberlain name. They made stops in Honolulu and Los Angeles en route for other business prior to Minneapolis. After completing business here, they would make business related stops in London, Dubai, Chennai, and Singapore on the return leg of their around the world trip.

"Your speaking slot was moved to tomorrow afternoon at 1 p.m.," said his personal assistant. "How long will it take us to arrive at the hotel?" Chen asked. "My leg is sore. I need a massage and dinner when we arrive." He was in town for a major medical device conference being held at the Minneapolis Convention Center. He joined 200 other speakers who would give presentations during the three-day event. "I also need to see the slide deck before I retire."

He directed this last dictate to his technical advisor. He didn't need an advisor but he never designed or wrote out his presentations. That was for underlings. He would be speaking about increasing IT security awareness in a manufacturing environment.

Chen's company and its subsidiaries had "won" contracts to provide IT security to the majority of automobile manufacturing in China. With his background in dot-com IT security in the U.S. plus his "expertise" in the manufacturing sector, he was a sought after speaker at events such as this. Most events he spoke at brought in business with new clients. Breadth of clients across a wide spectrum of industries was the motivation for Chen to take these trips often lasting two and even three weeks.

"Who is setting up the reception for tomorrow night? It needs to be perfect. Has everyone accepted our invite?" His marketing team had set up a series of meet and greets with C-Suite executives from numerous firms in the Twin Cities and surrounding metro area. Minnesota, and most specifically the Twin Cities, was home to headquarters of numerous Fortune 500 companies with industries spanning mining, manufacturing, agribusiness, medicine and medical services, retail, and consumer foods. Wide breadth, single area. Exactly what Chen was looking for. Program Golden Peacock had a target.

Chen turned to his personal assistant, "You set aside time for my other activities also?" Without looking up from his tablet the man replied in the affirmative.

It didn't hurt that he already had spies in many of these organizations.

He looked forward to making many more trips here.

Chapter 15

Years ago

Abdi Ali was Adnan Ali's oldest son. He was twelve when his father forced him to come to America with the rest of the family. Before coming to America, he was heavily influenced by the Shafi'i School of Islamic Jurisprudence. Muslims who had lived in the Middle East and returned to their homeland in the 1980's brought this dogma with them and forced it upon the Somali Muslims. It was the time of the "Great Reawakening" and many in Somalia reinvested in their faith by conforming to Islamic dress code and outward manifestations of the faith. Those who didn't were ostracized and many cast out. Adnan Ali and his wife followed parts of the new doctrine, such as the Islamic dress code, but the strictness overwhelmed them. Both were happy to be given the opportunity to come to America and be free from the harshness of their land, the government, and the despots running their beautiful religion into the ground. He fought often with his eldest child, Abdi, who believed all of the new ways.

When Adnan gathered his family to flee Somalia, Abdi was the last to be found. Adnan searched for days. When his father found him, Ali screamed, "I do not want to live in the land of the Great Satan. I am a Somali. I am a Muslim – a devout Muslim. You are not a true believer!" Adnan beat Abdi mercilessly. He felt he did what was needed to give his son the best chance to grow into the man he wanted him to be. To do that he needed to get him to America – the land of dreams.

Abdi never submitted to his father's way of thinking. Living in America angered him then and angered him still more than twenty years later. He vowed revenge when his father beat him and dragged him to America. In Somalia, he enjoyed participating in theatre. Mostly because he could change his "character." This early art of "deception" came easily to him. Abdi knew he had this skill. To get this revenge it would be smoother sailing if he used his skills. Abdi never again let his father see past the character he created to ease his internal turmoil.

Adnan loved America – so Abdi's persona would love America too. Abdi would learn English better than anyone else who came over. He would shed his Muslim identity to the extent that he could. He would assimilate and blend in. He would become another part of the patchwork quilt that made up America. This ensured his "invisibility." Abdi "played the game" – he was the most non-Muslim Muslim around. The fact that it pained his father that his son turned his back on the Muslim faith greatly pleased Abdi.

Abdi knew of Jamal Kusow because of his mother. He let Jamal become his mentor. If Jamal did it, Abdi was certain to follow. While Jamal did business, Abdi excelled in computers. He almost got into trouble by hacking into the high school grade book to change the grades of some of his American "friends" but he was able to quickly cover his tracks. That episode showed him where his skills in IT lie.

Al-Shabaab began seeping into the community soon after it became apparent Minneapolis was the largest of the refugee placement centers. Abdi heard of them and sought them out. He did not need to be recruited per se. The leadership of al-Shabaab saw something unique in Abdi – that he fit in. Therefore, he was taught to further fit in and hide in plain sight as a "sleeper." His mentor, Jamal, never figured this out.

After high school and at Jamal's urging, Abdi continued his schooling at the University of Minnesota where he studied computer science. This opened an entirely new world to him, one in which he felt totally at ease. Of the 50,000 students enrolled in the university, over 3,500 were international, many from mainland China. With some 2,500 students and 500 professors and researchers from China, the University of Minnesota makes up one of the largest concentrations of Chinese academics in the United States. Abdi found his closest friends from this group of students.

Chapter 16

Several years ago

Every metropolitan area has gangs. That's a fact. Ethnic and immigrant gangs top the list. A different agenda for each. Drugs, prostitution, power, money. They feed off the disenfranchised, the uneducated, those who cannot or will not assimilate, and those who found themselves simply in the wrong place at the wrong time and never recovered. Minneapolis was no different.

The common thread with all gangs is money. Like a corporation, a gang needs money to feed itself. A gang that provides for its members is a gang that grows. Growth needs to be consistent. Leadership in the most successful gangs tracks growth much like the C-Suite in a corporation tracks its quarterly earnings. A downturn, even for one quarter, is bad. Therefore, revenue streams are scrutinized. Poor streams receive attention and are removed before becoming cancerous and avenues for new streams are constantly being examined. College education in business, entrepreneurship, and supply chain management permeated the highest levels of leadership in the most successful gangs.

"This building is perfect." It had been empty for the past decade. "I want a hand painted business sign with the letters MKL-U-MD placed on the outside. I chose the name because is reflects the

Somali word for information – macluumaad. I want everyone to spend the next several days painting the outside, cleaning up the weeds, and generally cleaning up the lot. Understood?" The men in the pinstripe suits waved at their new employees prior to ducking into the limousine. Chen Li was impressed. He let the other man do all the talking to the Somali employees. He only spoke to the men he provided. Once they left, the combined Chinese and Somali management team resumed running the show.

A bus line ran close by and the number of employees was reasonable. The new management appeared to be cognizant of ensuring the lot remained well-kept. Very little "Cokes and Smokes" gatherings common to many businesses took place outside any of the exits. The windows were always clean and little activity happened outside normal business hours. The business kept to itself so much that no one knew what they did. There was minimal engagement with any of the other businesses in the area. Several vendors rotated with different catered food on a daily basis. Office supplies arrived via vans from big box stores. Nonetheless, the neighbors were happy. One less empty building to worry about.

MKL-U-MD was run by and employed minorities from several ethnic groups – Somalis and Chinese. More the former than the latter. Another success for the growth of minority businesses.

More people were employed by the business than most thought. The men and women who alighted from the buses and walked several blocks were learning a new trade. The clusters of tables and workstations contained computers, mobile devices, and other electronic devices. Once trained, the employees were sent into the field.

The core group of men and women who were always present were grouped into three teams. One team provided training, another the technical support while the third handled administrative and management activities. This was similar to many sales-type organizations. The Chinese handled the technology and much of the training whereas the Somalis provided the management and the majority of the field employees.

Passersby looking through the windows in the front of the building only saw several offices. Two large areas behind the offices offered fertile training facilities. Training lasted eight hours a day for several weeks. Often, the trainers would take small groups on "field trips." The field employees also went through a change in appearance. Initially, they arrived looking somewhat unkempt in baggy jeans and t-shirts. Women were visually easily identifiable as Muslims with their head and sometimes facial scarves. Throughout the training process a more business like attire was achieved. Gone was the facial hair for men. Stylized grooming replaced doo rags and bling. Even hygiene was attended to. Inspections each morning ensured compliance. Employees who could not follow instructions were given one opportunity to comply and then removed from the program. By the end of the transformation, the employees who went into the field looked like office employees anywhere. Some in business casual attire and others in more formal "executive" style attire. Stylish scarves designed to hang from the shoulders or be loosely wrapped around the neck, which could be placed upon the head should occasion require, replaced traditional scarves on many of the female trainees. The result? They too blended in. Their appearance made them look like they belonged – wherever they went.

The field employees spread throughout the metro area. They went to malls, athletic events, walked through the skyways of the downtown areas, into hospitals, universities, and in business parks. They went where people went. Always with their mobile devices. Always online, connected to headsets, faces firmly affixed to the screens. Yes, they fit in. Everyone else looked like that too. But what they were doing with their devices, walking around, was not the idle chit-chat of updating social media, making manicure appointments, negotiating contracts, or other mundane activity. They were gathering information.

Their devices were the same brands purchased by everyone. The apps and upgraded hardware on them made their devices more than a mobile phone. These were truly smart. As the employees walked around, ensuring they were always close to others, the RFID skimmers embedded in them would search and probe and obtain information from credit cards carried in purses, wallets, and money clips. Without their knowledge, everyday people, doing everyday activities, gave up all the information stored on numerous 2" x 3 ¼" slices of plastic with magnetic strips and chips on their person.

On a good day each employee would obtain literally thousands of unique pieces of personally identifiable information. Day after day, they radiated into the city to gather data, like squirrels gathering nuts at the onset of fall. Randomly, throughout the day, the app uploaded the PII to a server in a data center. The field employees need only to keep their devices on at all times. Software technicians in the back room of the office, connected to the data center, fired up additional programs which decoded the bits of information, grouping them into different categories. Credit cards, driver's licenses/passports, and corporate identity groupings were then sold through various intermediaries to organizations requiring them.

Credit cards, of course, needed to go out fast so they could be used for fast, high volume transactions prior to being cancelled, either by the credit card company fraud department or the individual themselves. Organized crime and foreign governments requiring real information for fake IDs purchased driver's licenses and passport information. This part of the business was all "off-book." The corporate identity card information, however, was a different story. The venture capitalist who provided all the start-up funding, technology, training, and trainers demanded this information. The information was the bonus payment made for the investment.

MKL-U-MD's Somali management team members could care less what the investors did with that information. They couldn't see any use for it. Business was good. Money was being made – lots of money. The money was the newest and most lucrative revenue stream for "The Man." Funding for al-Shabaab had never been so good.

Chapter 17

Six months earlier

"Celeste?" Abdi called out to grab her attention as he walked through the door of the Vice President of Operations at HyDek. "Can you sign off on those new security measures I mentioned last week?"

"Hi Abdi. Sit down and remind me what they do again," Celeste Van Dorn replied pointing to the chair in front of her desk.

"Sure." Abdi closed the door to her office and sat in the appointed chair. "The security measures will be the first part of an in-depth penetration testing process we need to do to increase our certification status."

"Oh yes. I remember that now. I have so much going on I can't seem to remember everything. Which servers?"

"The procedure requires loading new security measures on an entire batch of corporate servers picked at random. The servers chosen will be loaded based on an algorithm that I'll be writing. No one, not even myself, will know which servers would be picked. To make sure the software team doesn't figure out who is getting tested, the actual install itself will be embedded inside another security upgrade every server is scheduled to receive. One subset of servers will simply get an extra bit of code. I am a sneaky son-of-a-bitch, aren't I?" Abdi leaned in towards Celeste's desk as he reached the end of his response. "I already have approvals from all of the clients."

"Approved. Now how are the employees taking your last round of space inspections?"

"As you know, when I first started these inspections I routinely found cell phones, USB drives, and other media that people could use to steal from us or our clients or, heaven forbid, install backdoors for hackers. You know my background. I lived through a serious hacking attack several years back. I'm happy to report that because of the new screening done at the front entrance I have not found any more contraband."

"Yes, but how are the employees taking this? I'm tired of issuing insurance checks to you every time your vehicle gets keyed."

"I never will be well-liked and I can live with that. I do my job and I do it well. If there isn't anything else, then?"

"There is that one final thing Abdi. I need your recommendations when to implement the next round of layoffs. I already received personnel decisions from Dom and the other shift supervisors. Your security programs and successful implementation of automation programs are working so well we just don't need as many people anymore. I want you to know how much the management team appreciates everything you do."

Abdi reached into the stack of manila folders he carried, extracting one folder. It had a large red stripe running diagonally on the front and back. "Here you are, as requested. I provided three possibilities with a recommended timeframe highlighted in the last section of the finding."

Celeste took the report, thanked him, and excused him so he could go about his day's activities. Abdi rose from his chair, straightened his tie, and walked out of her office.

Abdi sauntered through the operations center. He stopped at a few operators' stations. Unlike Dom, he didn't chit-chat. He peered at the workstation environ looking for a reason to write up the operator. Finding nothing he moved on. One of the operators flipped him off behind his back while others made even more rude gestures. The contrast between Abdi and Dom was striking.

When he finally reached his cubicle, Abdi got down to the work he had been waiting to do all day long. He ran a report on all the servers in the data center belonging to MnMedDev. The report included type of server, hardware configuration, network routing configuration, type of network interface, amount of memory used, processor usage, and network usage over a period of three months.

"It is good to be the security guy," Abdi thought. He wrote all the security protocols and gave himself and Dom the ability to copy to and from media storage devices. Abdi wanted it for obvious reasons and Dom, well, he needed someone else to have the ability to make copies. He never told Dom about this, so he still had to be sneaky about it. The double sized cubicle helped.

Abdi copied the reports to a media convertor he made from a USB thumb drive. He grabbed for the coffee thermos inside his backpack. It wasn't his regular thermos but one that had a screw on bottom. He took a small screwdriver from his electronics work kit, inserted it into the lip of the removed bottom piece, and lifted out a small insert. Tilting it sideways he saw the small MICRO-SD slot and inserted the memory chip he removed from the media convertor. Reversing the process, he replaced the insert and screwed the bottom to the body of the thermos. After filling the thermos with steaming hot coffee, he could remove the data from the building. He saw this process in a movie years ago and had, as the Data Center Cyber Security Person, tested it out with every guard on every shift. If he was caught, it would simply go in the books as a security exercise and the guard who caught him would receive a bonus. No one ever asked to look at the thermos and when randomly scanned upon leaving the building, the data drive, too, went unnoticed.

This evening he would meet his old college buddies for a beer or two.

Das Rathaus recently opened after construction of the Green Line Light Rail route through the University of Minnesota. Named in tribute to many local German beer houses of yesteryear and with an off kilter nod to the university's mascot, it resembled the upscale and trendy eateries found in the hipster sections of most urban downtown areas. Forty years ago another bar with that name existed but it closed after a fire. The pool tables and "hidey holes" from the old bar, created by opening walls and expanding into rooms from neighboring buildings were now history. Also history, was the stank of decades of spilled beer and memories of another time – when spanking the waitress' ass was considered a right-of-passage. Now, new architecture, built to look old, with heavily lacquered rafters of old buildings given a new lease on life interspersed with a brick façade, invited clientele both old and young. Large glass garage doors leading to a sidewalk patio and a plethora of large screen televisions showcased any sport you could think of. It was snowing now though, the garage doors firmly closed, capturing the heat of the hustle and bustle inside.

A menagerie of booths, low tables for four or high tables for two created the main dining area. A series of twenty-foot long tables made from planks of wood and lacquered to a shine were placed in the bar area. They were designed for large groups of people watching the multitude of big screen televisions plastered on every wall.

Abdi found his buddies in one of the booths. Six of them showed up tonight, so the last two needed several chairs brought over. This group had been meeting for years. Most of the time there were ten who came, but sometimes as few as three. They missed the dark corners of their previous hangout in the Dinkytown neighborhood. One evening they showed up and it was shuttered, bought out by some large company. Months later a yogurt shop opened. This one had better food, though, so it would suffice. They couldn't even consider meeting across the street at the corporate owned restaurant.

As with any group of gamers, the laptops came out even before the beers arrived. Joshing and cajoling about skills ensued, beverages quaffed, and food consumed. Hearty laughs filled the air. Often, someone would pull out a data card and insert it into someone else's laptop to share code, a new game, or porn they obtained. They all belonged to the IT community and knew one another from their days at the U's computer science master's program. No one was concerned about security. After all, work computers were not allowed by an agreed upon and enforced set of rules. No one wanted to get fired for being stupid.

And so, MnMedDev server configurations were transferred from Abdi to the Chinese.

Present Day

Servers in the HyDek data center received data from MKL-U-MD's mobile apps via one of the programs cobbled together by subroutines the Chinese provided to Abdi. Another allowed the software technicians at MKL-U-MD headquarters to work on the data. The architecture of the system Abdi designed was similar to the massively parallel processing servers that typified open source projects like SETI. Each of the thousands of servers had a miniscule amount of data saved to its memory arrays. These arrays were accessed only when needed. This architecture and the vastness of the data center meant massive amounts of data was surreptitiously saved and shared. When the technicians were done using specific data it was removed and all logs cleaned. No one knew. No one suspected. MKL-U-MD then uploaded this information onto a server at one of Zhang Xe's front companies. A nominal invoice was sent, funds received, and taxes paid to the State of Minnesota. The amount of money coming into MKL-U-MD and reported to various government agencies was small. On paper, MKL-U-MD was, like most start-ups, hemorrhaging money.

Zhang's front companies further obfuscated the data within agricultural data and reports selling it to yet another of his front companies. The data that finally arrived on Chinese Security Service computers was decrypted providing corporate identities. This entire effort took only a matter of minutes as the process was computerized. Technicians on either end simply initiated and monitored. The Chinese were not spending all this money and effort to create new ID cards.

No. Obtaining the identity was only the first step.

Chapter 18

Several months ago
China

Zhang Xe explained, in basic terms, some of the concepts his team used to infiltrate corporations at a gathering of high ranking military officers to a fellow general. "Social engineering is a non-technical method hackers use to gain access to a computer by basically tricking people into breaking their normal security procedures. It takes time and a concentrated effort. It's generally just the first step in a more complex fraud scheme. Say for instance, you already have the identity of someone. You still need to interact with them and convince them to make a mistake. It isn't difficult though because people are 'click happy.' This makes our job easy."

"How many people do you need to do this to?" the general asked.

"The best comparison I can make is to a sales cycle. It's a matter of having enough numbers to go through to get the half of one percent to bite. So the numbers are large in that scenario. On the other hand, if you can obtain a name, email address, security clearance information, PIN numbers, and the locations those individuals are authorized to be in, well then, it's wickedly easy."

"Credit cards don't have all that information Zhang. What are you going after?"

"Look, the more security conscious a company is, the more information they load into the identity card handed out to an employee. In most countries the military leads the way with what's called a Common Access Card or 'CAC.' It's used not only as an ID, but also to access buildings and computers. Additionally, complete military records, orders, and even DNA information can be placed on these. We do the same here." The general fingered his ID card as Zhang explained this. "Many companies have followed suit, to some extent, and embed a great deal of information on ID cards. All in the name of security."

Several more peers gathered around. Zhang continued his explanation. "Who has heard the term skimming? It originated when electronic readers were placed over the normal card entry slot of an ATM. The reader grabs all the data from the card being used to access the ATM. Given this information, the person doing the skimming only needs to break the four-digit PIN associated with each card and presto – money printing begins."

"Yes, but isn't getting the PIN difficult?" another asked.

"Finding the PIN is just a matter of using a computer to run a program which algorithmically crunches through all combinations until the correct one is found. It sounds difficult," Zhang tipped his head to the gentleman who asked the question. "But security experts know out of the 10,000 possible combinations of four digits using 0-9, a specific 20 unique combinations, such as 1234 or 1111 or 0000, and so forth, made up 27% of all PINs. Additionally, patterns such as making straight lines such as 2580, or using the four corners 1397 make up larger percentages than people think." Many of the crowd surrounding Zhang appeared to lose skin color and fidgeted, looking at each other. Seeing this Zhang stopped and said, "Just go to a six-digit combination and change them often. OK? You'll be much safer then." He scanned the faces. Seeing relief washing over their faces he asked if they wanted to hear more. They did. "The algorithm I'm speaking about can effectively reduce the 'brute force' nature of the calculations. Once the data is retrieved, a card making machine embeds the data into the magnetic strip on a plastic blank. The 'new' card is as good as the old one. To get money, access a 'clean' ATM, enter the PIN you associated with it, and withdraw the max amount."

"Tell us more about these," the man asked as he held up his ID card.

"Absolutely. The only real difference between consumer and corporate skimming is the type of data being stolen. The theft of information from a corporate ID card is indeed similar. We replace the card reader providing access to a building or through a security checkpoint and mimic normal use. These skimming devices then either send the data being skimmed wirelessly or the data is downloaded when we remove it. Skimming in this fashion provides reams of information and data but it is more difficult to implement. Generally, we have someone on the inside to help with that."

Zhang stopped at this point. He wasn't going to tell them how his team really got the information. What he told them was true in a general sense and they seemed satisfied. He would tell them next year the progress his team in Minnesota was making. Time for someone else to talk. Besides he wanted an update on the other parts of the operation Program Golden Peacock was supporting. "Tell me Admiral, how are your plans going to increase the size and reach of our Navy?"

"Zhang, you honor me with your question. Please, gentlemen, if I could take some of your time to respond." All the men gathered around nodded in agreement. They too found these gatherings more informative than regular official news and were eager to hear what the Navy was doing. "The Guangzhou International Shipyards in Guangdong Province are more efficient than ever. Especially with the acquisition of the Russian carrier. Our overall goal is to support Chinese economic goals by protecting our shipping lanes. We are not yet a complete 'blue-water' Navy but are progressing."

"Excuse me," asked one of the gathered, "I don't understand blue-water navy."

"Certainly. Let me explain. A blue-water navy is one that is capable of sustained operations across oceans, able to project power far from its home country. That requires many ships and a competent logistics system for underway replenishment. You all understand the necessity of logistics for an army, correct? The Navy is no different. There are two ways to resupply a navy. One is to have bases scattered across the regions where you want to project power. The problem with that is two-fold. One, politics dictate where those bases can be, when they can be used, and even what can be resupplied. Second, bases are inherently unsafe because they are static. As soon as you build one, the enemy knows where it is." He looked at one of the generals who worked with the Army's nuclear warheads. "You prefer having mobile platforms over silos for your missiles, correct?" As expected, all were in agreement. "Good. We agree. The Navy needs mobile logistics also. That means the type of underway replenishment the U.S. Navy created in World War II and has since perfected. For that you need specialized supply ships. Our capabilities are close to those of the United Kingdom. We plan on passing them within the next ten years. Only the U.S. will have more. In the next few years, we will have ships displacing 23,000 tons capable of carrying 11,000 tons of supplies. Additionally, our sailors have trained extensively on how to resupply at sea in what is called underway replenishment or UNREP. It is now common to see our supply ships refueling two warships at once. Those that know how tricky this is appreciate how far we've come."

A waiter came by with hors d'oeuvres and drinks. Everyone in the assembled group filled their plates and grabbed for drinks. Many of these men were old enough to remember when the food served at meetings was not shrimp, lobster, and calamari; let alone alcoholic beverages. Once the waiter left, the Admiral continued.

"Coming out of the green water as a local defense force into the blue water means we can support operations and project power where we determine it is needed, not simply how far our ships can go before needing resupply. Does this answer your question?"

"Yes it does – with respect to logistics. But how about the warships?"

"Once again, if we look out over the next ten years, our plans are to have almost three hundred vessels. Of these, seventy to eighty will be warships, fifty-five to sixty submarines, fifty or so amphibious ships, around one hundred plus small missile boats in addition to the supply ships I already discussed. We project the U.S. Navy will be below three hundred combined vessels by that time. They continue to cut funding and reduce their capabilities. They will not be able to be everywhere at all times anymore. This opens opportunities for us at a reduced risk. Remember please, we do not have a long history of modern naval combat. The U.S. Navy has had ninety years to reach its current level of proficiency in aircraft carrier operations and the complexities of modern naval warfare with World War II, the Cold War, and the more recent Middle East operations."

"We operate three fleets now. The North Sea Fleet, based in the Yellow Sea and headquartered in Qingdao, Shandong Province; the East Sea Fleet, based in the East China Sea and headquartered in Ningbo, Zhejiang Province; and lastly, the South Sea Fleet, based in the South China Sea and headquartered in Zhanjiang, Guangdong Province."

"It sounds like you are taking up too much funding with all this growth. Why?" one of the generals grumbled with his mouth stuffed full of shrimp.

"Because we are a global player in the economy of the world. We rely on importing raw materials and exporting finished products. Look, in 2004, over 80% of our crude oil imports transited the Straits of Malacca. If we continue to let the U.S. Navy control that, neither you nor I get to play with any of the toys we have." The general almost choked on his food hearing this.

Zhang Xe smiled. He could not have asked his friend to explain things any better. Besides, no one asked him any more questions about his work. They were beginning to whole heartedly understand what they needed to do. Power projection was key. He quietly walked away. They were too busy discussing how to make sure they got more and more tanks, planes, and oil to notice.

Chapter 19

Present Day

Several months passed since Abdi provided the server configuration. Snow melted, flowers bloomed, and docks, boats, and water skiers replaced ice houses on area lakes. The baseball season was well underway and summer school in session. Normally a regular with the gamer crowd at Das Rathaus, his absence was noticeable. It couldn't be helped. The plan required his time and he did not need any attention drawn to him. Every now and then the jock crowd hassled the gamers, geeks, and medical students who came in for a beer. Testosterone levels, always high in the university bars, combined with alcohol provided fertile grounds for scuffles, fights, and ultimately the police. Abdi was never arrested though, mostly because he left quickly when things heated up. With the majority of students gone for the summer, things were better. He had been busy and trying to lay low. He still read the bulletin board daily though and this morning a message told him his presence was required. The message promised "more fun than you can imagine with ten fingers and a keypad." Message received.

He heard the group before he saw them. The crowd was thin and they were loud. Nothing like hiding in plain sight. He hollered his greeting and slapped several on the back as he approached. All of them had facial hair, well, at least as much facial hair as they could grow. Even in their 30's and 40's none of them had to shave every day. Many high schoolers in the metro had beards – something none of this crew would ever be able to do. No "Duck Dynasty" styled beards here. Something about the Chinese. Long and wispy worked, but big and bushy? He could grow more than they did and he let them know it. He longed to grow his facial hair to be "hadith" of "cut the moustaches short and leave the beard." This hadith – or saying – was attributed to the Prophet Mouhammad and Abdi ached to be a true follower. But his cover dictated otherwise.

"Hey, look who finally decided to bless us with his presence!" hollered one.

Another yelled, "Pull up a seat, oh late one." The nearest man shoved a chair his way. He and Abdi first met in a sophomore Java class that he was a T.A. for. Bei "Sam" Liping had approached Abdi after one semester and asked him how he felt about the infidels in class. It was a gamble to be so open, but it was a university setting and all views were "in the open" so to speak. He had been informed that Abdi was a sleeper so it was not as risky as other introductions he had made over the years. Sam moved his Galaxy S5 smart phone, which had been placed screen down, to make room at the table for Abdi.

"Better late than never – or I could just turn around and go back to work." Everyone laughed at that retort.

"Abdi, you have the lines but your delivery sucks," another shot at him.

"Yeah, you will never make it at the Comedy Club," yet another joined in.

"Ha ha ha." Abdi raised his arm, got the attention of the waitress, and ordered a round for everyone. "I hear you loud and clear. Last one here buys." A cheer arose from the table.

While this banter went back and forth Abdi set a Galaxy S5 smartphone from his pocket on top of Sam's phone - only with the screen up. The Near Field Communication (NFC) file transfer between phones was initiated when Sam appeared to drum his fingers on the screen.

After several minutes had passed, Abdi noticed what Sam was doing. "Hey, man. Did you get that wing sauce on my phone?" Abdi hollered at Sam. "Good God, man. That's disgusting. I can't trust you with anything. Who the hell put you in charge of the lab back in the day?" Abdi grabbed his phone, wiped the sauce off his phone, and put it back in his pocket. Once again, the entire table roared with delight. The waitress arrived with beers for all. The assembled men raised their glasses and toasted Sam's sloppiness.

The malware from Zhang Xe's team was now in Abdi's possession. This new transfer system was so much easier than swapping memory cards. Tomorrow would be a great day.

When it was time to leave, Sam and Abdi led the procession to the light rail station where he would catch the Green Line back to downtown St. Paul where he parked his vehicle.

The others took the Green Line in the opposite direction towards downtown Minneapolis.

Abdi reached into his pocket, plugged in his earphones, and turned on some music. Several stops later, he opened the text document that was one of the files he had received. It contained instructions. The document told him to encapsulate the code into a security patch he routinely wrote and have his software team upload and install as usual. The malware had already been tested on the sandbox servers built with the configuration files he provided earlier. There was no need to confirm installation as the code automatically initiated communications with a server the team monitored. They will know as soon as the code is live. The malware itself propagated from the servers in the data center to the servers running the machinery in the manufacturing facility. Once embedded there, it would reprogram, not only the actual manufacturing specifications, but also the QC program. In this fashion, not only would the medical devices be defective, the quality control process would pass them based on the faulty specs. All this took network bandwidth and processor time. Minimal, in fact, almost negligible; however, Abdi needed to have a back story ready in case someone suspected a memory or bandwidth leak.

When Abdi arrived in his condo, he downloaded the malware files to his trusty MICRO-SD card and placed it once again in the bottom of his thermos for transfer into HyDek. He destroyed the smartphone he had used for the transfer and scattered its shattered innards into the pond nine stories below the balcony of his condo.

Chapter 20

The skimmers from MKL-U-MD let their mobile phones do all the work for them. Many new credit cards have RFID chips that enables consumers to pay by simply waving their cards over a reader. No more hassle of taking the card out a wallet or purse. The MKL-U-MD software technicians built several apps that allowed them to act as mobile, virtual readers. All Zhang's skimmers needed to do now was enable the apps on their phones and walk within several feet of someone. The software technicians at MKL-U-MD had the benefit of working full-time for Zhang Xe's cyber unit. Years of research, trial and error, and testing went into these apps.

Fatima's MKL-U-MD employee number was 1008, since she was the eighth employee hired. She was their best skimmer. It helped that she was a master of disguise. Her skin was fair, her eyes light brown. She was of moderate height and weight and visually her age was unknown. Application of jewelry, makeup, shoes of varying height along with changes in clothes or uniform provided access that others could not attain. MKL-U-MD did not demand the disguises. She did it on her own – paying for clothing and what-not all out of her own pocket. MKL-U-MD, after all, invested in technology, not clothes or makeup.

Her latest assignment was MnMedDev headquarters on the grounds of the old Ford Assembly Plant in the Highland Park neighborhood of St. Paul. The headquarters campus was in a scenic setting overlooking the Mississippi River. As part of MnMedDev's desire to be good neighbors, there was no fencing and no secured entry into the campus itself. The design was similar to Google or Facebook in Silicon Valley. MnMedDev paid an outside consultant $1 million to conduct a study to encourage creativity when they were designing the facility. The consultant received another $10 million to create and implement what the executives called The Openness Initiative. To facilitate this, RFID chips were placed on employee ID cards. Security policy dictated how to wear the ID; hung around an employee's neck at chest level with a breakaway lanyard. A simple clear plastic badge holder with nothing attached to it held the ID card itself. The visibility of the ID gave everyone a sense of belonging, allowed people to identify one another by name, and ensured the RFID readers around campus would be able to gather the ID information in a straightforward manner.

The design and placement of buildings provided access to the inner courtyard areas. Fatima loitered near entrances to key card access doorways by smoking with other smokers – always closer than the prescribed twenty feet. She wore a fake corporate ID so no one questioned her presence. She identified the type of computing devices preferred by MnMedDevers on earlier reconnoitering trips. With that in mind, she brought a similar laptop and spent a period of time in the various eateries accessible on the campus. After five days her operation was complete. In those five days, her various disguises changed her appearance from lab technician, secretary, research scientist, to an accountant. She covered every physical location possible without risking someone identifying her.

Fatima's skimming resulted in 1,874 unique corporate identities being entered into the MKL-U-MD systems. One of these was the Vice President of Quality Control. Another was the lead project manager for the newer glucose monitoring devices currently being planned for production. The software technicians, both at MKL-U-MD's South Minneapolis office and in Kanming, China, went to work.

Dom sat down and returned to the printouts. He pulled up additional reports on data packet activity. Nestled between the thousands of lines in each report he knew lay an answer to his query. After three hours digging through and dealing with several High Priority alerts identified by his operators, he reached back for his thermos of coffee to pour another drink. He poured out the bottom dregs that had significantly cooled down. Seeing that his coffee mug was seriously lacking the required "get me up," he reached for his thermos. It was empty already. He needed more caffeine. His wife wouldn't approve, but she wasn't here. Gathering the printouts into a folder, he ejected the thumb drive he used for his research. *"Did Abdi really think he wouldn't figure out how to access the USB port?"* He wrapped the small chain attached to his thumb drive around a finger of the hand holding the folder and made for the break room with his thermos firmly held in the other.

"Is there any coffee or did the security guards drain it and not make any new stuff?" he called to Abdi Ali who was sitting at one of the tables reading something on his tablet.

"I just made some. Remember the coffee we used to get? This new generic crap is exactly that - crap".

"Agreed, but it's better than nothing I suppose. At least we aren't paying for it yet. I still can't believe they are making us pay for pop now. Is this a tech company or what?"

"I know. The measures being taken to increase profits are amazing. I have to lay off all the people assigned to work security updates now - like Amber upstairs. She doesn't know it yet. I need her to get all the latest patches in today and then show her the door. I have to do everything remotely now."

"Abdi, this is unbelievable." Dom slowly walked away from the counter, gazing out the windows.

"What's bothering you Dom? It's not like you didn't know some of this was coming down the pike."

"It's just that our people are still our best measure against cyber intrusions. They can think outside the box. They can see the bigger picture and make adjustments."

"No, no, no. I can't agree with that Dom. People are our biggest threat. People click on emails when they know not to, people bring Bluetooth enabled devices into the center when they know that is a huge security risk, and that old adage 'loose lips sink ships' is still germane. People get social engineered; computers and code don't."

"You may be right about that, but nonetheless, computers still don't work off hunches."

Dominic looked at Abdi with pleading eyes, searching for trust with his peer of several years. *"Can I trust you?"* he thought. *"I mean, really trust you?"*

"Remember when I asked about how to identify security breaches?"

"Yes, and I laughed. But I'm a good guy, so I showed you where to learn more."

"Let me show you what I've been looking into."

"Is that what's in the folders you have with you?" asked Abdi slowly.

"Yeah. They go with me everywhere. I just don't trust that my desk won't get rifled through when I'm not around." Dom turned and placed the thermos he just filled back on the counter. He returned to the table. "Move your tablet so I can put this stuff down." Abdi cleared the table off and let Dom spread his printouts, proceeding to voice his concerns.

He talked for thirty minutes straight, only occasionally answering a probing question from Abdi.

"When did you first start looking at this?" asked Abdi wearily.

"I knew something was up when all these cost-cutting measures rolled off Celeste's desk. I read somewhere once upon a time that a sailor who couldn't sense the wind shifting wouldn't survive for long at sea. I honestly took that statement to heart. Ever since then I guess I'm a bit wary of decisions that don't make sense when you look at the 'big picture.' With what you just told me about laying off more people I am even more convinced."

"Dom, I see how someone could maybe, just maybe, take all these issues and think something was not kosher so to speak. But this sounds more like ramblings of a paranoid employee who has conspiracy issues."

"Are you kidding me? Me paranoid? Conspiracy? You know me Abdi. I'm the most level-headed person around. The non-techie techie. I never even watched *Matrix*, let alone *Fifth Estate*. I mean my hobby is woodworking. I rarely even touch computers at home."

Abdi's eyes had hardened. He rose part way up, placed his hands on the table, and whispered to Dom. "I am serious. You are getting looney tunes with this. You really need to keep all of it to yourself.

I'm glad you came to see me first and haven't mentioned this to anyone else. Right? I mean anyone else hears this and your job is gone. Do yourself a favor, OK? Drop it. I won't mention it – but only because I'm your friend."

Silence.

Dom looked at Abdi.

Abdi didn't blink.

More silence.

Finally, Dom grabbed everything he had now spread across three tables. "You're right. You should forget I even brought it up." He wheeled around and practically ran back to his desk.

Chapter 21

The skyways of downtown Minneapolis ran a total of eight miles, snaking their way through 69 blocks of buildings, parking garages, over streets, and sometimes simply dead-ending at a locked door. What many people don't realize is the skyways are not owned, run, or maintained by the city. Each skyway is owned by one of the buildings it connects. The passageways internal to the building being connected are actually part of that building and, therefore, the owners of the building own that part of the skyway. Hours of operation within the system vary as dictated by these owners. Security within the system is also left to the individual owners.

Malick was in one of the few large open areas of the skyway. He spent several hours during the morning walking the system, loitering around ATMs. His target was the elevator access area around a building housing one of MnMedDev's downtown offices.

Malick was a new employee. Unlike Fatima, his face displayed the stereotypical features of an East African, at least those Hollywood chose to portray. Even though he was in fantastic physical shape, he looked gaunt. His eyes sank into his high and prominent cheekbones. His hair never quite looked professional even though the stylists at MKL-U-MD reworked it and showed him how to style it correctly. He normally wore a set of false teeth but he forgot them today. Malick had never graced the inside of a dentist's office, even when he broke several teeth in a gang fight.

Broken, misshapen and yellowing, his teeth invited no one to look at him more than once, let alone engage him in discussion; even to ask directions. Compounding this, his feet hurt. They hurt a lot.

He dressed in a tan suit, a light blue button down shirt, yellow paisley tie, a nice watch, and burgundy cap toe oxfords. He hated those shoes. No one ever made him wear dress shoes before. They pinched his toes, rubbed his Achilles tendon raw, and had created blisters on the balls of his feet. Malick's shift began only several hours ago. He did everything they had trained him to do – keep moving, blend in, act like everyone else, but he had to sit down.

He spied several lounge chairs in the lobby area. This area was technically not part of the skyway system, even though there were no signs. He sat, removed his earbuds, and bent over to loosen the ties on both of his shoes. He ran his hand over the back of his left foot where the topline had rubbed it raw. He felt it before he saw it. Blood. He did the same to his right foot. The same thing. Now both his hands were bloodied. The instructors who trained him and approved his attire did not provide him a handkerchief. A fatal mistake.

The security guards were alerted to Malick right away. They noticed many people every day – especially those who arrived in the lounge chairs via the skyway. Ninety-nine percent of the time after ten minutes or so, the interloper got up and left. Even though the area the lounge chairs occupied was not part of the skyway proper the guards long felt the hassle of keeping non-employees out of the chairs was too much of an annoyance and a PR nightmare. However, when the person in question didn't have a shopping bag, wasn't talking on a phone, accessing an iPad or tablet, or stayed for an extended period of time, the guard's internal radars perked up. Besides, sometimes no matter what, a person just didn't look like they belonged.

"Jasper. See that gentlemen in the tan suit? I'm going to see what he is doing. Keep an eye out, OK?" the shorter of the two guards said to his partner as he left the confines of the security area.

He approached within several feet of Malick, prepared to question the man.

"Hey there. How is it going?"

Malick looked up. This is not what he needed. He thought about just getting up and leaving but his feet hurt too much.

"I said, how is it going? Sir," the guard asked one more time with a more directed tone.

Malick knew he needed to reply. He slowly looked at the guard, shrugged his shoulders, and raised his hands in an outward fashion. Whenever the police questioned him, he always did this to show he held nothing. It generally did the trick and they left him alone. Not this time.

The guard saw the blood on Malick's hands. "Jasper, can you bring the first aid kit over here?" the guard spoke quickly into the microphone attached to his shoulder epaulet.

"I see you have some blood on your hands. Are you OK? I have a first aid kit coming if you need it."

"*Damnit. Just go away,*" thought Malick.

The guard stepped closer. Malick hated it when anyone violated his personal space.

Grimacing and choking back his desire to lash out at the chubby little man, he forced a smile. "Yo man, it's OK. Just leave me be. I ain't done nothing wrong. You banging me 'cuz I black?" Hinting at a racial bias suit when dealing with an authority figure never hurt. "New shoes. Don't that ever do it to you?"

The guard stepped back a bit. God, the man smelled awful and his teeth were terrible. His language certainly wasn't that of a businessman – at least not one in a legal business.

"Hey man, no sweat. I get it. I hate wearing new shoes too."

He turned to Jasper who had just arrived. "Thanks, for the kit. I got it. You can go back now and keep an eye on things." As he did this, he slightly tilted his head and shifted his eyes towards Malick. "Bad news," he whispered, "get the police."

He turned back towards Malick, dropped to a knee, and opened the first aid kit. "Let me take a look at your feet." He reached for one. When he did so Malick kicked at him.

Jasper called in a police request. Fortunately, there were several patrolmen just rounding a corner when the call came in for assistance.

"Hey, that is not necessary. I'll back off. Just settle down. Where did you say you worked?" the chubby guard responded while getting his feet back under him after landing on his rear to avoid the kick. He also placed his hand on the belt containing his taser. Malick had been tasered before. He still had the scars. Not by the police – it was part of his gang's initiation process. He saw the hand, the taser, and as he glanced to his left, the patrolmen that had been called.

The police worked their way through the crowd of onlookers which had gathered. They demanded an ID from Malick.

"Go to hell piggy." Malick spat on the policemen. He closed his eyes and braced his body for the beating that he knew would follow. Instead, he was forcibly raised from the chair, arms moved to his back, and handcuffs placed on his wrists.

"Sir, you are under arrest. Please come with us," the officer read him his Miranda Rights in a neutral tone and led him, untied shoes, bloody hands and all to the closest precinct – six blocks away.

Chapter 22

Abdi sat at the table and watched Dom leave the breakroom. He drummed his fingers on the table for several minutes. His hand went to the glasses he wore. His first desire was to break them. After all, he didn't need them – they were simply part of the finely-tuned character he created for himself. A man who was smart but appearing weak did not attract much attention. That's how Abdi was able to go places, do things, and no one ever knew he was there. He was simply part of the landscape.

Abdi left the data center through the main entrance and walked to his car. He jumped into his BMW and slammed his hands into the steering wheel with frustration. He tore off, wheels screeching in search of a place where no one would see him. It didn't take long. The corn fields were close by and corn was tall already. Two miles down the road, he turned his vehicle down a gravel road and pulled to the side.

Alighting from the car, he looked around to see if his chosen spot was secure. He saw no lights from the nearby road. There was a farm but it was not close and the moon was new. Before opening his door, he turned off the interior lights so Abdi was, for all intents and purposes, invisible. He pulled out a locked gun case from the trunk. It did not contain a gun though. The foam insert had been removed, leaving room for a collection of pre-paid cell phones still in their clam-shell wrapping. He took one, replaced the case, closed the trunk, and sat in the front seat of his car.

Abdi made quick incisions with a pocket knife freeing the contents. He plugged the phone into the power adapter, ensured the SIM card was in, and then he sat there agonizing over his next move. Dominic was an infidel, yes, but Abdi truly came to like the man after working so closely with him. He enjoyed spearheading the firing of the previous two supervisors. *"So what was the problem? Was it because they were still alive?"* He could not have these thoughts. Time was on his side when he forced those firings. Dominic, however, was a problem. Abdi knew Dom was stubborn as a mule. He wouldn't simply go away. He would continue to dig until he had the answer. Dom was smarter than he let on. A simple firing and expulsion from the data center was not an acceptable risk. Too much was at stake. There was no time left to start over. He turned the phone on and dialed.

"This is your landscaper. The grass is bad and needs removal." The phone number was all the identification the recipient needed.

"Understood" was the only response he heard and expected. It was done. He raised his head to the heavens and pronounced "Allahu Akbar" – God is the greatest.

Completing this task, he removed the SIM card from the phone and returned to the trunk. There he found a propane torch and a medium sized metal canister. The torch was purchased from the plumbing section of a local hardware store. Placing the phone, the clam shell wrapping, and the SIM card into the canister he turned on the torch and melted the contents into a puddle of plastic and copper. After letting it cool he threw the mess into the corn, replaced the torch and canister, and returned to work. He was gone for a total of twenty minutes. When he returned to his desk, he hacked into the security system and modified the building access logs to indicate he never left the building.

Chapter 23

Jon was just walking into the office when he received the call. The number was in his address book and the name appeared on the smartphone's screen.

"Roger, what's up. How is the gang unit these days? I saw on the news you had some shootings next to the river on the border area with St. Paul."

"Yeah, messy. Nice neighborhood. Five bangers splayed out in a park next to the biking path overlooking the river. But that isn't why I'm calling. I think I have something for you. Minneapolis PD took in a guy late this morning from the skyway system. Dressed in a suit but smelled something awful, teeth were bad, and his feet were bleeding. He just didn't fit in and when approached by security guards, things escalated. Anyway, when they got him in and ran his fingerprints, he popped up as a known banger. Member of the Riverside Thugs. That's one of your gangs, right?"

"Yeah. They're one of mine. He still at First Precinct?"

"No, he is already down at the Hennepin County Corrections Center. That's where I'm at. They called the gang unit in. Listen, he had a smartphone and earbuds. But I've never seen earbuds like this. Raised a red flag so to speak. We can't make heads or tails of it. Maybe you can?"

"Got it. I'll be right down."

Jon hung up the phone and grabbed his sport coat. "Rick, let's get going. Roger with the gang unit just called. They have a Riverside Thug in custody and thinks we should be involved. He mentioned the guy had some interesting electronics gear. That doesn't make sense. Riverside Thugs are just that – drugs and thugs. Nothing special. They haven't done much the last couple of years anyway. Let's see what we can make of it."

Chapter 24

"Hey hun, I'm going for a bike ride in town. I wanted to let you know I am, in fact, exercising and trying to take better care of myself. I'll be home later," Dominic hollered through the open door leading from the garage into the house.

"Ok, have fun. Don't get hurt. Love ya," his wife replied.

Dom shook his head – *"Don't get hurt – right."* He looked at the blister on his finger caused when he pinched it putting the bike onto the bike rack.

Dom got into his SUV, backed out of the garage carefully, using his rear view camera to see what obstacles his children left in his path on the driveway. Avoiding a skateboard and the rear wheel of his older daughter's bike, he turned his attention to calling his son's lacrosse camp coach. Last time he saw Jon he wanted to tell him about work but he didn't have enough information. Now he did. "Call Jon Wells, mobile," he said aloud. The integrated phone, navigation, and entertainment system in his vehicle responded by calling the correct number.

"Jon here."

"Jon. Its Dominic Seragosa. You know, Mike's dad from lacrosse."

"Hey Dom. Good to hear your voice. What's up?"

"I need to talk with you. Not over the phone. I'm coming into town now. Can we meet? It's extremely important."

"Uh sure. What is this about?"

"I said not over the phone. I'm heading in now and will be taking the bike path from Lake Calhoun to Lake Harriet. Can you meet me at the band shell in 90 minutes?"

"Absolutely. See you there."

Jon looked at Rick and said, "Rick, that was Dom Seragosa. His kid is one of the lacrosse players I work with. He said he needs to see me – now. Can you handle the gang banger? Maybe pull Reggie into it?"

"Sure, no problem," replied Rick.

Jon let Rick continue walking through the skyway to the Correctional Center and he turned around to get his car from the parking garage.

Forty-five minutes later Dom pulled his Ford Explorer into the parking lot on the northern edge of Lake Calhoun. He paid the parking fee, pulled his bike off the rack, and collapsed it so other vehicles could safely transit behind his vehicle. He put on a helmet and headed out on the path around the western edge of the lake. He immediately had to stop however, as the helmet did not fit correctly. "Damn it, grabbed the wrong helmet." He expanded the adjustable ring on the inside of the helmet and with great difficulty extended the strap at the buckle so it would no longer gag him.

The small back pack he carried contained the reports he earlier showed to his friend Abdi. He was no longer sure if Abdi was his friend though. The conversation was unlike any other they'd had. When Abdi's eyes met his, they seemed cold and empty.

Numerous bikers passed him as he struggled to progress at a decent pace. *"That's OK,"* he thought, at least when the bikers were teenagers or adults. When they were kids that made him feel, well, fat and out of shape. Sweat dripped off his hair and into his eyes. *"I just need to make it in one piece,"* he reminded himself. His view of the path was bad as the sunlight went in and out depending on the density of the tree canopy. He knew if he looked off to his left he would see the skyline of Minneapolis appear as if coming out of the lake. It was a shot the networks used often when broadcasting a sporting event. He was more concerned, however, with not hitting anyone on the path. At the southern end of the lake, he turned to cross one of the parkway roads. He didn't realize the small stop sign was for bicyclists and was almost run over. The bike path from Lake

Calhoun to Lake Harriet paralleled another road as it went up a small hill. His gear settings were too high. He crunched through several gears as he attempted to find the right ratio between forward and rear derailleurs. He didn't remember biking being so difficult. As he looked down he also didn't remember there being so many damn gears.

Chapter 25

Spring 2002
Avignon, France

They met in the courtyard area of the Palace of the Popes in Avignon, France.

The fortress was the seat of the Roman Catholic Church during the 14th Century. When Pope Gregory XI returned the papacy to Rome in 1377, the Papal Schism occurred. Anti-Popes Clement VII and Benedict XIII claimed authority over the church and continued to rule from Avignon until 1403. It was appropriate then, in the courtyard immediately opposite the entrance where tourists now entered, the two men seated at the table chose this as their meeting place. From all outside appearances, the two had nothing in common. Both, however, had a deep hatred for the same country. One man came from China, the other Saudi Arabia. Interestingly, both received their education in America and achieved what most Americans labeled success in the business world. Yes, they succeeded at capitalism, yet both held a desire to burn that country and system all down.

"I am overjoyed we agreed to meet here, in this place where my people, the Saracens, defeated the Christians in the 8th Century. It's also where the Christians almost ruined their so-called religion," the

Saudi gleefully announced while sipping his coffee. His sunglasses hid his eyes from the ever present bright sun famous in the Provence region of France. It was early summer, the mistral winds which blew down the Rhone River in winter were non-existent this day. "It is appropriate. Is it not?"

"If you seek to conjure the spirits of the conquerors I will not stand in your way. I, on the other hand, wish only to inflict a pain unlike any other the Americans have ever known. If the spirits help, so be it." Zhang Xe had no time for religious overtures. He had a plan. Men implemented the plan. The only spirits he believed in were those he drank. Nonetheless, the gentleman seated directly across from him was an integral part of the plan. Personally, he could care less what Ahmed Al Khadi Nihal's objectives were, but he knew that anything that kept the government spending time, effort, and money outside of his sphere of the globe was a good thing, and so here they were – compatriots.

"You desire money to fund your activities in the Middle East. Yes?" Zhang prompted.

"That is correct. There is great instability there and we cannot afford to let it improve."

"We? Certainly not I. You are talking about the Taliban, al-Qaeda, and the others who so superbly struck at America on 9-11." Zhang needed to ensure the man understood he would receive only money. Nothing else.

"Once again, you are correct. And you seek to disrupt the American's economy. To what end? Yours is growing faster than you can keep up with already."

"Confrontation with a country like the U.S. can only be done with deft strokes of deceit and coordinated thrusts of pain. You do not attack it directly. The Empire of Japan learned that. I believe that al-Qaeda will learn that also. I choose to use their own system of greed and desire and use their 24-hour news cycles to do the majority of the work. I will erode the consumers' trust in their companies so overwhelmingly the economy will crumble."

"In simple terms, how will you do this?" asked Ahmed.

Zhang smiled. "I will choose one industry and destroy it by extinguishing the consumers' trust in it. We go after a large company whose failure will be the first of many dominoes that will fall and eventually topple the entire economy." It was a brilliant plan, but he would never tell his partner the entirety of the plan. He needed a proxy to take the brunt of the condemnation and the wrath of community and law enforcement. Little did this man seated across from him, so full of hate, see his own demise.

They finished their coffee and began walking. The next part of the discussion needed to be done discreetly. Zhang never spoke to his network in hotels or other confined spaces. He preferred to randomly walk about in places of interest, pretending to point out interesting things and engage in what most observers would assume was an animated historical discussion between tourists. When they achieved their goals, the discussion would indeed be historical.

They walked north past the choir singing on the stairs of the courtyard. Stopping and pretending to listen to the music, the Saudi stated, "I'm assuming you need feet on the ground to achieve this." Zhang did not answer verbally. He nodded his head up and down in time with the rhythm of the music. He looked at the Saudi while doing so. The choral sounds brought a larger crowd by the minute. Zhang acknowledged the choir at the end of their song with a polite clap, nudging the Saudi to do the same. The musical selection completed, they continued their discussion while taking a "walking tour" which would take them down the stairs of Rue Pente Rapide through the narrow back alleys and passageways of the old town before turning onto Rue Limas and out the gate of Rue Ferruce. None of these roads seemed large enough to allow vehicle traffic and yet they had to avoid being run over several times.

The Saudi stated matter-of-factly, "Where and what will we attack?"

"That is the question indeed, isn't it? I have cultivated assets in California, Massachusetts, Illinois, Michigan, and Minnesota. Many of our supporters would probably like to see those little shits who make too much money in Silicon Valley fail. But I don't think that would cause the panic needed. There are too many companies ready to spring up and take their place, and besides it's all vaporware – just hire programmers and rework it. Additionally, there are too many FBI and other Federal agencies in California. Same goes for Illinois and Massachusetts."

Ahmed offered, "What about Michigan? You can't just hire programmers to rework the auto industry after all."

"No, Muslim extremism is too high there. This is a long-term investment and the extremism makes it too risky," replied Zhang. "I'm thinking of Minnesota and the hi-tech medical technology industry there. I have experience through my many companies in that field. I've been there myself on several occasions. There is a large Somali refugee community in Minneapolis. Are you connected there?"

The Saudi, now approaching the gate turned to Zhang smiling a broad smile, "Yes I am. In fact, I have a Somali in my employ. His connections in that community already run deep. I wasn't quite ready to use him but I see it now. So, Minnesota then."

They continued to discuss the specifics while on a bench facing the Rhone River. Before leaving, Zhang looked the Saudi directly in the eye. "The business front we create in Minnesota needs to be legal. The employees must be good citizens. No 'bad apples' as the Americans say. Everything above board, taxes paid, employees given benefits, no cash payments anywhere. A paper trail needs to exist."

Ahmed looked confused. "And why is that my friend?"

"Because hiding in plain sight is always easier. No lies to tell. You can increase the amount of money going to your interests if you embrace what I am telling you must be done. Think it over. I'm sure you will agree."

A tour bus arrived waiting for its seats to be filled with tourists. Zhang got on. The Saudi waited for an hour until his bus arrived.

Chapter 26

Present Day

A new ticket appeared in the software team's queue.

    Subject: Security Patch installation.
    Priority: High:

The ticket contained the listing of servers needing the installation. Abdi assigned it to Amber. He hated her the most and relished the thought of watching her get fired, at a minimum, or more than likely, thrown into jail. The code was uploaded to the software team's code repository for retrieval. They used a special program to retrieve and install code. It made falsifying the "paper trail" of who uploaded any piece of code more difficult, but Abdi liked challenges. In fact, he also planned to manipulate the logs showing Amber downloaded the code, added to it, re-uploaded it, and then installed it. All blame would go Amber's direction.

Amber was coming on shift soon so all Abdi needed to do now was wait for the install, run his "falsification" program to clean up the access logs, and go about his business.

Chapter 27

"Watch out jerk!"

Dom looked up in a panic only to see that he had not only crossed through the oncoming bike traffic but had also traversed the line delineating bikers and joggers. His negligence had forced several joggers off the path.

"Sorry," he yelled turning his head back towards the cursing joggers. He saw them cringe. He whipped his head back to the right and saw a group of oncoming bikes. He jerked his handle to avoid them but over-corrected. Sweat continued to drip into his eyes stinging them and further hampering his ability to control his actions. He never noticed the GMC Yukon that had been following him from his home until it was too late. The force of the vehicle as it sped up and rolled over him killed him instantly. One man jumped out of the car, ripped the backpack from Dom's bloody body, and quickly jumped back into the vehicle. It sped off jumping the curb, racing through the grass, and vanished onto a side street.

Jon was waiting 100 yards away in the parking lot of the band shell. He noticed people running to the top of the hill. Fearing the worst, he joined the fray. He pulled out his badge, identifying himself so he could get through the assembled crowd only to find the carnage of Dom's body and bicycle twisted together in an expanding pool of blood. He reached down and felt for a pulse. Nothing.

"Call 911," he shouted to the crowd.

He searched the surrounding area.

Nothing.

The park police were the first to arrive. They confirmed Dom's death and set about to interview witnesses. Jon offered his assistance after providing his credentials. When the Minneapolis police arrived, Jon provided them with Dom's wife's number so she could be contacted.

Robert Mitchell, Sergeant in the Minneapolis Police Department, now in charge of the scene, pulled Jon aside and asked why he was here.

"I knew Dom from his kid's lacrosse team. I help out when I can. Great kid. Dom called me a couple of hours ago and said he needed to talk. He wouldn't say anything else over the phone. He seemed really upset about something. A while back at lacrosse practice we were talking about this and that. He confirmed that I worked with the FBI. I asked him if there was something I needed to know but he didn't say anything else. I figured he was finally ready to come forward with something. I just don't know what that something is."

Sergeant Mitchell asked if the FBI was taking lead on the case.

"For now, you take the lead on the accident itself. I'm going to figure out why he wanted to meet. Let's connect tomorrow to share information. Fair enough?"

"Works for me," Sergeant Mitchell agreed and handed Jon his card. "Call me any time."

Jon breathed deeply and let a long breath of air push past his lips. It calmed him somewhat. "I get the feeling this is going to go in some weird directions before it's over."

Chapter 28

Reginald George Benkins, "Reggie" or "Reg" to his friends, was the lead technologist on the MPD Forensics team. He held court in the lab looking like a mad scientist with his ever present white lab coat, a wild afro that covered only the sides of his balding head, and a clipboard that looked thirty years old. He shook Rick's hand, but only after placing his can of Diet Mountain Dew – Code Red onto a table. Reggie was a local, hailing from the rough Northwest side of Minneapolis. He attended St. Cloud State University majoring in Computer Science and taking enough criminal forensics classes to minor in that burgeoning field. In fact, after several years in the MPD he took online classes from University of Maryland University College and achieved his Master of Science in Digital Forensics and Cyber Investigation. UMUC is recognized by the Department of Defense Cyber Crime Center. Reggie received multiple offers of employment in the D.C. area but chose to stay in his hometown. He couldn't leave his hometown teams. Under his lab coat was an authentic Minnesota Twins uniform jersey.

"Rick, thanks for having Roger send this over. How is Jon doing? I heard about his friend," said Reggie.

"Been better. Pretty pissed off and focused that's for sure," responded Rick. "What can you tell me?" Reggie provided assistance to the FBI on a consistent basis.

"I gotta tell ya, this is outstanding stuff. I wish I would have thought of it. I mean, if I were a criminal that is," Reggie exclaimed. "You owe me tickets to the entire Twins-Yankees series. I, the man with the golden fingers and mind of knowledge that has only yet begun to be tapped, have all that you need." Reggie was not shy about his skills. The rest of the team in the lab rolled their eyes, having heard this before. Some even faked putting their fingers down their throats to indicate a puking stance.

"Reg, calm down. What is so amazing?"

"Rick, see this? It looks like an earbud right? That's what I initially thought. I placed the cord and the phone on my examining table and wow."

"Wow, what????"

"The lamp illuminating my table flickered. That just doesn't happen – unless its burning out. I just replaced the bulb last week so I knew that wasn't the case. So some sort of electronic field is being generated. That caused me to take another look at the cord itself. I unplugged it from the phone and the flickering stopped. Once I plugged it back in, the flickering started up again. So I brought over an oscilloscope and BANG it went berserk. Earbuds don't do that. Look at the cord itself. See how thick it is? It isn't even an earbud, just looks like one."

Reggie plugged the fake earbud into a MP3 player and turned on some music, turning the volume up. "Go ahead, listen. Hear anything?" Rick placed the earpiece next to his ear and shook his head. "Me neither."

"So what is it, then?"

"Hang on. I'm getting there."

"OK. What about the phone?" Rick asked pointing to the device on the table.

"Glad, you asked. I was able to break in. The guy used 1111 as his code. I mean, really? There are no apps you would expect to find. The apps that are installed sure aren't something you'd get from any app store I know of. I downloaded the APK files to see if I could glean anything."

"APK files?"

"Oh yeah. That's the file extension for an application on an Android phone. Kinda like DOC is for a word processing file. Anyway, not much there. The files are custom-coded. Cool thing about Android phones is that you can write your own programs and install them without having to go through any approvals – like Apple. The flip side is, if you know what you are doing, you can make these do a lot more than they were designed to do."

"I went through the logs and this device – I'm not even going to call it a phone because that is NOT what its being used for – is downloading and uploading a TON of data. Normal devices don't do that. Not even my daughter used that much data when she found the NETFLIX app and wasn't on WIFI at her gramma's over the weekend while she watched ten hours of videos. She's now grounded from the phone by the way."

"So how is she going to call you?"

"I know, I know. Just scaring her for a day or so." Reggie grinned at Rick who returned a smirk.

"Glad she's a teenager Reggie?"

"You're funny. I'm going to laugh all the way to the bank when you finally buck up and get married. We'll see how well you handle a teenage girl. Back to the task at hand. Now the fun part. The oscilloscope is such a great tool. Now, see this credit card? It's a generic one we have on hand for credit card fraud testing. Watch the needle on the scope when the card gets close to the cord. See it move? When I turn up the tolerance a bit it moves when the card is within four feet of the cord."

"What does that mean?"

"We have an electronic skimming device."

"You mean the perp was going after credit card data?"

"That's what it looks like. Villainously sneaky bastard, I gotta give him that. I didn't know the Somali gangs were into this type of theft anyway. To be truthful this goes way over basic credit card skimming – almost overkill to be honest, but hey, looks like it worked."

"So was there an ATM close by?"

"Come to think of it, no. That's weird. Maybe just going after people exiting the office tower?" Reggie reached into a folder and extracted a sheet of paper. "Here's a list of companies who have office space in those buildings."

"Thanks Reg. Let me know if you find anything else."

Chapter 29

"Jon, Detective Bancroft with the Minneapolis Police Department. We need to talk more about the accident concerning Dominic Seragosa."

"Good morning Sergeant. Let me get you a chair. You want any coffee?" Jon gathered a chair from a nearby desk and walked over to the coffee mess. "Straight-up, flavored, or non-leaded?"

"Flavored? You have to be kidding. What is this — a Caribou Coffee? Straight up works for me. You feds get everything. Our budget still doesn't even cover coffee anymore. We all have to chip in. At least we got a coffee service to come in and bring in those packets that make it easy to brew coffee. No more sludge from the tin cans. Just rip open the packet, pour it in, and turn it on."

Jon walked back to his desk with coffee in both hands. "Hey, we're no different. No money in the coffee kitty from each of us every week and no coffee. Sounds like we have a better coffee service though. We get the carafe packets and single loaders. Makes the long nights easier that way. So what have you found out."

"Hey, I'm the one asking questions. Let me get those out of the way and then I'll fill you in," said the detective.

"Fair enough. Shoot," replied Jon.

"OK. Notes from Sergeant Mitchell say that you were meeting Dom. Can you tell me how you knew Dom and why were you meeting him?"

"Sure. Dom's son plays lacrosse. I played lacrosse in college – years ago mind you. Back in the day when the bucket-like helmets looked like polo helmets with face guards. It's hard to leave work but I needed a release. So, when I moved here and saw lacrosse taking off, I decided to find a school that would let me help out – but not be 'on staff'. You know how our work schedules are. Dom's son's team let me help out. That's how I met Dom and his family. Dom came to a lot of the practices. His wife and girls came around sometimes also. He was a good parent – kept quiet on the sideline about coaching. The only thing I ever heard from him were positive comments. 'Keep it up, Great job,' and such. He encouraged all the kids. Not just his son. So over the years I got to know the whole family a bit. One day, he showed up at one of the summer camps and just looked way out of sorts so I went over to say hi. He was really out of it so I talked up his son and how much he's improved – especially taking face-offs. Still nothing from Dom. Then he simply asked, or verified I should say, that I worked at the FBI. I said yes and specified the counter terrorism aspect. I asked him if there was anything I needed to know and he just grunted, said 'No, just wondering.' And walked off."

"That's the last time I heard from him until he called me."

"And he asked you to meet him – in a park – near Uptown?"

"That got my attention. I'm the one who always drives out to the suburbs. I mean, that's where they live so it made sense for me to do the legwork. He wouldn't say anything over the phone. He was adamant about that. He said we had to meet at the band shell on Lake Harriet."

"Why the bike?"

"Not sure. Dom wasn't the athletic type. I guess he used to be, but years of sitting behind a desk had caught up. So that surprised me."

"Why do you think he wanted to see you?"

"I'm still working on that. I know he was an IT geek but I wasn't real sure exactly what he did. He was a bit tight-lipped about that. I know he worked close to home because he had mentioned he no longer needed to catch a bus into town or drive the freeways anymore. I talked to his wife yesterday and looked into his background." Jon swirled the remains of his coffee.

"We did the same. What did you find?" asked Bancroft.

"He's been in the IT operations business for the past 10 years or so. He bounced around with various different companies, but a lot of IT guys do that so no worries there. He was at the data center that had the big breach several years ago with the retailer in town and then moved on to HyDek. He was a shift supervisor in the operations department. He pretty much ran things when he was there. HyDek is one of those new high-efficiency data centers that popped up recently in the outskirts of the metro area. You know the type of company. They play city governments against one another to get free land and no taxes with promises of high-paying jobs. Problem with these companies is that most of the full-time employees live elsewhere and the only locals to get jobs are janitorial, security, or part timers. We should be going after those companies for fraud or bait and switch, at the least, in my opinion."

"I hear you. My brother-in-law works for a competitor. If HyDek runs the same way they do, their MO is to undercut a large corporate IT department on costs, get the business, and then nickel and dime the client to death – charging them for anything not expressly written into the contract. They make a mint, but the cost of pulling out is often so high the client just sucks it up. The client makes money too, mind you. Since they no longer have as many employees, they can dump capital costs from their old server room costs, and so on."

"Sounds like you know a thing or two about finances. That explains the expensive suit and tie." said Jon. He was starting to like this detective even though he dressed like a banker.

"I wasn't always a cop. Started out as a bean counter, got my MBA, and then saw the web of lies corporate finance is. They can make anything look legal. So I got out, joined the force, and worked mostly financial crimes. Occasionally they throw me a simple case involving a death to keep my credentials on the up and up. The department felt this was a simple hit and run when they assigned me."

"What do you mean a simple hit and run? Have you been able to track down the SUV that ran Dom over? And what about the guy who ran out and grabbed his backpack. Simple hit and runs don't stop and steal stuff before driving off." Jon was now re-evaluating just how much he liked this guy.

"Whoa, Jon. I'm on your side here. Like I said, that was the initial thought, but now I think it's more. What was it you said to Sergeant Mitchell at the end of your talk with him?"

"Something like, this is going to go in some weird directions before it's over."

"I agree."

"So what about the SUV?" Jon needed some definitive answers.

"We checked for closed circuit surveillance, but let's be real, the incident was in a park. The only video surveillance is around the band shell itself. We looked at that but it only showed people running off in the direction of the accident. We know, from eyewitness accounts, the SUV sped off, turned around in the grassy area, went back down the road it came in on, and hung a right on Richfield Road heading in a northerly direction. This is a nice neighborhood so we canvassed the area for closed circuit video."

"How about social media? People with smart phones are always uploading stuff these days. The more gruesome, the more uploads and views. Believe me. This was gruesome. I was there."

"We actually found a lot. Let me show you." Bancroft pulled out his laptop, powered it up, logged on, and pulled up his browser. A series of photos taken from various video cameras appeared on the screen. "You're right, in that social media went 'nuts-ville' with videos and pictures. Most of them don't show much more than the crime scene photos we have since they were from the assembled gallery of 'looky-loos' after the fact. No, not much there, however, there was one video, which looks like it came from a Go-Pro on a biker's helmet that captured the entire incident. It's not the best from a cinematography perspective. The camera was bouncing around, so no luck on the license plate – BUT we know the make and model of the SUV. We also have proof positive that this was not an accident – as you most emphatically stated."

"Great. But where does that get us?" asked Jon.

"Let's get back to video surveillance from the surrounding neighborhood. Going north on Richfield you have Lake Calhoun to the west and Lakewood Cemetery to the east until W 36th Street. St. Mary's Greek Orthodox Church has a ton of cameras around it. The artwork and statuary in the building and on the grounds are invaluable so they have an extensive security system. They let us tap in and review their feeds. We didn't pick up the SUV heading north on either East Calhoun Parkway, which is what Richfield Road turns into at W 36th St, or Irving Ave S which runs on the east side of the church's property. That means they had to head east on W 36th St itself. There are many businesses and small apartment complexes along that route. The main entrance to Lakewood Cemetery is also on that road and we grabbed numerous images of the SUV progressing down the road. None of which got the full license plate. There were enough images, however, for our forensics team to stitch together a complete plate. We tracked that down to a Somali restaurant in Minneapolis, owned by a Jamal Kusow."

"Jamal?" asked Jon.

"You know him?" Bancroft looked up from the laptop screen.

"Yeah. He's my main connection into the Somali community. We relied on him to get a handle on why young Somali men were willing to join the terrorists in the Middle East."

"I think someone needs to talk to him." Bancroft closed his laptop, got up from his chair, and slowly walked around Jon's desk.

"Jon, am I missing some valuable piece of information? Is there something you're not sharing yet? Why did you think this was going to get weird?"

"It's not that, Detective," replied Jon. "Yes, there are some things we are investigating right now, but up until the point you found the connection to Jamal – and we are not sure if it is actually a connection yet – there was no concrete linkage. I don't want to take over the investigation just yet, although I may end up doing just that. How about this? For now, we work the case jointly. Can you and your team find the SUV and see what else ties Jamal to the SUV other than the registration. I can't see him being involved, but I guess I have to be open."

"The boss isn't going to like it, but I agree. Can your boss call mine? What are you going to do?"

"Yeah, I'll have Tony call your boss. Just leave me his number. After I'm done updating Tony, my partner, Rick, and I are going to head out to HyDek and see what we can find out."

"Hey, you never said why you thought Dom called you."

"I can't tell you that until I run everything by Tony. There is something there and if it's the connection I think it is, this goes way beyond a simple hit and run."

Detective Bancroft eyed Jon and threw up his hands. "I just handed you what we agreed was a JOINT CASE, Special Agent Wells, remember. It's my ass on the line."

"You'll know as soon as I clear it with the boss. Not my rules, not where this is heading, understand? I don't want to step on your toes, steal any thunder or anything like that, but we are talking big here, so just trust me."

Bancroft, who had placed his hand down on Jon's desk and leaned over it to show his displeasure, now backed off. He straightened his suitcoat, looked squarely at Jon, turned around, briefcase in hand, and walked towards the door.

"My ass, not yours Jon. Remember that. So keep me in the loop."

Chapter 30

Jon and Rick drove from downtown to the corn fields on the outskirts of the greater metro area. The drive was long enough and the traffic light enough for Jon and Rick to review the case. Rick took notes while Jon drove.

"What is it that we know?"

Rick read from the notes he was keying into the laptop.

"A Data Center Shift Supervisor, Dominic Seragosa, wants to talk to the FBI about something – something he won't talk about over the phone."

"He gets run over by an SUV owned by Jamal Kusow. "

"Occupant in passenger side of SUV jumps out and steals Dom's backpack after running him over."

"SUV has not been found."

"Jamal is our main conduit to the Somali community in the Twin Cities."

"Gloria said there was chatter that there was Chinese cyber terrorism on the rise and that there was a connection to terrorism in Minnesota. This is why she wanted to read us in to what she and her team had discovered."

"So we have some leaky connections; cyber, data center, terrorism in Minnesota, Somali connection, Jamal, and the death of a data center/cyber type shift supervisor tied to Jamal. Anything else?" asked Rick.

"Not that I have right now. The linkages are weak but not the weakest start to a case I've ever had."

"Let's see what the folks at HyDek have to say. How far out is this place anyway?"

Jon and Rick pulled into the parking area at the HyDek facility. "What a dismal place. I've seen prisons that look nicer. All they're missing are the guard towers," Rick noted as they exited the vehicle and walked towards the entry.

Once in, they were greeted by an executive from HyDek. Rick and Jon both introduced themselves. "And your name, ma'am?" Rick asked.

"I'm Celeste Van Dorn, Vice President of Operations. Thank you for calling ahead and letting me know you were on your way out. It gave me a chance to get some information gathered," the executive reached her hand out and shook both Rick and Jon's hands. She signed them in and gave them their guest passes. "Please, you'll need to have these on to go in. Also, I need you to leave any computers, phones, or data storage devices with the guards. They'll be returned to you once you depart. My office is inside the secured area."

Rick looked sideways at Jon. "It all looks secure to me."

"Thank you. Our clients deserve only the best. We strive to provide the best in data security. The physical security is only the first step. If you can't get in, you can't do anything bad. Personally, I think it's a bit overkill, but it sells. So...just don't tell the clients that." She winked at Rick as she completed the last sentence.

Once they settled in Celeste's office, Jon looked at Rick giving him first chance to start with the questioning. He normally let Rick handle the base coverage questions while he preferred to watch how people answered. Jon felt he often gleaned more information watching how people responded.

"Celeste, thank you for your time today. As I mentioned on the phone, we are investigating Dominic Seragosa's death. We understand he was employed here. What exactly did he do?"

"Why is the FBI investigating his death and wasn't it an accident anyway?" Celeste replied.

"I am not at liberty to discuss the particulars of the investigation but suffice it to say that there are some extenuating circumstances.

The Minneapolis Police Department requested our assistance. Now, if you could please answer the question."

"Dom was a shift supervisor here. He reported directly to me," she replied curtly.

"What do shift supervisors do?"

"What do they do? What don't they do really. They are in charge during their shift. Everything goes through them. They act as the representative of HyDek to the client on an operational basis. For instance, should an alert happen on a client server, the shift supervisor makes the determination as to what severity the alert is. Now, there are standards for what each type of alert is and those are followed, to the "T" mind you, but the responsibility still lies with the shift supervisor. Communications with the client are initiated per the SLA, excuse me, the service level agreement until the alert has been properly addressed. Once again, per the SLA. Nothing really happens, that is not covered by an SLA; however, every once in a blue moon, something comes up that was unexpected and the experience a shift supervisor brings allows them to take appropriate actions and keep all interested parties informed. The last thing I need is for a client to call me and ask what is going on with their servers and I don't know. I count on my shift supervisors to keep me in the loop and out of trouble."

"So they know everything that goes on during their shift and communicate the shift's activities to the clients and you?" Rick confirmed.

"Yes."

"Who are your clients?"

"That is privileged and confidential information. No one gets that information without a warrant."

"Fair enough. We'll come back to that later. What can you tell us about Dom? Did he have any friends here we should talk to? Was he a good employee?"

"Dom was one of the best. He had a ton of experience and had a way with employees. He was what we called a 'big picture' guy. Techies, you see, often get lost in the minutia of their daily tasks. What concerns them too often is the 'cool and neat' of technology. Well let me tell you, 'cool and neat' doesn't pay the bills. Once you learn that and are able to see the money end of the business the big picture appears. We need more of those in IT. He was also always bringing in little wooden presents he made for people. In fact, his last day here he brought in a wooden lacrosse stick that he made for his son. He wanted to show off a little I guess," Celeste's face went ashen all of a sudden.

"Oh my God, his family. How are they? He has three kids and another on the way you know. How is his wife? Must be just sick with grief. I can't imagine...," she collected herself after a moment and continued, "to be honest, I'm not sure how we'll replace Dom here. I mean, we'll hire someone to fill the seat, but it won't be the same. We are going to miss him."

"What about friends?"

"He and Abdi Ali, our security expert, worked together at various places for years. In fact, we hired Dom based on Abdi's referral. His office, cubicle really, is right over there." She said pointing in the general direction of the main operations floor. "I'm assuming you want to speak with him?"

When Jon replied in the affirmative she picked up her phone. "Abdi, this is Celeste. There are some gentlemen in my office who have questions regarding Dom and his accident. I said you were friends and they could talk with you. I'm bringing them over." Celeste returned the phone receiver to its cradle. "Gentlemen, if you'll follow me."

"Abdi, let me introduce you to Special Agents Rick Anderson and Jon Wells, FBI. They are the gentlemen I told you about." They each shook hands introducing themselves to one another. Celeste turned to Jon and Rick. "If you have nothing else for me, I'll leave you with Abdi. He'll answer any questions he is allowed to and sign you out." She did not wait for either of them to say thanks before she left.

"Wow. She's a piece of work," exclaimed Rick upon Celeste's sudden departure.

"Abdi, thanks for seeing us. Although it seems you were unaware of our visit. Is this an appropriate place to talk?" asked Jon.

"Yes, it's fine. Did Celeste say FBI? Why are you looking into Dom's accident?"

"Oh, just a little inter-departmental help. We do that every now and then. We understand you and Dom were friends?" Rick deflected Abdi's query with his own line of questioning. Jon noted how well Rick did this. *"He's getting really good."*

124

"Dom and I worked at various companies together over the past ten years or so. One of us would start someplace, then refer the other, and pick up a referral bonus. We each took turns. Our little scam to get more money out of 'the man' so to speak. But we didn't do much outside of work if that's what you are asking."

"That's all right. Getting back to Dom. Did you notice if he was upset about anything recently?" Jon watched Abdi's face and eyes while Rick continued with his line of questions.

"Dom was pretty even keeled. He always saw the 'big picture.' But now that you ask and given his unfortunate accident he did seem a bit unlike his normal self lately. But then again, Donna, his wife, is pregnant again. I think this one was a surprise. Donna went back to work two years ago when their youngest started junior high. I guess that would be enough to freak anyone out. Just couldn't keep it in his pants I guess."

"So his being 'unlike his normal self' was not due to work – just having a surprise baby on the way?"

"Yeah, I guess. You know babies cost a lot of money. And then Donna will probably need to quit her job. That had to be a load on his mind."

"I see. You aren't married I take it?" asked Rick.

"No, I'm not. Why do you ask?"

"Oh nothing. Just making an observation."

Jon, sensing this was going nowhere fast thanked Abdi and asked him to escort them to the entry. They gathered their electronics, signed out, and turned back to Abdi.

"Abdi, thank you for your time today. We may have to talk with you again so stay available. Say, what is the nationality of your name Abdi anyway?" asked Jon.

"It's just a Muslim name. Nothing special. Why?"

"Oh just curious. I'm a bit of an onomast, that's all." Jon shrugged his response and left with Rick looking somewhat confused.

"An onomast? What the heck is that?" Rick asked when they reached their vehicle.

"It's the study of name origin. I knew it was Islamic. Who wouldn't. I just wanted to see his response. I didn't get a good vibe from him from the start of our questioning. That's why I let you ask all the questions."

"I agree with you."

"I think Mr. Abdi Ali is going to have his life explored in depth and we'll be the people doing the digging."

"Do you think…."

"Yes. I do think. Make sure you capture the conversation and our thoughts in your notes. I'll work on the warrant so we can get the list of clients."

Chapter 31

A fire was reported coming from a cement plant just north of the Crosstown Commons where I-35W joins Minnesota Highway 62 for several miles on the border of South Minneapolis and Richfield. The area is highly industrial with the cement plant, an energy company yard, several large scale landscaping facilities, and a rail line abutting the 14 lane, grade-separated freeway into downtown Minneapolis. The bright light of the fire was not the reason it was noticed; the acrid smell was. A bicyclist with a keen sense of smell called it in when passing by on her way home from work.

The vehicle was a total loss. The Fire Department took its time in responding as there was no danger to human life or property. Once the fire was extinguished the police investigators began piecing together why a vehicle had been torched. Inquiries to ownership of the cement plant indicated the vehicle was not one of theirs. Nor could they provide a reason for it being on their property. The fenced portion of the facility was further in from the gravel parking lot area where the vehicle lay smoldering. The scent of gasoline filled the cabin. It was easy enough to see the ignition point of the fire. The doors of the vehicle were discolored. Bubbles had formed on the exterior panels and soot covered the inside of the shattered glass of the driver's side window.

The suspicious nature of the fire was further corroborated when an investigator determined the VIN had been ground down, rendering it unreadable in the field.

"Wasn't there a bike accident several days ago by the band shell on Lake Harriet involving a vehicle similar to this?" hollered one crime scene investigator to the other.

"Yeah, I read a report on that yesterday. Do you think this vehicle could be the one involved? I don't recall reading they found the vehicle or the suspects."

"Guess we better take this one downtown for further testing."

Chapter 32

"We have a serious problem!" Matthew Scoggins rushed into the office. Matthew was the Vice President in Charge of Quality Control at MnMedDev.

MnMedDev, one of the largest medical device manufactures in the world, was headquartered in the old Ford Assembly Plant high above the Mississippi River on the eastern bank. A dam, built for Ford in the 1920's, still provided all the power needed for the new medical device manufacturing plants. Unlike many corporations today, MnMedDev located all divisions of the company here in Minnesota – most in the metro area. MnMedDev started out 70 years ago and held the lead in specialty medical devices ever since. The company believed control came from "owning" every part of the process. But leadership changes in the past decade brought forth new ideas less conservative than those forging the company into the behemoth it had been. The economy over the past decade forced leadership into interesting decisions. As a result, some of its ancillary service divisions outsourced small parts of the company. The company, for the first time in its history, laid off 1,000 IT employees seven years ago. Then they outsourced the entire IT division. The market reacted positively resulting with a 15% increase in the share value of the company's stock. Leadership was enthralled with the results and vowed to find more ways to reduce employee headcount to increase the share value of the company.

Most recently, the C-Suite sent one of its senior vice presidents in charge of process improvement to Germany. His directive was to improve profits by fully integrating computer systems throughout the manufacturing process. MnMedDev was once a leader in automating distinct parts of manufacturing. In other industries robots machined metals to tolerances people would never attain and computer aided high-speed photography sped up the quality control process as parts made their way through the mechanized assembly process. This was not an automobile plant and the board had been reluctant to move towards limited human involvement, but global economics dictated much of what large corporations did.

The VP of Process Improvement hired a German consultant who spent the previous five years in China creating automobile assembly plants as part of a joint venture. In China, the job force was still not highly educated. Therefore, they learned the key was to increase automation and to completely integrate sales, design, engineering, manufacturing, and quality control divisions. His team removed the human element as much as possible, wrote programs to completely automate repetitive tasks, and incorporated the same engineering specifications entered in the front end to provide QA testing values. He also outsourced IT to control the entire process. Outsourcing provided impartiality, therefore providing a separation of sorts between engineers and QC. This streamlining jumpstarted the Chinese automobile industry and propelled them to lead the global industry in number of vehicles produced each year. Minnesota provided a wealth of highly educated and experienced workers. Certainly, the concept and implementation of highly-integrated systems would provide even greater results with a work force skilled in their fields.

The lure of money was too strong and MnMedDev's Board relented. Automation meant fewer employees, which improved the bottom line. So more highly skilled employees, in manufacturing, engineering, process control, and human resources, were laid off, but not before the German process engineers brought in to manage and provide oversight to the implementation gleaned all process knowledge from them. The same team outsourced more software engineers to install the new IT infrastructure and write the code for the new processes.

Money was saved and one more time, the market smiled upon the great thinkers within the C-Suite and Board, by increasing the value of the shares by 20%. All was well.

Nancy Pillery, Senior Vice President of Manufacturing looked up from her desk and over the top of her glasses. Outwardly, her face showed nothing. Internally, she felt only disdain. She did not like problems. Problems led to failures. Failures led to job loss. True, the golden parachute she negotiated guaranteed her $10 million dollars at termination of employment, regardless the reason, but Nancy Pillery did NOT fail.

"What are you taking about, Matt," she muttered as Matt plopped himself into a chair. His face was red from running, papers stuffed at odd angles burst from the manila folders he was holding, and his always immaculate appearance was disheveled.

"I never wanted to go all out automatic. It just isn't right. Not enough checks and balances. I knew it then but I was too afraid to speak up. I should have. I just can't believe I sold out and let this happen. Oh my God! What is going to happen to me? I'm going to get fired – maybe even thrown in jail!"

"Calm down. Take a deep breath and I'll be with you shortly." Nancy rose from her chair and walked to the door. She slowly closed it. She exuded calm and grace. Nothing would change that. Her red tartan belted dress, hemmed at the knee, black heels, and dark grey jacket framed her well-toned body. The door clicked shut. Moving to the left, her hands slowly closed the blinds of the glass that was the only interior wall to her office. She had an oddly-shaped corner office with outside windows on three sides designed to allow maximum sunlight in while offering exceptional external views. The headquarters building received numerous architectural awards, from most unique corporate design to the coveted LEED Platinum certification for sustainability.

Nancy sat next to Matt and leaned in close so she could speak softly. She had learned that with men, when you leaned towards them with a small sneer on her face and spoke in a smooth, soft, even-keeled tone, she could shake most men to their core. They were putty in her hands afterwards. "Now Matt," she said. "You can't just burst into my office like that. What will everyone think? Appearances often outweigh reality. And at our levels, appearance is everything."

Matt looked at her with incredulity.

"Matt. I mean it." She leaned even closer. "You need to get control of yourself. If I think you can't," she leaned back, "I'll call security and the appearance will be that you have had a breakdown." Once again she moved in. "You...WILL...be...finished. Have I made my position perfectly clear?"

"Yes, you have," Matt replied fighting back his fear. "I'm in control." He took another deep breath.

"Good. Now tell me, slowly, what brought you in here today." Nancy sat back, removed her glasses, crossed the temples of her glasses partway. She rolled the tips back and forth – depending on her reaction to what Matt said. This was another of the strategies she employed to control a potential situation. It worked on both men and women.

"All glucose monitoring device lines have production issues. The tolerances are off – the devices are failing." Matt looked Nancy in the eye. She did not bat an eyelash.

"Like I said earlier in my haste, I never liked the process of integrating the software packages of the engineers with the robots making the devices AND certainly not with the QA equipment. The checks and balances that we lived with for years went right out the window." He took another breath to keep his heart rate down as he described what he found.

"My job is to figure out why the problems are occurring and make sure it doesn't continue. As a mechanical engineer I know how the entire process should work and where problems tend to crop up. I know engineering. I know machines. I know how they work. I even know, or at least once upon a time I knew, how to program the machinery to do the work. But now, with all the damn integration and the software programming being done elsewhere, by God knows who, it's harder to nail down the problem."

"Continue," was all Nancy said.

"My team has gone over everything. The only thing we can think of is that somehow the tooling machines are not doing what the engineering designs dictate they do."

"Shouldn't your QC team catch that?" Nancy asked.

"Yes. I agree. So fingers can be pointed that way. But the parameters being fed to them for testing are the same parameters the tooling machines are receiving. Therefore, everything passes.

The kicker is the logs show that the parameters are the same as those on the engineering designs. I don't understand how that can be and we don't have the forensic skill to dig any deeper. Then, this morning, I took an exemplar of specifications for the newest glucose monitoring device to the Chief Engineer and asked him to review the data. Ranju said the specifications are off."

Neither Nancy nor Matt said anything for several moments. Matt shifted uneasily in his chair. Nancy stood and walked over to the windows overlooking the only true gorge along the entire 2,350-mile length of the Mississippi River. It was one of her favorite and most relaxing views. She did her best thinking looking out this window.

Matt broke the silence. "I think it's the IT system. My gut tells me we've been hacked, but I can't back that statement up. The IT division is outsourced so you know what that means. They will stonewall that accusation. I need your help to figure this out."

Nancy held up a finger indicating she heard him. After a few more moments, she slowly turned around and said, "I know who to call." She proceeded to her desk, sat down, worked out the wrinkles in her dress, reached for her personal cell phone, took a calming breath, and finally made the call.

Chapter 33

The Riverside Thugs was a Somali gang. Jon put several members behind bars for ties to al-Shabaab. Now that they had a link to a known Somali gang that had ties to terrorism, receiving a warrant for more information at HyDek was a slam dunk. Rick was busy with the MPD forensics team. Jon invited Detective Bancroft from the Minneapolis Police Department to join him at HyDek. Jon gave his word he would keep MPD in the loop, especially Detective Bancroft. Besides, maintaining a good working relationship with the metro's largest police department was always a good thing and he needed that. The warrant was being served outside of Minneapolis so additional paperwork was needed. Paperwork was always cumbersome and something to be avoided when you could.

Jon and Detective Bancroft, whose first name Jon found out was Tyler, had no problem gathering the information they needed this time. Celeste Van Dorn, Vice President of Operations at HyDek, was more than accommodating. What was troubling, though, was the fact that one Abdi Ali, Security Expert, was not on the premises and, according to Ms. Van Dorn, left shortly after Jon's previous visit. He had not returned.

"I don't know why he left or when he will be returning. I have to say this is unusual. I called him several times but only reached his voice mail. I'm more than a little upset about all of this," the VP of Operations told Tyler. Tyler asked for phone records for Abdi. They reviewed the printout but did not see anything of interest. "You know," said Celeste, "this is a bit strange. Abdi is always talking to someone."

"There is not much on the report about calls on his corporate line," said Jon as he scanned the report.

"True, but Abdi was the one person allowed a cell phone inside the secured area. That's what he used. He was always walking and talking. It pissed everyone off he could do that. I just assumed it was all business-related. Our clients never complained about his work. As long as the clients are happy the employees can get a little pissy and I'm fine with that."

"Celeste, what can you tell us about Abdi? You said clients never complained about his work. Anything else?" Jon asked.

"Well, he was extremely conscientious about security. But that's why we hired him. In fact, he was a bit anal about it. OK, more than anal to be truthful." Celeste went on the say that Abdi had a "bug up his ass" about employees here at HyDek. The executive team felt Abdi was doing a fantastic job. His attitude towards security significantly reduced liability in their view. And that increased profit. But it did have its drawbacks. Employee turnover was higher than anyone was comfortable with.

"No one around here honestly liked him, except Dom, come to think of it. I guess that's because of how he approached his responsibilities. Look, no one ever likes the cyber security person anyway. Sort of goes with the territory," Celeste went on to say.

"Hi," a voice from outside Celeste's office whispered. "Are you here about Dom? Man that is so weird, him getting run over riding a bike and all. He hated riding his bike. His wife wanted him to ride it to work, to – you know – lose some belly fat. But Dom, just didn't want to. Anyway, can I help?"

"And you are?" queried Jon.

"Oh, that's Bradley. He was Dom's number one operator. He's taken over for Dom until we hire someone new."

"Bradley. Come on in. What else can you tell us? Did you know Dom well?" directed Jon.

"Oh yeah, sure. Me and Dom, we were like this man," Bradley indicated by crossing his index and middle fingers in a juvenile manner to show closeness.

"Well then. What about Abdi. How well do you know him?"

Bradley looked at Celeste. "It's OK Bradley, go ahead say what you want."

"He's a real asshole. Celeste, you know he's the reason no one wants to work here."

"I think that's over stating it."

"No it isn't! Jesus! He even got into an argument with Dom the other night in the breakroom. They'd been gone for a bit and a HI PRI came in. You know, a High Priority issue? Important like. So I went looking for them. I walked back to the breakroom and heard them even before I got there. I poked my head around the corner. I was just going to barge in, but then thought better of it. I turned around and took care of the HI PRI. I mean, hey, I've been doing this a long time too, ya know? Figured with them being friends and all I'd just let it pass. By the time I took care of the issue, Dom returned to his cubicle. So I updated him and went back to the breakroom to get a pop. I saw Abdi leaving the building then. I saw him later in the shift though. They both looked pissed so I just did my own thing."

"When was this?" asked Tyler.

"You know the other night. Actually, come to think of it, it was the night before Dom got killed."

"Was it a personal issue or -"

"No way man," Bradley cut Jon off. "It was work-related. Dom was upset about something. He had papers spread all over the tables and I thought I heard him say something about a 'conspiracy' or something like that."

"Anything else?"

"Nah man, that's it. I better get back to work. Later." Bradley spun around and waltzed out of the room.

Tyler and Jon looked at one another and then towards Celeste who said, "Sorry about that. He takes a while to get used to."

"Not a problem. Did you know about this argument?"

"No, not at all."

"Abdi said that Dom was 'not himself' lately. And what of this 'conspiracy.'"

"Special Agent Wells, right? I don't know about a 'conspiracy' or anything like that. Bradley is well, you saw him; he's a bit weird. Great operator. Never late. Always here. You can count on him to do his work. But he'll never make supervisor if you know what I mean. But right now, I have no choice. As far as Dom being 'not himself' I wouldn't say that. I didn't see anything to indicate he was anything but himself."

"Is it possible to view the security logs without Abdi?"

"Yes, let me pull them for you. I have access to all that." Celeste typed in some commands on her keyboard.

"OK. Here is the report." She turned her monitor so both men could see it. "Wait a minute, this is interesting. The report shows Abdi never left the building until his shift was over. Hmm. Let me pull up Dom's report. He does this thing he calls, I mean, called a 'walkabout'. He walked through the entire building saying hi to everyone, chatting with them, and checking things out. He often left the building and checked outside also. I asked him why he did this. We have cameras and access logs. He felt it was his way of connecting with the team and showing them he cared about what they did. Also, according to Dom, everyone knew he did this so no 'hanky panky,' so to speak, could go on during his shift."

She shifted her attention back to the screen. "Christ almighty. What the hell is going on. This is NOT right!" Celeste pounded her keyboard. "Sorry. But this has never happened. The log shows Dom left the building the same day we're looking at and never came back. That's not right. I know it isn't. Let's check the video feeds." She stood up from behind her desk and sped out of the office without a word. Jon and Tyler had to jog to catchup.

Celeste ordered one of the guards at the front desk to pull up security footage for that week. She gave him the dates and times in question. When Celeste, Jon, and Tyler looked at the videos what they saw contradicted the access logs. Dom did, in fact, return from his walkabout. The guards on duty happened to work that shift. Celeste asked them if they both remembered Dom being there all shift. They did. A quick look through the login records confirmed he logged in and unlocked his computer shortly after the video showed him returning. The video also showed and the guards remembered, Abdi left for about twenty minutes that particular evening. Just like Bradley said.

"Celeste. We need these reports and videos. We also need Abdi's computer for forensic evaluation."

137

"Jon, glad you're back. I went down to the Minneapolis Police Department Forensic lab like you asked. They have a 2015 Black GMC Yukon that was torched down by the Crosstown Commons. Looks like they connected the vehicle to Dom's death."

"Rick, tell me you have more," responded Jon.

"The forensics team conducted numerous tests confirming the vehicle fire was purposefully set by igniting gasoline poured over the driver's seat. A further investigation of the scene produced a red two-gallon gasoline container in the area. Fortunately for us, the vehicle didn't burn very well."

"Why is that? Did they find more?"

"Oh yeah. They recovered blood from the front grill and bumper area. The blood matched Dominic's. Also, they identified paint chips from Dom's bike." Rick read from his flipbook notepad, "the paint chips were Pinot Noir Black Metallic Color Code: WA103V/GWU for a 2015 GMC Yukon. That pretty much confirms the vehicle was the one that ran over Dominic Seragosa."

"That's what I like to hear. Anything else?"

"Yep. Even though the VIN had been tampered with, the team was able to recover it by using an etching reagent to raise the numbers. They made a cast impression of the VIN for evidence with modeling clay. The recovered VIN is registered to Jamal Kusow. This confirms what we already knew."

"I want his mouth shut up!" screamed "The Man." He had received a report that Malick was missing when his device no longer sent in data. Further investigation provided information that he'd been arrested. "Who trained him anyway? This is exactly why they didn't want bangers involved in the first place. It's my ass on the line here, I convinced them you were perfect." He was beside himself with rage. When he gathered his composure, he looked at Guled and said, "Here is how you're going to fix this. Get someone inside and shut him up. Kill him if need be. I don't care how you get it done, cause a riot somewhere or something and get several of you in. Something like that should work. I need it done now!"

Detective Bancroft needed a win. The investigation into Dominic Seragosa's death had reached a dead end. The videos and forensics on the truck pointed them to Jamal Kusow. But he was a pillar in the business community. He also collaborated with the FBI and MPD Gang units to break apart the terrorism funding and recruiting ring. No one wanted to go down that route. His superiors told him to let the FBI handle Jamal.

Bancroft was establishing a rapport of sorts with FBI Special Agent Jon Wells. He didn't like sharing information with the Feds but nonetheless knew they had more resources than he. Still, he felt they were not as forthcoming with the information those vast resources were obtaining.

MPD discovered that the credit card skimmer was a gang banger. During his first interrogation session Malick was proud, angry, and refused to cooperate. He kept mumbling over and over that Allah was good, Allah was great, death to the infidels, and that something wonderful was happening. The police felt a night in the general correction center population would help him see the error of his ways.

The next morning, bright and early, Malick was brought back into the six by six square windowless room. The evening in jail had not gone well for Malick. He was bruised, his eyes were bloodshot from lack of sleep, and he had even less teeth than he did when arrested. The detective's second attempt to find out who was in charge of the credit card skimming was much more fruitful. Malick told the detectives he and several other members of the Riverside Thugs were on their first attempt to gain credit card data.

"Guled ran the entire thing man," said Malick.

"You mean the leader of the Riverside Thugs?" asked Tyler seeking clarification on who this "Guled" was.

"Guled run the gang every day but you know he still reports to someone. No one knows who. But Guled, ya, at work man, he run everything. Him and the Chinaman. They promised me new clothes. They told us how to blend in and not be noticed, ya know?"

"Yeah. Well, we noticed. That didn't go so well did it?" remarked one of the other detectives.

"Fucking shoe. That and the Chinaman trainer got sick. They gave us only half our two weeks' training. Promises, promises, just fucked me man. Now I'm here. Can't even have my own money."

"What do you mean by that?"

"Man, they made me set up a bank account for direct deposit and employment paperwork so taxes be paid and everything be legal. You believe that? Me legal. Ha. I don't think that smart so I don't do it at first. That when I got these." Malick showed them the burn marks on his arms. "Bossman pissed, say next time I fuck up I'm a goner. So I did the bank thing and I sent them money they paid me where they said it had to go. I knew I was gettin' taken. Make me be legal, pay me big money then I gets to only keep a bit of it. That's not right. Make me wear those stupid ass clothes. You know I had to buy those fuckin' shoes with my own money man! They didn't have any my size. They should go buy them for me."

Malick turned away from the men and refused to answer any more questions. Tyler and the other detective briefly stayed in the interrogation room after Malick was removed. They used this time to review each other's notes from the session. It had taken the entire day, but the second day of questioning was now completed. Malick was cooperating, but only so many questions could be asked. It was a pain-staking process of asking the same question multiple times in multiple ways to make sure his story was solid.

"I want him in solitary confinement," said Tyler. "You heard what he said about what would happen if he messed up again."

"I'd classify getting caught and thrown into jail a major mess-up," the detective sitting across from Tyler replied. "Major fuck up indeed."

During the all-day session of questioning and unknown to Tyler, an unexpected outbreak of civil unrest in the city occurred. A series of protests against police corruption and cruelty erupted in several neighborhoods. The cells in the correctional center overflowed with protestors. The jailers did their best but Tyler's request to have Malick placed into solitary was lost in the paperwork shuffle of the evening. Malick was placed back into the general population cell. That evening, a brawl broke out between protestors. In the chaos no one noticed the three men with beards and skull caps who shanked Malick twenty times in the lower back, neck, and chest. He bled out within minutes. That's what happened to gang snitches.

Tyler still had some unanswered questions. Namely who the Chinaman was and where he received his training.

With the only lead now dead from suspected gang retaliation, all indications were the Riverside Thugs were moving in an unexpected direction. Tyler's supervisor determined MPD needed to gather up as many members as possible and figure things out from there. It would not be easy. The gang had a history of violence – especially when interacting with the police. Once the word was out the cops were looking for Riverside Thugs they would go underground. It had happened before. No one saw any Riverside Thugs for a complete month during one disastrous round-up. Police were divided on how to proceed. Detective Bancroft led the group promoting a raid on the gang's known major residence. His side won. The raid was on.

"Jamal, I'm investigating the death of Dominic Seragosa."

"Who is that?" Jamal responded from behind the counter at his deli-style restaurant.

"Just a guy I knew who was on his way to see me and run over by a truck registered to one of your restaurants."

"What do you mean a truck of mine ran someone over?" Jamal was tired of being on the wrong end of accusations. He waved a knife in the air from behind the counter. Not at Jon, but he was showing it off nonetheless.

"Jamal, I'm serious here. You and I go back a long way and have always been on the up and up with each other. Let's continue with that. I have a job to do and I have some questions I need to ask." Jon was in no mood to be messed with today. "Do you own a Black GMC Yukon with Minnesota plates UHK 612?"

"Jon, my company has around eight vehicles if you count the ones my parents and I use. Sure, one of them is a GMC Yukon. I don't know for sure that's the license plate of my vehicle though."

"Jamal, I know the vehicle is yours, OK? We looked it up in the DMV records and that is why I'm here."

"OK, OK. Where and when did this accident occur?"

"Last Tuesday by the Lake Harriet Band Shell in William Berry Park. A Black GMC Yukon with those plates ran over the victim, a man jumped out of the vehicle, grabbed the victim's backpack, and returned to the vehicle. It then fled in a northerly direction. The vehicle turned easterly on West 36th St. We found it later, torched."

"Fine. I will look into this." Jamal motioned for another employee to take over making lunch for the paying customers – Jon was not one of those. He walked back to his office. Jon followed closely seeing the knife was no longer in Jamal's hands. Jamal searched his computer for vehicle records and responded. "Yes. That vehicle is mine. Or I should say, I use that vehicle for pickups and deliveries for all my restaurants. It's actually very new to us."

"What do you mean, it's new to you?"

"I have several investors that help out with finances. One of them just purchased the truck and delivered it to us several weeks ago. It has really come in handy. It's one of the ways he invests. Periodically, he needs to use it and I let him have it. So far it's worked out."

"Did this person 'borrow' the vehicle during the time in question?"

"I guess you need that now?"

"Please."

Jamal looked at Jon for several moments before responding. "Let me check," he reached for his cell phone and made a quick call.

Jon reviewed his notes while Jamal engaged in a heated conversation in a mixture of Somali and English. When he hung up Jon questioned the tone of the conversation. "You know, I couldn't understand much of what you said, but it sounds like you are angrier with them than you are me."

"That was the manager at my flagship restaurant." Jamal threw up his hands in an exasperated manner. "You aren't going to believe this. The vehicle you want to know about is missing. The son-of-a-bitch didn't want to tell me. He's been looking for it, covering his tracks with other vehicles for work. I just don't understand how not telling me helps him."

"Jamal. Look, I'm sorry to have to ask you these questions. You are not being personally implicated in any wrongdoings, especially the hit and run. It was just a vehicle registered to you." Jon and Jamal stared at each other. Each standing his own ground. Neither willing to budge. Finally, Jamal took a step back and sat down.

"What do you need to know?" asked Jamal.

"Does your manager know who took it?"

"No. Get this. The keys are still at the restaurant."

"That means whoever took it didn't get the keys, or need the keys."

"Agreed. The only people who have the keys are me, the restaurant manager, and Abdi. I know I have mine."

"Abdi? Who is that?"

"Abdi Ali. He's the investor that bought the truck."

"How do you know him Jamal?" Jon was frantically searching through his notes while Jamal answered.

"Why?"

"Please? I'll tell you when I find it in my notes," responded Jon.

"OK. He was one of the first kids I mentored. Great kid. He excelled at computers. I managed to get him enrolled in the U of M with my connections even though his grades were not the best in high school. But hey, lots of kids don't see why grades are important if their parents aren't involved. Abdi's parents are OK, but he has five other siblings so he didn't always get their attention. Abdi got into his share of trouble, but it was the type of trouble more associated with normal high school stuff. Anyway, after college, he got jobs in IT departments at a number of different companies here in town. He jumps around a bit more than I think he should, but he tells me it's just part of the IT culture to move around a lot."

Jon looked up from his notes. "What does he do in IT?"

"Cyber security and network stuff. In fact, he's done all of my computer work. That's how he first got involved in the company. Now he mostly provides funding and stuff like the truck. He isn't married and doesn't have any kids. He helps some of the Somali kids out – once again very quietly. He also gives me names of kids to hire. Not sure how he gets the names. As far as I know, he rarely comes to Cedar-Riverside, attends mosque, or has other connections with the community."

"Do you know where he works now?"

"Why so many questions about Abdi?"

Jon looked Jamal in the eyes and said, "just tell me where he works, Jamal."

"OK. Last I knew, he worked at some data center out in the sticks. I can't remember what it's called...HyVee, no that's the grocery chain. It's sounded like that though...."

"HyDek?" Jon offered up.

"Yeah, that's the one."

"Shit."

"What's wrong Jon."

"Dominic Seragosa worked at HyDek."

Chapter 34

Nancy actually dated Jon Wells several times as an undergrad at Cornell. Nancy was never one to get caught up in a romantic relationship, even in college – too much at stake professionally. Even so, they remained friends over the years, each tracking the others progression through their career paths. Those paths crossed again when Jon was assigned to the Twin Cities and they were able to meet more often. The friendship was great and Jon certainly had a way about him. A catch in college, she was surprised that some lucky lady hadn't caught him. And he certainly had matured with gravitas. She enjoyed the banter and friendship and every so often allowed herself to think it would be nice to end up in the morning with Jon next to her. At least every now and then. Her feelings were getting the best of her and uncharacteristically she felt flushed. *"See this is exactly why I didn't - and don't!"* Nancy chastised herself for allowing daydreams to distract her at a time like this. *"Get it together, isn't that what you are going to tell Matt to do?"* she thought.

Nancy knew making a call to the authorities without going through the corporate channels was risky, but Jon would know what to do, how to do it, and would keep things quiet as long as he could. His handling of the Somali Terrorism Ring showed that. She moved away from the window and told Matt she knew who to call. She picked up the phone and dialed.

"Jon? Hi. It's Nancy. No time for chit chat."

"What? You? No time for chit chat?" Jon too enjoyed the banter he and Nancy shared.

"We have an issue here and I need to talk to you about it. Can't discuss this on the phone yet."

"Guess that means it's serious. Should we come down?"

"Oh God, no. That would cause a ruckus. That's exactly what I am trying to avoid. Get my drift? Meet me at Pig's Eye Grille across from the "X" in St. Paul in an hour. I know the owners. They'll find an out of the way spot for us. Just tell the hostess who you are and they'll take you to me. Just you Jon. No one else."

"Got it. See you there."

Jon shared the conversation with Rick and told him to check into anything he could find out about MnMedDev. Jon's boss wasn't in so he would have to call him on the way. He looked at his watch. Fifty-five minutes left to get from downtown Minneapolis to downtown St. Paul. On a good day it took 15 minutes to drive the distance once you got on the freeway. Ten minutes on each end to walk to the car, find parking, and walk to the restaurant. That gave him twenty minutes or so for bad traffic – always a consideration with the construction that MN Dot continuously seemed to be doing.

Nancy looked at Matt. He was in sorry shape. *"I'm so glad I never married a feeble man like that,"* thought Nancy. *"Jon on the other hand...stop it!"*

"Matt. You need to pull it together. Continue to gather as much information as you can find without causing alarm. Do NOT say anything to anyone until I get back. And for God's sake Matt, look like you're in charge and quit acting like a victim! Holy shit." Nancy directed her anger full force at Matt. She was angered with Matt, at the situation he just presented, and at herself for allowing what felt like a schoolgirl crush to muddy her thoughts. She gathered herself, opened the door, ushered Matt out, and walked over to her administrative assistant.

"Alissa. I'm going out for a while. Clear my schedule for the rest of the day. I am not sure if I will be back during working hours. Do not forward any calls to me until I call and tell you otherwise. Thank you."

With that, she pivoted and walked away before Alissa could say anything.

Jon's cell phone rang. It seemed like some days the damn thing never stopped ringing. Jon knew it was an important tool for his work, but sometimes he seriously wished he could throw it away and just enjoy the day. Driving in this traffic sucked enough without talking on the phone too.

"This is Jon," he snapped at the person invading his space.

"Detective Bancroft. Holy shit Jon, bad day?"

"Sorry about that. Sometimes I hate my phone."

"Oh, don't I know that feeling. My wife hates it even more – except when she's the one doing the calling. Say, the reason for my negligent interruption of your time is…" chortled Tyler.

Jon interrupted Bancroft and joked, "Yeah, Yeah, Yeah. Do you have something for me or did Rick tell you to just piss me off?"

Laughing on both ends of the phone line ensued. Jon continued, "Thanks. Actually, I feel better now. What's up Tyler? You have something more on Dom's investigation?"

"Not exactly. I got pulled into the electronic skimming case once you guys grabbed the data forensics found. Reggie's in a pile of crap by the way. You'll need to fix that later. Since we were already sharing info on Dom's investigation, I guess my name just rose to the top and the Chief grabbed at it."

"Sorry about that. I'll help out Reg."

"Thanks. Now that we've concluded our foreplay, here is some information you need to have. I dug into our boy Malick a bit more. We both know he is a Riverside Thug but he also has a job. He worked for a firm called MKL-U-MD. We exercised a warrant to check his bank account and some other areas. He has been getting a hefty sum of money every two weeks from them. We called them and they verified he is an employee. They lawyered up real fast though and wouldn't provide any more information – not even about what they do. So we dug harder."

"Go on," said Jon.

"I checked that company out. It's a fairly new company in South Minneapolis that, whether they wanted it or not, has received a lot of attention. They are minority run, employ minorities, and the neighboring businesses are happy to have them around. They've even been recognized as an example of a successful immigrant business. They have some sort of connection with one of the governor's economic trips to China also. They pay all their taxes and have never been cited for anything. All in all, they look like an honest company. I almost dropped it until I cross referenced the names on the business license."

"I'm not following."

"The business license filings with the City of Minneapolis have names of some shell companies that actually own MKL-U-MD. We were able to identify several people who appear to be running the day-to-day activities. One of them is a known member of one of the Somali gangs in Minneapolis. The other name didn't track back to anything other than being an alumni of U of M and a member of a Chinese society there. That is not enough to get a warrant to access their computer network, bank accounts, and tax records. One step at a time I guess. Oh yeah. One last thing. Malick, the gang banger, is dead. He got shanked."

"Thanks Tyler. I've got a call to make of my own." Jon hung up from the call and dialed Gloria's number.

Gloria did not answer her phone. That was not unusual. She was always getting pulled into meetings. Jon left a message with her to check into everything MKL-U-MD, as they employed the skimmer they had discussed earlier.

"I'm Jon Wells. I was told you would know who I was and take me to my colleague."

"Right this way." The hostess turned and motioned Jon to follow. She wound her way through several doorways that looked as if they had been cut out of the brick wall separating what used to be different stores decades ago. All the tables were filled with patrons and the going was slow. "*Looks like a game night at the 'X.' I didn't think the lunch crowd was this heavy. I need to get out more,*" thought Jon. He followed her down a back stairway to the basement. The walls had that old chiseled rock face look of a cave; however, the ambience was anything but cave-like. More of a speakeasy meets hipster feel. He saw Nancy seated in a button tufted, maroon, back corner booth with only a single Nokia pendant providing minimalistic lighting.

The half-circled booth faced away from the stairs. Nancy looked fantastic. He could see she was worried about something but that didn't diminish her beauty. If anything, she was better looking now than twenty years ago in college, and that said a lot. *"I wonder if...."* Jon thought, *"No. Probably would never work. We both have our careers. Still..."*

Jon eased into the booth and gave Nancy a small peck on the cheek. Continuing to hold her hands he looked into her eyes. *"Snap out of it Jon. She asked you here for a reason. So get on with it!"* He rebuked himself, let go of her hands, and addressed her. "Nancy. Given the cloak and dagger involved in this, there is either a surprise party in store for me a la our college days or you're scared. As much as I'd prefer the former, my guess is, it's the latter. What's up Nanc?"

"What do you know about MnMedDev, Jon?"

"Just what you've told me. You manufacture numerous medical devices for a multitude of purposes. You are one of the largest U.S. firms in the industry and you have sales in the billions annually."

"Close enough. We are a major player in the U.S. medical device industry. The industry in the U.S. alone employs 1.8 million with a payroll of around $113 billion."

"OK. Thanks for the economic update. What are you driving at?"

"We have a major problem with our manufacturing, Jon. When I say major – I mean it."

Jon kept silent. It was clear that Nancy was deeply upset by something that she had not yet opened up about. Over the years Jon had learned the best way to dig deeper was often to just stay still and keep quiet. People generally wanted to tell you more than they thought they could.

"Remember when Ford shut down their facilities in the Highland Park neighborhood?" Nancy began, "St. Paul was clamoring for something significant to replace it with. Preferably an employer with high-paying jobs. About the same time, we were looking to upgrade our manufacturing facilities, so we negotiated a sweet deal with the city, state, and even the feds. The site was on the superfund list and we got the city to clean it up. Then we built our new plant. Win-win for everyone. Well, almost everyone. The C-Suite, you know, the people with a 'C' in front of their title - CEO, COO, CFO, and CIO, also took it upon themselves to automate many of the manufacturing processes and streamline the design-build process with a new IT system in the new plant. We brought in the same German engineering company who had done this at their new facilities in China. It paid off handsomely. But the board wanted more profits and the shareholders demanded even higher stock prices. So we took it a step further, adding Quality Control into the new processes. Finally, we outsourced the entire IT department. Lots of high paying jobs ended up being lost when we finished everything. Profits and the stock price hit the roof."

"We knew the state wouldn't be happy with us with all the outsourcing and job layoffs after they invested so much in tax abatements and the like. So when we moved all our servers offsite, we chose HyDek's new data center out in the exurbs. The state, while not exactly happy, was placated."

"The problem with all this is that we lost a lot of control. Right now, I think we are paying the price for our short-sighted behavior. None of our manufacturing lines in the Highland Park facility are making devices that we can ship. They are all defective – and have been for the past week."

"Jon, three years ago the national economic output in the U.S. for the industry was $381 billion. If the industry took a $3 billion hit the economy would lose 39,000 jobs and suffer a $8 billion hit in the economy. If we can't fix our lines, we'll go under. It won't be just a $3 billion hit. MnMedDev created a third of that $381 billion figure I mentioned. Now do you see why I am worried?"

Jon shifted in his chair. This was definitely a significant event that needed some type of intervention, but he didn't see why Nancy didn't go to the FDA with this.

"Nancy. I'm sure I'm not the only person you've discussed this with. Who else have you talked with and what did they say?"

"Matt, the VP of Quality Control is actually the person who came to me. He is old school and didn't trust the software that connected engineering to manufacturing and also QC. He felt we had removed the checks and balances that non-connected teams inherently bring to the entire process. Mind you, it costs more because it means redundancies. But those redundancies and separation are required to be completely effective. He went out to the line and did some manual spot checks on devices. He found defects, even though the software says everything is fine. Matt thinks the software got hacked. That is why I called you. You know the kind of people that can figure this out – and quickly. I'm shutting down all lines for "unexpected maintenance" or something else – I haven't quite figured out what to call it. But you know how the markets react to these things. The same boneheads that ordered this system will want me to just 'fix it' and start up again."

"Hacked you say? How would someone access your system?"

"I've been struggling with that ever since Matt told me this morning. As far as I know, but I'm not an IT expert mind you, it has to be an inside person either at the plant or where the servers are."

"How do you access your servers from say, your office, Nancy?"

"Through my laptop. Why?"

"No, I mean, how do you log in? I noticed the ID card you have not only has a magnetic strip but also one of those chips on it. Do you use your ID card to access your computers?"

"Yes, we have a card reader on every computing device. Not only do the cards have all my security privileges on them, we have readers throughout the facilities that keep track of us. In some buildings, doors automatically open based on how those readers interpret who is in the room and heading towards a door."

"When did you go with this type of ID card?"

"When we opened up the new Highland Park facility. The facility itself is a real game changer for us. We've been able to recruit higher-quality scientists and put all our manufacturing under one roof, so to speak. We still have some satellite offices in most major downtown areas for sales types and conference facilities when people travel. When we show off the Highland Park facility we always show the capabilities of the ID Card. People think it's neat."

"Can the cards be spoofed?"

"I don't know. I do know this though. If you lose one, you have to report it immediately. You are placed on probation for one year, you have to shell out $200 for a new one, and if you lose it again, you are fired – immediately."

Two hours later, Jon left the restaurant and placed calls to Rick and his boss. Tony grudgingly gave him permission to bring Gloria at NCJITF into the case.

"Jon, Reggie here. Pull up Skype. I need to show you something. We can do it via Skype faster."

"OK, Reggie." Jon fumbled with finding the right program icon. He logged in, gave Reggie his username, and accepted an invitation to open and video chat with Reggie. "OK, I'm in. Can you see me?"

"Yeah I can see you. Go ahead and hang up the phone."

Jon did and called Rick over to his desk to listen in.

"Hey Reggie, Rick here. What do you have for us?"

"Remember the gang banger we brought in who was credit card skimming?"

"Yep," Rick and Jon replied at the same time.

"Remember I said the technology being used was overkill? Well that bothered me a lot. So I kept digging in and what I found needs to be shared."

"You mean he was going after more than credit card data?" queried Jon. Rick briefed him on Reggie's findings earlier so he knew what was going on.

"Like I said, I initially thought just credit cards, but I kept digging in. I opened another one of the unique apps that I told you someone wrote. First off, see this?" Reggie held up what looked like a blank credit card to the front facing camera on the tablet he was using."

"What's that?"

"Hang on, let me show you. Let me walk you over to the other side of the room. Can you see the readout from the DMM?"

"Reggie. You'll need to tell Jon what a DMM is OK?" Rick said.

"Oh. Right. Sorry Jon. A DMM is a Digital Multi-meter. It's kind of like an oscilloscope but way cooler. It takes digital reading instead of analog readings."

"Thanks. OK Reggie. Please continue," Jon replied while somewhat glaring at Rick.

"I left the card I showed you next to the DMM. OK I'm going to head back to my desk and grab the phone while you watch the readout." Reggie ambled over to his desk, tapped the phone's screen a few times, made sure the fake earbud was still plugged in, and slowly walked back to where he left the tablet, card, and DMM.

"Here I come. Watch the readout. Slowly. Do you see a spike?" Reggie looked at Jon and Rick with glee on his face when he got back to the table and looked into the camera. "Cool, right?"

"Reggie. You've now gone over my head," Rick said. "It looks like your phone picked up something electronically. Was that the card you showed us?"

"It not only saw, but look at the app on the phone," Reggie held up the phone so the screen was facing the camera.

Jon and Rick looked at their computers screen and saw the following displayed on the phone's screen:

```
First Name: Reginald
Middle Name: George
Last Name: Benkins
Department: Forensics
Company: Minneapolis Police Department
Access: Segment T1X-6
```

"Did the phone read that off your card?" exclaimed Rick.

"Yeah. The earbud read this from ten feet away and added it to a database on the phone. And that's not all. Just like the credit card data, this database gets sent off somewhere in internet land."

"Have you looked at the data on the database?"

"Yep. And you aren't going to like it. Check your email. I just sent a file with what it captured."

Jon opened the email and saw that the database contained security card and access data gleaned from several hundred employees that worked at the building Malick, the Riverside Thugs Somali gang member, was arrested in front of. The companies ranged from retail and insurance, to finance, and a medical device research and manufacturing firm – MnMedDev.

"Reg, what is the purpose of getting this type of information? I can think of a lot of things and none of them are good," asked Jon.

"Well, I suppose you could use the information to create an ID card so you could access the building, but why go to the expense needed to create this for that. I mean, just hire a pick pocket to swipe one, use it for whatever you need, and dump it before its reported missing. Why go to all this trouble? The data you saw from the card I made to explain and show you was colossally basic. If you look at the raw data in the database, you'll see a lot of additional information. Most of it doesn't make any sense. Some of it looks encrypted. My gut tells me, whoever is behind this, is looking for some type of information. The end game, though, I don't know."

"I'm going to send this off to D.C. and let Gloria Ransik look at it. You remember her, don't you? No offense but she has more resources at her disposal."

"I figured you'd do that. My boss isn't going to like it, but I agree. There's only a few of us here who can do this so go for it. I remember Gloria and she definitely has the chops to get this figured out."

"Thanks Reg. Let me know if you find anything else and don't worry, everyone will know you found this."

Chapter 35

Winter 2008

Ahmed's flight into Minneapolis was five hours late. He was not in a good mood. Volatile more appropriately described his demeanor. The extended stay at Chicago's bustling O'Hare Airport added immeasurably to his disdain for all things American. The women in their slutty clothing, the ever obnoxious and pandered children – "I want, I want, I want," the suffocating excess of people who knew no pain. He would give them pain. Pain where an American felt it most – their pocketbook.

As the taxi took him to the dilapidated house, he forced himself to settle down. The gentleman he was meeting was an acquaintance and had lived here for many years. He was referred to in the community only as "The Man." His particular specialization was revolt. "The Man" knew what buttons needed pushing. He knew how to cajole, prod, and if needed, force the awakening with the Muslim youth of America – especially those from immigrant communities. Many of these young adults were childlike in their understanding of the Muslim heritage and the need for Jihad. While disaffected, they lacked the inner strength to understand their duty. They needed guidance, a mentor, a coach to move them forward and attain enlightenment. He was that man. Ahmed knew it and also knew that while he was in charge and was funding this endeavor, he must submit himself to "The Man." A great leader knows when to let others take charge and Ahmed felt he was a great leader. Besides, "The Man" was a Somali and the targeted community was Somali.

The two a.m. hour came before he entered the house. Ahmed was dressed in jeans, tennis shoes, a hoodie, and a large winter coat to combat the temperature of twenty below zero. This was not the attire he wore for travel. In fact, he didn't know how long he could remain in such putrid-smelling clothing. These clothes were left in an airport locker. The key slipped to him in a classic brush pass as he walked through the baggage claim area. In a bathroom handicap stall he changed from his Armani suit to better fit in. He did not need to be remembered by a taxi driver or anyone else. He would throw these clothes away as soon as he could. He wanted to burn them but the resulting smoke would infuse even more stink upon him. The front door was unlocked and Ahmed entered as if he belonged.

"The Man" greeted Ahmed and led him to the front room. Lights blazed throughout the dark of the night and into the early morning hours. "The Man" knew the playbook. He ran it for Ahmed in other cities throughout the world. He even had his own disciples running it elsewhere. This mission was different though. The two-pronged strategy required his presence. The first prong was his forte. The second was not. Ahmed focused his energies in this second area. Ahmed's benefactor had been adamant that funding was only available through its success. Ahmed assured "The Man" outside assistance was available. "The Man" insisted a new gang of Somalis of both sexes needed to be formed. He convinced Ahmed what Zhang didn't know would not hurt him. Zhang didn't understand the Somali culture and besides, it would be a different type of gang. The normal thuggery would be downplayed. The clan warfare aspect brought from their homeland would be subdued. They would be trained to make good decisions. Under the radar and in plain sight must be the mantra. The business was to be formed in legal fashion. It took hours, but Ahmed finally acquiesced. The benefactor, a Chinese acquaintance of Ahmed's, would provide a business advisor, half the workers, and the business strategy. "The Man" needed to hire a CEO as well as filling the rest of the workers from the new gang. Ahmed provided the name of a local Somali IT specialist "The Man" needed to convince to be the CEO. His benefactor had given him the name.

Planning continued throughout the afternoon. They created complex as well as simple strategies to move corporate funds from the new business to ISIS – all the while staying within the loose business rules of the state. Finally, they agreed upon communication protocols. The meetings now concluded, Ahmed exited through a back door carrying several grocery bags. He headed in the direction of the light rail line with a small detour into the local drug store. This particular drugstore chain provided public restroom facilities without the need for a key. Ahmed changed into the set of clothes in the grocery bags. They were more akin to a casual business worker. After dumping his old clothes into the restroom garbage he bought a small can of body spray with cash and exited the drug store. Rounding the first corner he sprayed his entire body with the spray. Unfortunately, the stink of the previous evening did not abate. Frustrated, Ahmed threw the nearly empty can in the general direction of the trash container and ran across the four lane street to the nearby light rail station. Luckily for him, a train arrived shortly. He boarded it and headed towards the airport.

He walked into the terminal and retrieved his suit and shoes from the locker he used the evening before. His ticket was on his phone and he easily passed through security. Ahmed spied the new spa and salon in Concourse C and bought himself several hours of pampering. He showered the grime away while the staff cleaned and pressed his suit. After his shower and massage, the feel of his Armani suit reminded him the first class seat on Emirates Airlines to Dubai was only a short flight away. Dubai. There, he would be as close to his homeland as he ever got. Certainly not a bastion of Wahhabi life, it was close.

Chapter 36

Present Day

"Jon? Gloria here. Do you have some time?"

Jon was at his desk finishing up from the video conference he and Rick completed with Reggie thirty minutes earlier. "Sure, what do you have for me?"

"The team and I confirmed that there was indeed an intrusion into MnMedDev like your friend Nancy surmised. We only know that it commenced from their server farm located in a data center on the edge of the metro area. It's called HyDek. Do you know anything about them?"

"HyDek? Yeah, that's where my friend Dom worked. He was killed in what the police officially are still saying was a hit and run early last week. Rick and I don't agree with them. What else do you know? Is this connected to our earlier conversation about the Chinese?" Jon waved Rick over to the desk and put Gloria on speakerphone.

"Hi Gloria," said Rick.

"Hey there. We don't know much more right now and I haven't found a connection to the Chinese yet either, Jon. Tell me more about your friend. What did you say his name was?"

"His name was Dominic Seragosa. His son played on the lacrosse team I work with. He called me the morning he died and wanted to tell me something. He refused to say anything over the phone. That's never a good thing. He was on his way to meet me when he was killed."

"Sorry to hear that Jon. Have you been out to his work or are the locals handling everything?"

Rick jumped in to the conversation. "Jon and I went out and spoke with Dom's supervisor – a Celeste Van Dorn. She's the VP of Operations at HyDek. She wouldn't share anything work-related without a warrant, which we expected. We obtained the warrant so Jon could go out later. He let MPD tag along in the interest of cooperation. The VP did, however, let us speak with a friend and coworker of Dom's. His name is Abdi Ali – he's their IT security expert. Gloria, this guy Abdi didn't seem on the up and up when we spoke with him. Jon tell her what happened when you went back with Detective Bancroft."

"Thanks for the lead-in Rick. Gloria, Rick is spot on about Abdi. Turns out he is a bit of a 'bad apple,' always causing problems with people at work. He's had a bunch of people fired for 'security reasons' and was seen engaged in an argument with Dom the night before Dom was killed. Evidently, Abdi said something about a 'conspiracy' according to the witness."

Gloria said, "That's interesting. So the IT security guy at the same data operations center we are looking at for the intrusion into MnMedDev has an argument about a conspiracy with Dom, who happens to be a shift supervisor at that same data operations center, the night before he is hit by a vehicle and killed – on his way to see you about something he was evidently too scared to talk about over the air."

"Yep, and get this," said Jon. "Abdi purchased the vehicle that ran over Dom."

'No shit!" exclaimed Gloria.

"Exactly. There's more."

"Really? What?"

"When Detective Bancroft and I went back out with the warrant, we found out this guy Abdi hadn't been back to work since Rick and I were out there the first time. We looked at the security logs at HyDek and discovered someone tampered with them the same evening Dom and Abdi argued. We know Abdi left the building during his shift but the logs don't show that. The logs also show Dom leaving and never returning, even though the security guards swear he came in after what Dom called his 'walkabout' at the beginning of his shift. He was there for the entire shift. Ms. Van Dorn was visibly upset that the logs were messed up."

"I bet. Doesn't look good for her. What's your thinking on this Celeste person? You leaning one way or the other yet?"

"Detective Bancroft sure thinks something is going on, but it's more in a corporate greed – profit over people or quality processes sort of thing. Celeste seemed deeply concerned about Donna, Dom's wife, and the kids. So I don't see any connection with Celeste to Dom's accident. I suppose anything is possible so we'll check into that."

After a short pause Gloria responded, "Jon, what I didn't tell you about what we found out, was what we didn't find."

"Gloria, you have an awkward way with words, you know."

"Well then let me explain. The NCIJTF team investigates many instances of potential and valid cyber threats to the U.S. We are made up of experts in many fields. This expertise sometimes comes from hackers that we catch. If they are the right type of person we can turn them and incorporate their knowledge into the team. Often, these particular individuals don't have any formal education past high school when they pop up on our radar. With only two options – prison or employment – the vast majority take the option of being a government employee. It's an eclectic group we have here, Jon. Some even take advantage of the education benefits offered and get their degrees - bachelors, master's and, in a few cases, even doctoral degrees. My lead analyst, Dr. Jasmine Gomez is one of these. She's been with us for years now and is one of the premier analysts in NCIJTF, not just my team. She is the best, probably in the world, figuring out who could crack into a system like this. Right now, she is not sure who is ultimately behind all this and how they accessed the systems. In our experience Jon, access like this means you generally need someone's credentials."

"How do you get those?" asked Jon.

"Either through brute force cracking or some other manner of social engineering. We didn't see evidence of a brute force crack so…that leaves an inside job, or theft of credentials," replied Gloria.

Rick looked at Jon. Could this be connected to the discussion they just had with Reggie?

"Gloria, what do you know about skimming?" Rick blurted out. "Give me some perspective."

Jon began, "A little while back MPD arrested a guy who was causing a disturbance in the skyways. Turns out the guy is a Somali gang banger, so they called me. You remember Reggie Benkins in their forensics unit?"

"Yes I do. He's still there? Good technician," responded Gloria.

"Yes he is. So Reggie was going through the guy's things and found a smartphone and earbuds that just didn't look right. Turns out the earbuds, which were thicker than normal, were actually an antennae used to electronically skim data from people's wallets and purses."

"I've heard of that. So what's the connection?"

Rick took over the explanation. "Turns out he was not just skimming credit card information. He was also gathering data skimmed off of corporate identification cards. Plus, MnMedDev has offices where he was doing his deed."

"Did you get a download of what he skimmed?" asked Gloria.

"Yes we did. Reggie sent it over to us. Rick and I were actually just going to send that off to you. None of us were sure what to think of why he was doing this but figured you could help out. I hate coincidences and this is a big coincidence in my book," said Jon.

"I agree. Maybe, just maybe, the team here can see if this is how they got the access I was talking about. Do you think you could get a real ID card from Nancy and send it to me?"

Chapter 37

Officers from MPD gathered every computing device they could from Abdi's cubicle at the data operations center. They brought it all back to the MPD forensics team on direction from Detective Bancroft and Jon. HyDek management also provided everything they could think of without waiting for additional warrants, including phone records from Abdi's office phone. A quick review through these did not glean much information. Celeste identified all but a few numbers as belonging to their clients. A combined team of cyber forensic specialists from Minneapolis PD and the FBI was given the task of figuring out what was on his equipment.

"Reggie, you called. What have you found?" Jon barked as he blew through the doors of the lab.

"Abdi wrote a lot of code and ran a ton of reports."

"Tell me something useful Reg. He was the security guy. Isn't that part of his work?"

"Yes, but copying extracts of reports from server configurations to a USB drive and copying code onto computers from a USB isn't. HyDek has a strict policy against that."

"He's the security guy. Doesn't that generally mean he is allowed more leeway in what he can and can't do? You said server configurations? Could he simply be taking work home?"

"I suppose, but once again, it isn't allowed. We called HyDek to confirm. It's never allowed. If fact, most of the computers on the floor don't even have functioning USB ports. You have to log in with special privileges, such as those Abdi has to override the settings in order to use the USB ports. Remember the scanner you had to walk through at the entrance? They look for stuff like that. We don't even do that here."

"You wanted to know about the server configurations? Those were all for everything one particular company had at HyDek. Initially I thought maybe Abdi was assigned to identify a weakness or vulnerability for that company's servers. We called HyDek again and no such tasking had been assigned."

"Do you know what he copied back to the computer from the USB?"

"Just code written in Python. By the way, that is the favorite language of the hacking community. We are crunching through it. We'll figure it out soon enough. Funny thing though, it was in the clear. Just plain ol' code. Mind you, there is a fragment here, another fragment there. It isn't even all put together. You would think if this was malicious, it would be encrypted. But then again, we didn't see anything on his computer that would decrypt code, so…"

"What else did you find?" interrupted Jon.

"Looks like he went about his business the rest of the day he copied the code. Normal stuff. He wrote a software patch, created a ticket, assigned it to the software team, and some other things. Same type of stuff he does every day. Looks like the patches were installed without any issue. Nothing is out of the ordinary. HyDek said this was all normal."

"Reg, you need to find out what the code does."

"Roger that. We'll figure it out."

"When did all this take place anyway?"

"Six months ago. It was a fluke that we found it. One of the newbies just read an article about device configuration changes and how to identify them. So we ran a report specifically looking for that type of activity. I've ordered another report run on all the devices just to see if this happened anywhere else."

"You said one company?" asked Jon.

"Yes I did. The name of the company is MnMedDev."

Jon turned away deep in thought when he heard the name of the company.

"Does anyone know anything about why he was looking at MnMedDev's servers?" asked Bancroft. "They make medical devices at the old Ford plant don't they?"

Jon looked up and said to both of them, "I think we just found a connection point with Dom's murder and the electronic skimming case."

Chapter 38

Minneapolis and St. Paul Police Departments joined forces with the FBI through its Safe Streets Violent Crime Initiative. This created the Twin Cities Safe Streets Violent Gang Task Force replacing Minneapolis's Metro Gang Strike Force. That entity collapsed several years ago due to extortion, financial, and other misconduct. This team, along with members from the Minneapolis Special Weapons and Tactics or SWAT team gathered in the Minneapolis Armory to review the afternoon's raid on a house in the Little Somali section of Minneapolis. The house was the de-facto home to the Riverside Thugs, the largest and most radical of the Somali Gangs in Minneapolis. The raid was to be the culmination of the investigation into credit card theft by members of the gang.

The team had 20 members, two large UPS-sized trucks for suspect transport, five vehicles, and a helicopter on standby. The Lieutenant in charge issued instructions and handed out photos of the thirty individuals that needed to be rounded up in the action. Thirty minutes prior to the designated go time he sent the troops out in their vehicles. The transport vehicles would be called in after the round up was completed. No one wanted Twitter or other social media outlets to let the gang members know something was afoot.

The house in question was a late 19th century American Foursquare style structure that had not been taken care of in many years, if not decades. As the name implied, it was in essence a square box with two stories above ground, plus an attic, and a basement. Four basic rooms on each floor. This particular home had an addition in the back containing the kitchen and a stairway to the basement. A gravel driveway was on the east side going back to where a garage used to be. Like the house itself, the backyard was in a general state of disrepair. Couches, clothes, and other odds and ends were strewn all over. The front porch contained the main entry to the house. The second entry was in the back off the kitchen. Shades were lowered on all windows and no lights appeared to be on.

Two task force vehicles drove into the alley behind the house, with the remaining three stopping several houses down. Fortunately, there were large oak and maple trees on either side of the block and directly in front of the house. The back yard also contained numerous large trees and overgrown bushes hiding, for the most part, the alley and the houses beyond. The foliage provided cover for the teams. The majority of the task force members approached the house without fear of being seen. Those remaining shut down traffic on either end of the block or coordinated the efforts of the Task Force from the command vehicle. Both teams stacked up at their respective entry points; team one on the front porch and team two in the rear.

"Team one ready."

"Team two ready.'

Having heard ready calls for both teams the Lieutenant gave the go signal through his tactical headset. Team two's breacher broke open the kitchen door with a battering ram. The next team member in the stack approached and threw in a flash bang grenade. The breacher and his partner entered using a combination technique where the breacher button-hooked to the left to clear the area not immediately visible. His partner went right utilizing a crisscross technique to clear the remainder of the kitchen. Team one followed suit in synchronized fashion. The movement of each breaching team was serpentine, allowing members a clear vision of all areas of the rooms. Each team cleared their assigned rooms and met in what was once the sitting room in the middle of the house.

"Team one, clear main floor."

"Team two, clear main floor."

The flash bang had done its job on the first floor. Ten Riverside Thugs were in various stages of stupor. Some holding their ears, others in modified fetal positions, moaning and grimacing in pain. Three members from team one guarded them while team two returned to the kitchen to root out anyone in the basement. The remaining five members of team one backtracked to the main stairway heading to the second floor and attic.

An open railed stairway was on the far side of the living room. As the lead rounded the corner and strode to the stairway, he was felled by a barrage of fire.

"Shots fired. Stairway to second floor, front. Man down."

One team member grabbed the downed man by the handles of his bulletproof vest and pulled him to safety, the remaining three returned fire in two short staccato bursts of three rounds each and ascended the stairs. The M-4 tactical assault rifles were perfect for this type of house breach. Two suspects were hit. One rolled partway down the stairs. Team members jumped over the body and continued their ascent.

Additional task force members entered the front door after hearing the shots fired call. That made the total number of police in the house now fifteen. Four of these immediately ascended the stairs. One moved the limp body from the stairs making for a safer access route.

Seconds later voices shouted from the second floor, "Stop firing! Stop firing! We give up!" Team one cleared ten people from the second floor. No one was found in the attic.

Team two was descending the back stairway when they heard the shots. Seeking to avoid a similar situation they loosed a flash bang down into the darkness. They waited for the flash. The smoke hung in the air as they made their descent and spread throughout the damp and musty smelling basement. "All clear, basement, no bad guys," team two leader announced.

The task force medic entered the house and attended to the policeman hit by fire. Once stabilized, he moved to the two gang bangers who's ill-advised shooting foreshadowed their demise. Both were dead. Shots to the chest and head guaranteed that.

"Task force leader, team one leader. All clear. One friendly injured but ambulatory, medic onsite. Two bad guys dead, 18 bad guys in custody. Request ambulance and transport."

"Task force leader, team two leader. Confirmed all clear."

"Team one leader, team two leader, task force leader. Confirmed all clear, ambulance and transport en route. Begin clean-up."

The 18 remaining gang members were rounded up in the sitting room, arms placed behind their backs, and plastic flexi cuffs affixed to their wrists. Several were still experiencing pain from the flash bangs while others had not come out of their stupor from the raid. No one was going anywhere.

"LT, no one fires at us when we breach like this unless there is something or someone to hide," team one leader said to the task force leader when he and team two leader met for a quick after-action debriefing.

"Agreed. Make a quick sweep through the house but don't touch anything. I need the detective and crime lab personnel to gather all evidence and ensure chain of custody."

"Roger that. I saw a lot of computers, credit card blanks, stacks of money, and what looked like money transfer receipts in the left-side back room upstairs. I'll have one of my people stay there until the crime lab arrives. One other thing, do you notice how normal the interior of this place looks? I mean, when we went through the closets looking for bangers, I didn't see many bangers' clothes. Mostly professional looking outerwear – almost like a costume shop for a theatre group. Weird."

Chapter 39

"Donna. I'm so sorry. Can I come in?" Jon looked into the tear-swelled eyes of Donna Seragosa. He made the trip out to their house the day after Dominic was killed. Yesterday, they spoke briefly at the police headquarters while the Minneapolis police embarked on their investigation. Time was not on Jon's side then so he tabled further discussion until today. Donna only agreed because her oldest, Mike, needed consoling and she had two younger girls, Laura and Kylie, plus a pregnancy to deal with.

Jon followed Donna down the stairs of the modified split level house the Seragosa's purchased when Mike was three. The mortgage was almost paid since they chose the 15-year option. The extra cost limited vacations, newer cars, and nice furniture until Dom's last promotion at HyDek. The past year finally brought relief to that austerity in the form of a remodel of several rooms, two nice new cars, and the wood shop Dom always wanted. Dom made the furniture showcased in several of the rooms and just finished a new project specifically for Mike.

Donna showed Jon down the hall to Mike's room and stood outside the door. His was the only occupied basement bedroom. Being the oldest, he no longer needed the closeness of his parents during the night hours. Laura, at age 13, felt she should be able to move into the second downstairs bedroom but her parents did not want to separate the girls until the baby was born.

"Hi. Can I come in?" Jon poked his head through the doorway.

No reply.

"Mike?" Jon entered the room. The lights were off and the shades were pulled most of the way down. He almost tripped over an overturned chair. A dark form lingered in the corner. Had this been a sting, Jon's gun would have been pulled for safety. But this was a condolence call on a young man he knew and worked with on the lacrosse field for the past several years.

"I won't cry." Mike's voice was barely audible. His breaths vacillated between deep cleansing and short staccato. Broken only with the inevitable anguished moan.

"Why did he have to die?"

"I won't tell if you cry. It's OK." Jon spoke in a quiet and reassuring voice as he navigated towards Mike.

"We can talk or I can just listen. We could simply sit and be there for one another if you want."

A shaft of sunlight from the mostly covered window illuminated a long wooden object in Mike's hands.

"What's that you have in your hands?"

Silence.

"Mike? I'd like to know what that is. I'm here for you."

"My dad was making it for me."

"Great. What was he making?"

"It doesn't matter!" Mike hollered, rising quickly from the bed. He leapt forward, smashing the object on the desk, sending shattered remains across the room. Mike crumpled to the floor sobbing uncontrollably.

Jon moved to the side. He'd seen this type of reaction before and knew it was not directed at him. Once Mike was on the floor, Jon quickly moved to him, but not before turning on a desk light that escaped the recent physical manifestation of grief.

"Mike. That looks like an old fashioned wooden lacrosse stick? It looks amazing. He loved watching you play, you know."

Mike rocked himself back and forth, arms draped over his pulled-up legs. After several minutes of this and without any more questions from Jon he slowly unfurled himself. He crawled around on the floor picking up the shattered remnants. He stopped, slowly raised his head, and looked at Jon. A wave of emotion engulfed him.

"What have I done? It's the last thing he ever made for me and I broke it!" Mike tossed the remaining shaft to Jon.

When Jon caught it, a small metal and plastic object fell out of the end where the webbing was once attached. Jon picked it up. It was a USB drive – with the name JON WELLS written on it.

"Mike, we'll fix this up and you will always have it as a memory of your dad. OK?"

Mike rocked back on his haunches and after a moment of thought bobbed his head in agreement. He saw Jon had something in his hand other than the shaft and asked what it was. Jon replied with a question of his own. "This looks like a memory stick. Is it yours?"

Mike shook his head slowly in the negative. "Why?"

"I think it came out of the lacrosse stick your dad made. That's why. Weird." Mike moved closer as Jon rotated the stick length-wise, examining both ends. "Look here. There is a space just large enough for this."

Mike took both the lacrosse stick and memory drive from Jon and examined them himself.

"Did your dad ever say anything about that?"

"No. The lacrosse stick was a surprise. I didn't know anything about it. Mom brought it down and gave it to me an hour ago."

"Hey Mike, you are going to be fine. I'm here for you. I'll help you fix the lacrosse stick if you want. Can I have the memory stick back? I have to take that back to the office. You know who I work for, right?"

Mike nodded.

"I bet this will lead us to the people that murdered your father." Jon turned and exited. He saw Donna as he left Mike's room.

"Did you say murdered?" she gasped.

"That's what it's beginning to look like. I'll keep you in the loop."

Chapter 40

Nicole increased her speed for the last hundred yards of her daily morning run. Fog was quickly burning off the small lake on the property as the sun's rays heated the air in rapid fashion. Not many caught the beauty of a 5:30 a.m. sunrise in the middle of the summer. It looked to be a warm and muggy day in Minneapolis. Five years after her last competitive cross country meet at Bethel University, she continued her routine, albeit the length of the runs had diminished somewhat. The running kept her body in the same toned shape she enjoyed as an undergrad. Her mind relished the freedom to wander. The rest of her day as a social worker for a small outreach facility left little time for her own thoughts.

She completed the run by slowing to a nice easy jog and stretched for twenty minutes before finally walking into the apartment she shared with her boyfriend. He was a musician and played gigs late into the night. *"Would they ever go to bed at the same time?" she wondered.* Nicole grabbed her diabetic medical bag and a glass of cold tap water, opened the door to the deck, and sat down on the plastic chair. It was part of a patio set she and Zander grabbed from a lawn when they first moved in. She shook her head and thought, *"I have a college degree. Why can I only afford furniture that has a 'Free' sign taped to it. Should have studied business. Should have done that at a state school."* The $25,000 in student loans ate up a large portion of the $12/hr. social worker job she'd had since graduating. Nicole, or

Nicky as her friends called her, was starting a new job next month, with an increase in pay. The patio set was the first thing she would replace.

She smiled, thinking about her future. Neither she nor her boyfriend were able to afford medical insurance, but the new job would provide medical benefits, at least for her. And she needed it. Last winter, Nicole was one of the many who contracted the flu virus. It hit her hard. Out of work for almost a month, she and Zander had barely scrapped by. The worst part was, the doctor at the free clinic discovered that the flu virus attacked her pancreas, limiting its ability to create insulin. This, in turn, caused her to develop Type 1 diabetes.

Because of this, her glucose needed to be tracked. She could not afford a large outlay of cash, so the new continuous monitoring devices were out of her reach. She enviously eyed the patients in the doctor's office showing off their new devices, connected via Bluetooth to their sparkly new smartphones. So, she stayed with the tried and true manual injection testing packages that ran $20.00 at the local drug store. She knew she was spending more over time than those with the more expensive devices. That was aggravating. She just never had $500 at any one time to pay for those devices; let alone the newer smartphones required to use them. Maybe when the medical insurance kicked in with her new job, she could look into those again.

The pharmacist was aware of her situation and recently recommended changing to a different system. It would save her $3.00 per package and last twice as long. This new system was from MnMedDev. It was a local company and the system was finally available after years of testing and approvals. Nicole always shopped local when she could.

This system required her to use a lancet to pierce her skin. The lancet was small and not easily manipulated, even for Nicole. Her fingers were raw from repeated skewering. There were several other spots on her body that she could use, some of which required a good amount of body manipulation. Nicole was thankful she had kept in shape. She couldn't imagine how some of the people she saw at the doctor's office could reach some of the places recommended for piercing. The lancing device, about the size of a large pen, made it easier to hold when pricking her skin. God, that little prick packed a wallop of hurt. She'd rather twist her ankle. Nicole placed the drop of blood onto a test strip and then inserted it, narrow end first, into the small opening in the side of the blood glucose meter. The meter itself was the size of a large automobile key fob with an LCD readout and several control buttons. The test strips and the electronics inside the meter were like a key and lock for the system. If either was damaged, inaccurate results could occur.

Unfortunately for her, the system she purchased came off the lines at MnMedDev's Highland Park facility just last week. The test strips from that week were missing an entire layer containing glucose oxidase. The absence of this layer threw off every result since the required electrochemistry was not per standards. The production run that week also contained devices whose micro-electronics programming had been hardwired to display not only a variety of random results within the normal range, but also erroneous out of range results with a high rate of frequency.

She looked at the results. Crap. She hadn't seen results this high in several months. She glanced at her logbook. Nicole was somewhat anal when it came to recording things. It was one of the reasons her soon-to-be-new boss hired her. The only time she had seen levels like this was when her friends had taken her out for her birthday and gotten her royally drunk. She was so hungover the next day she forgot to give herself any insulin. Nicole dutifully recorded her results along with her temperature, the time, and notes about how she felt after her run.

Rules were rules and she was a rule follower. So a high reading meant an injection. She reached for her bag, prepped the injector and site, and gave herself the dose required by the meter results. It was the beginning of a catastrophic series of events. The dosage required for the results displayed on the meter was in actuality a huge insulin overdose.

Even with Nicole's best intentions she always woke Zander when she returned from her runs. This morning, he heard her return but dozed in and out of sleep for another forty-five minutes before finally extracting himself from the mattress and stumbling into the bathroom. After relieving himself, he walked to the kitchen and stopped while he yawned and stretched out. He knew Nicky liked relaxing out on the deck in the morning after her runs. The blinds were closed going out to the deck. She was thoughtful and always closed them so as to not interfere with his sleep. She was unaware the screech the sliding glass door made when she opened it woke him every day. Zander never said anything though; he didn't mind. Besides, when she came back in and undressed in the bathroom she always turned the lights over the mirror on and left the door ajar. Often, he was awake by this time and watched her. Sometimes he even joined her in the shower.

Their second story apartment overlooked a marshy area of the lake she ran around. He opened the sliding glass door to the deck. "Morning babe, how was the run?" Something didn't look right. The patio set was overturned. Items from her medical kit were strewn all over the deck and Nicky was nowhere in sight. He knew she went out on the deck. He heard the screech loud and clear this morning. The deck was not large so it didn't take him long to end up next to the railing. Something in his gut felt wrong and he didn't want to look down. Even so, he forced himself to look and saw what caused that feeling. Nicky was lying askew in a large pool of blood on the pavement below. The blood was from a large gash on her head. She didn't look like she was breathing and the blood had congealed. Zander immediately ran from the deck, through the apartment, down the stairway, and out to the parking lot. He slid over the gravel encrusted concrete ending up on his knees and scooped her into his arms. Her eyes were still open but there was no life left. He screamed.

Someone in the complex called 911 after hearing his screams. The police arrive a short time later. They found Zander, now sitting, holding Nicky's head in his lap. Tears streamed from his face. By this time his screams had abated somewhat. He rocked back and forth, pounding the ground, splattering blood over himself and Nicky. It took several policemen to extricate Zander from the scene. They took a look at the situation and immediately arrested Zander. Clearly, they thought, this was a case of domestic violence.

"I did not kill her. I loved Nicky. She came back from her run, like normal, and went out onto the deck. She does that every morning when it's nice. She checks her blood levels and gives herself a shot if she needs it. I can't watch her do that to herself. It hurts her when she has to prick herself or give herself injections. I hate it when she winces in pain," Zander adamantly objected to their claims.

The coroner found no evidence of bruising associated with domestic abuse or those associated with being pushed, so Zander was released. The coroner reported cause of death was a subdural hematoma due to hitting the pavement after the fall. He hypothesized that Nicole tripped over the railing and fell to her death after suffering a seizure induced by an extremely low blood sugar level. According to the blood work the coroner's team did, Nicole's insulin levels were off the chart. When the coroner provided this information, the detectives assigned to the case returned to the apartment to question Zander about Nicole potentially committing suicide. It wouldn't be the first time someone with diabetes had committed suicide due to depression. Once again, Zander objected. He stated she had just been hired for a new job that would pay more and provide her with medical benefits. She was happy. It was the step forward she needed. With her diabetes she needed medical insurance. Zander backed this up his objections with the meticulous record keeping in Nicole's logbook.

The detectives gave the logbook to the coroner since they couldn't make heads or tails of it. It wasn't difficult for the coroner and he asked for Nicole's medical kit after seeing the last entry in the logbook made the morning of her death. His wife was also a diabetic and this case was not making sense. Was the blood glucose meter working? Some of the people he went to medical school with worked at MnMedDev. He'd have to call them.

Chapter 41

Gloria heard the chirp of her phone over the music she was listening to while stuck in the notorious Washington D.C. traffic. Why didn't she take the Metro today? She didn't live that far from the FBI Headquarters and the Navy Yard Metro stop was only blocks from her condo in the recently reinvigorated Capitol Riverfront neighborhood. Like Jon in Minneapolis, her condo had a view. While his was great, hers was incredible. Out her living room window was the United States Capitol building. The route driving home was simple in theory and the view it gave her was generally worth it. She'd lived here for several years now and still loved driving by the grandiose buildings of the federal center along the Mall. Leave the Hoover Building, left on Pennsylvania Ave, right on 3rd St NW, head south. Through the National Mall, wave to the Capitol on the left. Turn left at the National Museum of the American Indian onto Independence Ave NW, quickly change lanes for the almost immediate right turn onto Washington Ave which moved her in a diagonal direction to South Capitol St SW. The Capitol Dome would be in the rear view mirror as she continued under I-695 and even in bad traffic she still felt like pinching herself when she saw that view. But not today. She had progressed only several blocks in thirty minutes. All she could see were six yellow school buses on one side of the road and nothing but cars, SUVs, and tourist buses in front of her. Even the ten perfectly-spaced Corinthian columns on the east side of the National Archives were not worth this traffic. She had been there long enough to read the inscription below the roofline and above the columns - *This building holds in trust the records of our national life and symbolizes our faith in the permanency of our national institutions.*

Should have taken the Metro. Of course, if she was in the Metro, which was underground here, she couldn't answer the phone. The phone. Shit. It was ringing. Gloria selected the button on her steering wheel, answering the call in hands-free mode.

"Hello?"

"Gloria, Jon here. I'm glad you answered. I was afraid I missed you. Are you still in the office? I have something you absolutely need to look at."

"Well, hi there yourself Jon. So many questions. You sure sound excited. I am not in the office right now. I'm stuck in traffic by the Archives. Someone important must be headed somewhere. Lights are blazing all over and I know nothing serious is going on."

"Head back to the office, now," Jon said in a tone that sounded like an order.

"Why? What happened."

"I found a USB drive that Dom had stashed."

"Your friend Dom who was killed?"

"Yes, that Dom. Remember where he worked?"

"HyDek, right?" Gloria said.

"Exactly. I found the USB drive in a lacrosse stick. It has my name on it."

"In a lacrosse stick?"

"I know. Actually, it came flying out of the lacrosse stick when his son smashed it."

"Smashed it?" Gloria was confused.

"Let me explain. Dom relaxed by doing woodwork. He made an old fashioned wooden lacrosse stick for his son, Mike. That's one of the boys I coach. He was going to give it to him as a surprise for being a great kid. I stopped by to check in on Donna and the kids this afternoon. Donna took me down to Mike's room. She had given him the lacrosse stick earlier. It is unfinished, but still…Mike isn't taking his dad's death well at all so I went in to talk. Mike got all upset, grabbed the lacrosse stick, and smashed it onto his desk. Then he threw what was left. I happened to be in the trajectory so I caught it. When I did that the USB drive fell out."

"Gloria, the only thing I can think of is that Dom made a copy of something at work and was going to give it to me when he got hit. I think that's why the guys in the truck got out and grabbed his backpack. They were looking for the USB drive. He wanted to tell me something and was afraid to speak about it on the phone. You know, I think that's how he got the USB drive out of the data center. I remember now that the VP of Operations mentioned that Dom brought it into work the last day he was there. He showed it off to everyone. I examined the end of the stick where the USB drive came out from. There was a space carved out of the wood and, come to think of it, the space was lined with something shiny. I think he downloaded something at work, put it into the lacrosse stick to get past security, and brought it home. He must have made a copy in case anything happened and put it in the lacrosse stick."

"Oh my God Jon. That makes Dom's death a murder. Not an accident."

"My thoughts exactly."

"When can I have the USB drive?"

"I'm in my car coming back from Donna's. I'm not close to the office yet. What is the best way to get it to you? Do I simply upload it? I'm not comfortable with that. What if I screw it up?"

"Reggie is still in the doghouse with his boss, right?"

"Sure is. I owe him still."

"Let him handle it. Given it's more likely a murder investigation now, MPD will need to be pulled in anyway. I'll make sure Reggie's boss gets an atta-boy from my end. That should fix things." Gloria always had a way with the higher ups.

"Thanks. Will do. Gotta go and call Reg now. Bye." Jon hung up and called Reggie.

"Reggie, my turn to return a favor...."

Chapter 42

A day later 10 p.m.

"You did get the warrant, right?" Jon asked Detective Bancroft. "Any issues with the Edina Police?"

"Yes, I did. I have it right here and no, with the FBI in the lead, the Edina Police are not going to get in our way. See over there? They're our backup tonight."

"Great. Because after that disaster with the Riverside Thugs we can't screw this one up. If he is in there, we take him quietly." Jon looked directly at Tyler. Then he continued, "If not, we see what we can find. Can the Edina Police check the garage, find his vehicle, and open it up?"

"Sure, I'll direct them to take that action." Detective Bancroft left Jon and Rick at the entrance to the seventeen story condominium and walked over to talk with the four officers Edina PD had provided. The building was a combination condo and hotel across the street from the Galleria at Southdale, the most expensive assemblage of stores in the metro area. They didn't call people from Edina "cake-eaters" for nothing.

"This is a pretty ritzy place for a thirty-five year-old don't you think?" Rick was eyeing the marble encased entry complete with its own concierge and valet. "I sure couldn't afford it. Maybe staying single is a good thing when it comes to money. I looked at the prices for these and a two bedroom, two bath condo here goes for $1.3 million. Can you believe that? Well, maybe you do. Your pad is pretty sweet."

"Focus Rick. My guess is the money is coming from his interests with the gang."

"True. Hey Detective, everything set with EPD?"

"Yes, they are heading into the garage as soon as we go in the front."

"Roger that, let's go."

Jon was not taking any chances tonight. Both he and Rick had additional ballistic plates embedded in the front pocket of their bulletproof vests. The term bulletproof was not absolutely accurate, but when you added the ballistic plate and if the assailant was kind enough to hit you there, well then, you were just fine. If not, well the vest wouldn't help in that case anyway. The raid the MPD executed on the gang house in Little Somalia did little to ease his apprehension that this would be anything but a routine execution of a search warrant.

The concierge and building security were notified of the plan earlier. At EPD's direction, the concierge quietly cleared the condos around Abdi's on his floor and those immediately above and below. If shots were fired, they did not want a stray bullet hitting someone.

Jon assigned Rick the task of ascending the stairway with his team while he and two others entered the main elevator. He kept it open until everyone was in place. The building engineer disabled the second elevator and placed it in the default position on the first level of the garage. A quick final check of security cameras verified Abdi was not in an elevator, in the stairway, or in the garage. His silver BMW 328i was in his assigned parking space on the top garage floor, but he was nowhere to be seen.

"This is FBI team lead. Execute, execute, execute," Jon said into his headset. He pushed the button for the ninth floor after hearing affirmatives from the team and waited impatiently while the elevator rose towards its destination. Weapons drawn, the three exited on the ninth floor, turned left, and walked the fifty feet to Abdi's door. Jon knocked three times on the door and bellowed, "Abdi Ali, this is the FBI. Open up. We are executing a search warrant." Jon counted to five. Hearing nothing, he stepped back allowing one team member to unlock the door using a key provided by building security. The other stood ready with bolt cutters in case the door had additional security or chains. It didn't. They opened the door and the three entered the condominium.

The entryway was small with only enough space to turn around once. One went straight into the kitchen while Jon and the other turned right and headed for the dining room. The lights of the chandelier danced around the walls. Mercifully, the blinds were closed. The large floor to ceiling windows would have acted like funhouse mirrors with the chandelier on and the lights of the city and mall below.

"I thought this was a three-bedroom condo? I only see two."

"Looks like the office area must be counted as a bedroom." The team continued, meticulously searching each room for Abdi or anyone else.

"Clear." Jon heard from each of his teammates. "FBI team lead, all clear topside. Status garage and stairway." Jon heard all clear from the garage. Just then, Rick and his team entered the condo. "All clear stairway and we are in the condo."

"Team lead this is team two. We are searching the exterior of the BMW for potential explosives. Will advise."

"Roger," replied Jon.

Jon looked through the drawers and cupboards in the office. Rick took the kitchen, living, and dining rooms. The drawers and closets in the bedroom received the same attention.

"I think I have something here." Rick heard Jon over his headset. He moved into the office. Jon had pulled out a large container and opened the top. Rick looked in to see four laptops and a bevy of burn phones still in their clamshell casings. Papers on the desk appeared to be programming code of some sort along with notes and comments penciled in the margins and on sticky notes. A whiteboard on the wall was full of drawings and terminology neither understood with the exception of two words – HyDek and MnMedDev. One other heading stood out, but only because it made absolutely no sense – MKL-U-MD.

Rick found a paper shredder underneath the desktop behind the chair. It was only partially full. Evidently Abdi rushed the last bit of shredding. The paper shredder was a simple one; strip-cuts only with a maximum of six sheets. When Rick took the top off, the last shred was still attached to the blades. He slowly maneuvered the shredder top and gently laid the still attached strips on the desk.

"Jon, I think I know who wanted Dom dead."

Jon looked over and easily saw Dom's name with a big red 'X' through it with a date next to the name.

The next morning 4 a.m.

No one was in the building. But then again, it was four o'clock in the morning. The raid on Abdi's condo the evening before led them here. Maybe, just maybe, they would find him here. Infrared scopes were negative, laser microphones picked nothing up other than the normal mechanical noises associated with air conditioning. The team had been in position for sixty minutes. No one had left or entered any of the building's three entrances. Jon routed the architectural drawings to his team. The drawings were date stamped several years ago when MKL-U-MD commenced operations. All changes made at that time were on this set of drawings. The layout could have changed, but no building permits had been let in the preceding timeframe. As far as they knew, MKL-U-MD did everything by the book. That assumption was made after pulling all records associated with MKL-U-MD. The possibility that an unknown underground exit or a panic or safe room existed and off books was negligible. Then again, experience showed that anything was possible.

Judge Singer signed the warrant just as she had the warrant for Abdi's condo. She was Tyler's go-to judge. Tyler didn't ask for quick decisions often, which she appreciated. The ties to murder, gang activity, and the potential of corporate espionage were probative and the warrant granted. Rick called Gloria while Jon and Tyler worked on obtaining the warrant. Jon needed Gloria's team ready to connect to the computers in MKL-U-MD as soon as possible after the raid. He also made sure Reggie was ready locally at the MPD Forensics lab.

Jon and Rick were the only FBI personnel. MPD was leading this as they did the raid on the gang house. They too, needed a win.

Two MPD officers watched the back door. That left two doors in the front of the building. The windows on the sides of the building were barred. A quick check verified the bars were intact and no one could leave via them. The two front teams entered in unison. Four a.m. was a tough time for anyone on guard duty. Night was almost over, but the sun was not up yet. It was a good time to attack when he was in the Army. Using the same philosophy, it should be an even better time for a raid like this. With that in mind, Jon made the decision to enter using non-lethal weaponry. The shootings at the gang house were deadly. Answers were needed and the dead don't provide those, at least not in a speedy manner. Even though it was still early dawn and dark out, no night vision gear was being used. Powerful directional flash strobes worn in place of the night vision gear would disable and disorient. Beanbag shots and tasers would bring down anyone attempting to fire or flee. If the action went south, the rear man in each four-man team had a Glock. Jon needed more information than he had, but he wasn't leaving his teams unprotected.

"Go. Go. Go" Jon gave the order. The teams made their entries. The entryway and two front offices were clear as expected. The second front door opened directly into one of the office spaces which acted as the public face of the company, complete with a receptionist and several lounge chairs. This room had two doors, one to the rear area and the other connecting to the adjoining front office. The large rear room, which took up most of the remaining space in the building, was clear also.

Jon, Rick, and Tyler were across the street watching the entry. The sight of the flashing strobes moving through the building briefly gave Rick a slight nauseous feeling. He had forgotten to put on his goggles. Stupid. Jon and Tyler had donned theirs. They entered the building after receiving the all clear from the entry teams. No bad guys in the building, basement included. Rick followed after the queasiness left several minutes later. He did not want to know what it felt like to be blasted full bore with the strobes. He experienced all he needed.

Jon entered the reception room and immediately turned into the adjoining office. He guessed it was the manager's office. Three desks and several chairs occupied the space. No whiteboards to write on, no easels to show charts and graphs or to write down ideas. Just computers, printers. No office phones either. Interesting. Maybe all communications were via smartphones. Many homes had dumped landlines, so why not an up and coming business?

Tyler and Rick examined the large room in the rear of the building. It gave the appearance of a combined electronics lab, server room, and meeting room. Three racks of servers occupied the side area closest to the reception office. Two large electronics workbenches complete which shelves, racks, pegboards, and organizer cabinets served to complete the remaining side wall. Rick noticed the supersized circuit panel on the rear wall. The power consumed by the server racks since the inception of MKL-U-MD was more than the building had probably used in the fifty previous years combined.

MPD provided one computer forensics specialist who immediately connected Gloria's team in D.C. to the servers. The computers and servers would ultimately be removed and shipped to Gloria but Jon needed information now.

"Reggie, are you online?" Jon asked after walking over to the video screen the computer forensics specialist set up for him.

"Yes I am. Have them hook up a mobile camera and walk me around the building. OK?"

Jon grabbed the Bluetooth enabled camera the specialist gave him and slowly walked around each room in the building. This allowed Reggie to get a head start on identifying if this was where the smartphones and earbuds had been modified into the electronic skimming devices. He did this until Reggie said he had what he needed.

The entry team was sent back to headquarters, their job accomplished. Two squad cars arrived to arrest any employees who might still show up for work later that morning. Jon thought chances of that were slim to none. The raid on the gang house and Abdi's condo last night had to have let the cat out of the bag that law enforcement was onto them. But hey, if they were able to grab some people and glean information from them, why not.

Jon evaluated the raid. Abdi was nowhere to be found. Goal number one of the raid down the drain. Gloria's team had access to MKL-U-MD computers. Goal number two achieved. Not bad. While Jon really wanted Abdi, his capture was the secondary goal. Now, who was behind this? Find Abdi and he would know. He had put out feelers to the community. Maybe they would see him and call. Another longshot.

Chapter 43

"Jon, get in here and tell me where you are with the MnMedDev intrusion," barked Tony Suarez, Assistant Chief, FBI, Minneapolis office, into the phone. "You've been out of the office so much I'm beginning to wonder what you are up to."

Jon walked Rick and Detective Bancroft into Special Agent Suarez's office.

"Who the fuck are you and why are you in my office?" Tony glared first at Detective Bancroft and then, even more intensely, at Jon.

"Detective Tyler Bancroft is from the Minneapolis Police Department. He is assisting with Dom Seragosa's death investigation.

"What the fuck? I told you to back off that once already. I need answers to MnMedDev, not some bicycle accident. You think the public will accept the FBI spending valuable resources solving a bike accident in a park? For fuck's sake."

"Glad to see you in a good mood today boss." Rick tried to lighten the mood.

"Fuck you."

"The Seragosa case is tied to the MnMedDev case. That's why we need Tyler here. He has been working with me. Plus, his boss is allowing their forensics team to work on both cases. Gloria and Jasmine at NCIJTF and Reggie Benkins here in Minneapolis.

They've established a great working relationship and they've made a lot of progress."

"Reggie? He worked with Gloria before she was whisked off to D.C. right? OK. Now, tell me about this progress," barked Suarez.

"Dom was killed by Abdi after he found out Abdi was infecting MnMedDev servers at HyDek. He was on his way to give me proof when he was murdered. MPD found the truck and tracked it back to Abdi. There was a connection to a Somali gang that we didn't quite have figured out at the time," Jon began going over the case specifics.

"At the same time," Detective Bancroft interjected, "we, MPD that is, arrested a guy who was skimming credit card data and corporate identification card information from the skyways downtown. MnMedDev has an office there. This guy was a gang banger also. Same Somali gang Jon was talking about. We kept him overnight because the interrogation was taking so long. The second evening, he was shanked by other cellmates. You know what that means. The killing led us to raid the gang house. While there we found evidence of a high number of large money transfers to the Middle East. We collected a number of cell phones during cleanup."

Jon now reclaimed the lead in the conversation. "The cell phone find was significant. Detective Bancroft organized a combined raid with the Edina Police on Abdi's condo soon after the gang house raid. We found several significant things in Abdi's condo and car. First, we found multiple cell phones still in their clamshells. The burn phones had sequential numbers, except one was missing. That missing phone number turned up in the recent calls list in one of the cell phones MPD found in the Somali gang house raid. The call was less than 15 seconds and took place the night before Dom was killed. Cell towers indicate the call was made close by HyDek and the time of the call coincides with the time right after the argument Dom and Abdi had at work. We checked security logs. Those were the logs that had been scrubbed. Remember, Abdi is the security guy there. The navigation system in Abdi's car shows him leaving HyDek going to a field close by, stopping for ten minutes, and returning to HyDek. He was gone no more than twenty minutes. Video feeds at the front desk confirm this. Looks like Abdi tried covering his tracks but missed the video. Good for us."

"Second, we found a partially shredded piece of paper with Dom's name on it and a big red 'X' through it." Jon saw his boss getting frustrated with the direction the conversation was going. "Boss, I know both of these findings are more related to the murder."

"Just fucking get there Jon," snarled Tony.

"I will. Third, the names MKL-U-MD and HyDek were scrawled on another note we found. We executed a warrant on MKL-U-MD this morning in conjunction with MPD. I have Gloria's team at NCIJTF doing a computer forensic search and analysis on their computing equipment. That analysis and the code from Abdi's computers should shed light on everything.

Rick jumped in now. "I took a look at records from the gang members Tyler and the team picked up. Abdi knows a lot of them. They grew up together. That ties the gang and Abdi to the intrusion and the murder. Boss, we're close to busting this."

"You're fucking telling me a bunch of gang bangers pulled off a hi-tech security escapade like this. What the fuck are you assholes smoking? Jesus. Unbelievable."

Jon had had enough. Tony was an asshole, but that didn't mean he had to treat his people that way. He walked slowly over to Tony until he was face-to-face. "Tony, you are the boss and I know you have a deep-seated sense of duty. Having said that, you lack loyalty, you show little or no respect, you are not selfless – in fact you are the opposite – you are completely selfish. You exhibit a disregard for honor and integrity. I don't need you to apologize, because I don't think it would change you. Just stay out of my way. We have this handled. Never, and I mean, never, speak to me, my people, or anyone else for that matter, that way again."

Jon pivoted and marched out the door. Rick and Tyler joined him in rapid fashion. Tony just stood there; he had no clue.

Rick and Tyler caught up with Jon in the elevator. "Thanks Jon. You have balls. That's for sure."

"He never would have made it in the service. The FBI has leadership classes we have to take, right?" Jon said after taking several deep breathes.

"He had a point Jon. This gang never could have pulled this off," Tyler offered up.

"I know. Someone is behind this. Gloria needs to figure that out."

Behind them, in his office, Tony Suarez collected himself, reached for his phone, and made a call.

Chapter 44

Jon and Rick met Detective Bancroft in the parking lot adjacent to the eastern edge of the Cedar-Riverside Complex. Jon's feelers had panned out. They received verified reports from members of the local Somali community that Abdi Ali was hiding in the complex. The community, as a whole, was like most other American communities. They despised bad apples. They wanted only the best for their children and would do anything to protect them. Once word was out that Abdi was wanted in connection with a murder, the phones began ringing. Besides, his parents still lived here and people of all races and religions often run back to mom and dad when in trouble. MPD units were dispatched to their apartment in case he was stupid enough to encamp there. Jon knew MPD had that area under control. He knew, from experience, Abdi's capture in his parent's apartment was a longshot. So he directed his search into the bowels of the complex.

Jon hustled through the courtyard of building one. Rick was close behind. Tyler circled around and entered through the parking garage. A central steam plant located two stories beneath the main level provided heating to all the buildings. Access to this area was not straightforward. Tyler trotted down the ramp towards a loading dock located at the back end of the parking garage one level down from the street. The maintenance staff normally used a door next to the grade school located on the pavilion level. Jon and Rick chose that route. They climbed the pavilion steps, scooted across the pavilion, under tower number two, and to that door. It was locked. Rick used a breaching device to open it. Guns drawn, they entered the stairway one at a time. The concrete stairs had deteriorated over the years. Salt residue from three decades of snow and ice removal chemically attacked the now pitted and crumbling treads.

One flight down they reached another locked door. They burst through into the steam plant and maintenance facility. Yet one more stairway. This time it was fabricated from steel. The paint was chipped and smeared with grease and grime. The grated stairs and interior rails offered a view to the floor three stories below. It was dimmer that expected even though the sun was directly overhead and no clouds were in the forecast. The courtyard above had multiple sections filled with colored glass blocks ostensibly designed to light the maintenance area below. Three decades of grime and cracking blocked most of the light before it had a chance to reach its potential illumination.

"That must be Detective Bancroft," Rick said when the noise from the cargo elevator's doors opened with a screech and whine. Movement in the opposite corner caught Jon's eye. "This way," he motioned to Rick, before taking the metal grate stairs two at a time in an attempt to reach the person responsible for the movement. Tyler popped out from the cargo elevator and waited for the others at the bottom of the stairway.

Earlier, when on the pavilion level, several people had pointed to the power plant door when Rick had questioned them about Abdi or anyone they did not recognize. Both Rick and Jon felt the noose was tightening around their quarry. Even with years of training and numerous other suspect captures their heartbeats increased with anticipation.

Jon jumped out to an early lead in the race to corral Abdi. The sounds of shoes on pavement and short breaths echoed off the walls. A loud crash reached their ears from just ahead. Someone had knocked over metal objects, probably tools or a work bench. Jon reached the end of the short hallway and stopped at a crossing. Rick and Tyler were approaching the same junction from the right. The noise came from a room directly in front of them and to Jon's left. Rick motioned for Jon to enter and go right while he provided cover. Tyler entered second and peeled off to the left side of the room.

When Rick entered he could see that Jon and Tyler were the only people in the room. There was only one entrance into the room and they had just used it. Where had Abdi gone?

Rick saw a light switch close to him and turned on the remaining two light panels. A bench had indeed been overturned and tools were scattered all over. Tyler motioned for Jon to approach his side of the room and for Rick to stay. "Do you see this?" he pointed to a metal shelf unit. "It has a back panel. None of the others do. Also, see the scoring on the floor? I bet the shelf moves and a door or hole is behind it."

"Nice work. Rick, cover us while we move the shelf. It looks like he went this way." Jon and Tyler holstered their weapons and pushed the shelf to the side. It made a loud noise similar to what they heard earlier. A cool, dank draft immediately hit them. Sure enough a hole had been punched through the wall.

"Does everyone have a flashlight?" asked Jon. He grabbed his from his back pocket, turned it on, and shined it in the hole. He saw only another hole at the base of the first and what amazingly enough looked like a cave.

Abdi heard the shelf unit scratching the floor as it was moved. A light vainly attempted to reach him. He had scampered far enough through the cave for it to be unable to illuminate him. "The fools. They have no idea what they are in for."

During construction, the entrance to this cave had been inadvertently revealed. It was part of a system of limestone caves that ran under parts of Minneapolis and St. Paul close to the Mississippi River. Many of these had been used for storage of beer and liquor during prohibition. Now they were mostly a nuisance to construction companies and their engineers. Pilings were driven into the caves to provide support for the buildings unfortunate enough to be raised above them. In this case, the engineers determined no pilings were needed. The construction foreman was lazy. Rather than fixing the opening per building codes, he simply told his employees to cover the access up. No one checked – or said anything if they did.

Over the years, water seepage and high heat chipped away at the cement. Children from the complex, eager to find new and interesting places to hide, ultimately found the hole, squeezed in, and claimed this area as their own. They placed a shelf unit in front of the entrance and effectively hid it from the adults. Some of the same children, who once played here, grew up, joined a gang, and used the caves as a secondary hideout. Abdi was one of these children. His gang membership made him proud. Not many knew of his membership; his lieutenants saw to that. He ran the Riverside Thugs. He was their leader, the president, the number one. He knew this was against what his al-Shabbab handlers wanted but the pull of the clan was too much. He needed the gang.

Abdi reached the first of three caverns. This, being the largest, also had furnishings. In addition to the benches and tables, three large metal chests were located here. These contained hand guns, night vision gear, a couple of helmets, and some climbing rope. The gang had explored most of the cave system in this part of town. The largest and most accessible portion contained the three caverns. The remaining tunnels were no more than crevices almost too small to pass. Ropes were needed for safety since the depth of the crevices was much deeper than the width. Additionally, water continuously ran through the caves making the limestone facing and footings slick. While no one died, several sustained serious injuries.

Abdi was in a hurry and knew his way around, but he was being chased. In his haste he chose to only take a gun, three clips of ammo, and a set of night vision glasses. The glasses would allow him to navigate the twists and turns of the cave ahead.

Jon followed Abdi into the cave, pistol and his Maglite flashlight lighting the way. He sent Rick and Tyler topside before he entered the cave. Jon knew these existed in the metro area but didn't know about this particular vein. He also knew that the university's library placed its archives underground in tunnels. Water treatment and runoff systems also crisscrossed the area. The U of M was only six blocks away so theoretically this system could meet up with the tunnels where the library archive was located. That's where he sent Tyler. Rick, on the other hand, had the more challenging task. If, in fact, this cave system joined with the water runoff system, they would find themselves exiting through a cliff overlooking the Mississippi River a hundred feet below. Rick needed to find where the runoffs exited and have troops guarding those areas.

Jon was not new to tunnels. He chased terrorists in tunnels bored into the mountains of Afghanistan. That's when he discovered he suffered from claustrophobia. He survived the constrictive nature of those tunnels by convincing himself that by facing and overcoming his fears he was making a difference in the world. He told himself this would be no different. Forward. Ever forward he went until he entered a good-sized cavern. He shined his light all over. Several chests were on the floor as well as some furnishings. One of three chests was open. Guns and night vision gear. Jon grabbed the night vision gear and turned it on. Shit. It didn't work; neither did the other pairs. He would have to continue without them. *"Did Abdi have a pair that worked? I bet he knows the terrain down too,"* Jon thought. He had to assume Abdi's night vision gear worked. That meant he needed to make haste and not fall any farther behind. He trusted Rick and Tyler would have their areas covered. He didn't trust the cave would hook up with those tunnels though. Keep up hope and move forward. Don't think about how tight the tunnels seemed. *"I'm still walking after all. It's just..."* There. *"What was that?"* A noise up ahead.

Five years passed since Abdi last entered the caves. He let his underlings creep around here. He preferred the life he led as the leader. BMW's, condo in Edina. This was not where he, the leader, should ever come. How did his plans deteriorate so fast? He wasn't even able to execute his exit strategy. Just then, he slipped on the slime where the floor met the cave wall. Water and limestone. Slime was ever present. He twisted his ankle flailing around in an unsuccessful attempt to keep upright and he found himself lying on the floor of the cave. Wet and slightly injured. Worse than that, his night vision gear was no longer on his head. He looked around. He couldn't see anything. He rose to his knees and felt around with his hands. Nothing. Shit. Must have broken. He didn't even have a flashlight anymore. He had one when he entered the cave but had left it in the cavern when he grabbed the goggles. The second cavern was not far ahead.

Jon found the exit the noise had come from. He pointed his flashlight ahead and entered the next section of the tunnel. The tunnel's height was sufficient for walking as long as he bent forward slightly. Hopefully the ceiling had no protrusions. Hitting one would be painful. The floor was slick and he almost fell several times. Once, his flashlight went skittering in front of him when his hand shot out to right himself. The sound of the small object careening off the cave walls caused Jon to stop dead in his tracks.

Abdi heard the noise behind him. He was upright but walking with a noticeable limp. His hands reached to the side and ahead to guide him on his way. Not far. There. The side of the tunnel was no longer on his hands. He reached up. He could not touch anything. The cavern - finally. There was another lockbox here. Where though? Reaching back into his memory. A faint light flickered off the walls. Yes, he heard something from the tunnel behind him. Shit. The lockbox. Abdi stepped to his right. His foot hit something. There it is. The sounds were louder, closer. He knelt down, his fingers feverishly worked to open it up. Open. Hands inside. Would the light still be there? Yes. He grabbed it and amazingly it turned on.

Jon reached the second cavern as Abdi's new flashlight turned on. He bolted towards the light. Abdi stood up completing only a partial turn when Jon's shoulder slammed into his midsection. A perfect tackle except Jon didn't wrap up. Instead he rolled over the top allowing Abdi to once again reach his feet. Both flashlights were now on the floor of the cavern casting earie shadows as the two men danced around looking for a weakness to exploit.

Jon reached for his gun. It was not there. Must have fallen out of his holster when he rolled over the top of Abdi.

This cavern was smaller than the first. Probably the size of his boss's office. Just enough space. Abdi made the first move. When Jon tackled him earlier he grabbed some loose mud from the floor of the cavern. He threw it into Jon's face and followed with a right hook. Jon ducked to the right to avoid the mud. Abdi's punch connected with Jon's left shoulder. Not well placed. No damage. Jon moved laterally and countered with a jab to the face. Abdi staggered back. His warrior fighting styled practice sessions came with headgear. He wasn't used to being hit without padding. His lip split. Abdi righted himself. His head ached and blood gathered in his mouth. He blew blood-drenched spittle toward Jon. "You asshole," he managed to say before launching himself into Jon.

Jon caught the full brunt of Abdi's body in his chest. Abdi's momentum crashed Jon's back and shoulders into the wall. An outcropping rock jammed between his shoulder blades expelling the air from his lungs, stunning him. Abdi continued the attack with a barrage of uppercuts. Jon fell to the ground. Abdi backed off and searched for the closest light.

The uppercuts Abdi threw at Jon did not affect him much, but he needed to catch his breath from the body slam into the rock face of the cavern. He feigned defeat, falling to the floor. When Abdi retreated Jon made his move. He lunged at the light. Abdi expected Jon to attack. He felt the air around him shift as Jon lunged. He had the flashlight firmly gripped in his right hand. He pivoted and brought his hand down in a smashing movement. The end of the flashlight protruding from his grip hit Jon's head hard.

Jon briefly lost consciousness. Waking, he reached with his hand to the source of the pain shooting from his head. His other hand somehow found the flashlight of its own volition. Blood from the head wound appeared on his hand but was by no means covering it. Good. Jon knew that even though head wounds bled like a son-of-a-bitch this particular wound was not life threatening. It would just hurt. He looked around focusing on the lockbox. Good, he could focus. He shined the light quickly around the cavern, found his gun, checked to see the magazine was still in place, and took off after Abdi. He couldn't have gotten far.

Abdi's ankle was worse. It swelled and the pain that radiated was excruciating. Progressing past the third and final cavern he now approached the narrow portion they had dubbed the "Yar Yar" as teenagers. Here, you could no longer stand, or even hunch over. Forward movement was on hands and knees and then on one's stomach. Was he still small enough? Yar Yar meant tiny after all in Somali.

He wiggled through the crevice. He had to crane his neck while pushing one shoulder through. At this stage only continued pressure from his toes moved him forward. His ankle sent shards of pain through his body yet he persevered. The shoulder made it through and he articulated the rest of that arm so it could follow suit. His hand passed by his face, then the elbow. He pushed. Stuck. He pushed harder. The limestone walls here were unstable and the outcropping pinning him in collapsed. Abdi fell forward in a heap surrounded by the pieces of limestone that had broken. He pulled the rest of his body through the now much enlarged opening. Just ahead lay the water run-off tunnels. He could use them to escape.

Jon slithered forward. On his hands and knees just a minute ago, the passage quickly closed in around him. His heart beat faster and faster. His old adversary, claustrophobia, was gaining ground. It didn't help that his head throbbed with pain and his body was getting numb from the dampness and water in the tunnels. This had to be the way. He didn't remember seeing any offshoots Abdi could have taken. His flashlight illuminated evidence of Abdi's passing on the ground. Gouges in the mud-caked floor marked the way. Finally, an opening appeared. Abdi must have broken through as clumps of limestone were lying on the ground and the ceiling was jagged instead of smooth. He heard noises again. It sounded like someone was running. The cave was ending. Thank God. Jon needed to get out.

Abdi lowered himself into the concrete waterway. The city runoff system gathered rain and snow melt from the neighborhood and directed it to the Mississippi River gorge. He knew this tunnel well. He was directly under the U of M West Bank campus. Further in, the system contained overflow tanks where large volumes of water could gather before rushing through the rest of the system. This provided relief during summer storms that otherwise would overwhelm a system that only had tunnels. Several choices presented themselves now. Go upstream and exit using a manhole cover. That was dangerous as the manhole covers opened in the middle of busy streets. He didn't need to get run over by a vehicle after coming this far. Alternatively, he could try to access the university's Library Archive. Unfortunately, thrill seekers had done this too many times over the past decade. Security systems now made access mostly impenetrable. That option was the least viable. The last option was to continue to the end of the waterway. Noises. He heard noises. How could that be? The FBI man was behind him in the cave. These noises emanated from upstream in the waterway. Homeless? Kids? No. The sounds were too uniform in nature. It sounded as if more than one person was coming his way. Shit. The choice had been made for him.

Rick was with twenty police officers on the grass one hundred feet below the road deck of the Washington Avenue Bridge which spanned the thousand-foot wide gorge of the Mississippi River. The two-tiered bridge connected the East and West Banks of the University of Minnesota. Rick sent several into the brush leading up to the side of the gorge. While not a cliff, the hillside was extremely steep and technically unpassable to the top. Approximately two thirds the way up several water runoff system tunnels protruded from the ground. Erosion and mudslides the past several years had exposed them. Rick's focus was on these. If Jon was right and the cave system was as expansive as he thought, Abdi could, theoretically, try to escape this way. When Rick set up this reception party, he also sent teams into the system from five different manholes. He knew Detective Bancroft did the same in the Archives. If Jon didn't apprehend Abdi, Rick or Tyler's teams would.

The two policeman had entered from S 4th Street near Ted Mann Concert Hall. Others were entering the system further back and yet more from other access points. Running as fast as they could, they were not attempting to be quiet. Flushing the quarry out was the tactic being employed. The lead held up his hand with a clenched fist. Both stopped. A flickering light could be seen ahead. They had him. Redoubling their efforts, they increased the speed of their approach. Several more minutes. That's all that was needed. They could get him. There, up ahead they could see him now silhouetted against the sunlight streaming in. It wouldn't be long now.

Abdi reached the end. He slowly edged out. The floor of the tunnel flared out several additional feet on each side while the top and sides simply ended, leaving him exposed. He shielded his eyes from the sunlight with his left arm. His right hand still held the flashlight. He peered over the side and saw the police below. He heard the noises behind him. He was trapped.

The two policemen in the tunnel stopped and assumed a ready position with guns pointed ahead.

"Stop right there!" a voice from behind shouted. He pivoted to his left. His right arm swung outside his body proper as he pivoted.

"Gun!" shouted one of them.

Both fired a three shot burst into the body of Abdi Ali.

Jon heard the gunfire and hung his head. Two guns, six rapid fire shots. The police had fired at Abdi.

Please don't let him be dead.

Rick saw the man at the end of the tunnel turn. The body convulsed and ever so slowly fell backwards. Abdi Ali's body fell twenty feet before hitting the hillside and tumbling into the brush. If he wasn't dead before he fell, he was now.

Jon was going to be pissed.

Chapter 45

"Gloria, I have something you will definitely be interested in," Jasmine said over the cubicle wall she shared with Gloria in what was affectionately called "The Pen."

"What is it?" Gloria rolled her chair out of her cubicle space, around the fabric covered wall, and into Jasmine's space. She had learned over the years to drop what she was doing when Jasmine wanted to share something.

"I can't figure out what MKL-U-MD was set up to do as a cover. At first glance, it looks like they gathered and sold a bunch of retail and consumer preference data. That in itself isn't much. I'm glad MPD set us up with a direct connection into their network. I had Shannyn look at accessing it externally. The network would have been a real bitch to get into. Talk about encryption and firewalls. And they employ active monitoring of their network. I don't know many companies this size that do that. We had enough hoops to jump through with access protocols even being on the inside. I accessed their accounting software in order to follow the money trail and see where it led. It didn't take long. MKL-U-MD only does business with one company. A Chinese company. Remember the chatter we picked up on how the Chinese Security Services have stepped up their cyber-espionage effort? The hack at MnMedDev caused problems with their manufacturing, right? That correlates

200

with the chatter in my book. MnMedDev's intrusion led us to HyDek and Abdi Ali. And now, we've landed at MKL-U-MD."

Gloria thought for a moment and then said, "The electronic skimmer case Jon had us working on also pointed to MKL-U-MD, right?" Jasmine nodded her head in the affirmative. "That means MKL-U-MD is at the center of all this. We need to address the Chinese connection more. Does that Chinese company do business with anyone else in Minnesota?"

"I'm glad you asked. Because they don't. It took a while but according to what we found out, that company only does business with MKL-U-MD. No one else, and when I say no one else, I mean all over the states. Looks hinky to me. No one does business with only one client, who by the way, only does business with you. My first guess would be money laundering, but there are better solutions to money laundering than this. That, and MKL-U-MD has employees that they are paying. By the way, they pay the employees more than any of us get paid, and I'm a PhD!"

"Follow me back over to my cube. I need to think out loud," Gloria said as she backpedaled out of Jasmine's cube and next to hers. Gloria often re-hashed what she knew in an audible murmur so people could correct any mistakes and she could quickly change tact. When she did this, her eyelids half covered her eyes, her mouth opened slightly, and she raised her head slightly. It almost appeared that she was entering a trance or prayer state of some sort. It took co-workers awhile to get used to, but she was the best and, of course, the boss.

She muttered out loud, "So you've found that MKL-U-MD is doing some sort of business in Minneapolis and has only one client, a Chinese company – in mainland China no less. A company that employs and significantly overpays known members of a Minneapolis based Somali gang. MKL-U-MD's computer network has the security of a bank. Their employees appear to gather credit card data and corporate identification data. It would appear this is what they are selling. Have you checked what they are invoicing?"

"Let me check." Jasmine looked through various records, quickly accessing the answer. "Get this. The number of invoices being sent out is incredible. They invoice every hour and the invoices say the same thing every time, no variance - 'Services Rendered.' Does that make sense?"

Gloria pondered the question for a moment. "Well, generally when a new business starts out they often have a small number of quality clients. But rarely just one. That's just asking for problems. You should always have enough clients so that losing one of them will not sink you. It's that age old business plan decision. Either go deep with a client and mine them or have many clients each with smaller accounts. The former is risky if you lose the client but the latter is risky also, especially in the beginning, because it costs a ton of money to get new clients. How long did you say they have been in business? What else do the corporate records show or am I simply spinning my wheels here?"

"You talked about business plans and how marketing is important. I saw nothing in the computing files to show they even have a sales or marketing arm. No list of potential clients – nada. Has anyone dug into the employees yet? Jon said the task force members found money transfer receipts at the gang house."

"Have one of the business analysts pick up what you were doing. This is all fantastic information but it isn't the most important part. With that said, I want you to shift gears and see where the money goes after leaving MKL-U-MD." Gloria picked up her headset and spoke into it. "Get me Reggie Benkins with the Minneapolis Police Forensics Unit. Patch it directly to me when you get him. Yes, it's urgent."

Gloria stopped Jasmine from leaving prior to picking up the headset. Now that she was waiting for Reggie's return call she said, "Before you scamper off, I need you to hear me think out loud more. Besides, I'm sure you want to hear what Reggie has to say."

"We know that MnMedDev's ID card data was skimmed. Reggie is still figuring out what was on Dom's USB drive – I'm sure that will enlighten us. We know the intrusion into MnMedDev came from HyDek. We know the security guy at HyDek was not on the up and up. There was writing on a whiteboard in his condo that seemingly connects MKL-U-MD with both MnMedDev and HyDek." Just as she was finishing her phone rang. "Reggie, Gloria here. I have Jasmine with me. Let me put you on speaker. We've been going through MKL-U-MD computers trying to connect the dots. We're hoping what you've been working on will help with that. What can the USB tell us?"

"Mostly, the USB contains a shit-load of reports that Dom ran over a three-week period. Normally it would take me dang near that long to interpret what all the reports meant, but fortunately for us I also found a README.TXT file. Mostly, you see those attached to a program letting you know how to install it. In this case, Dom basically left a diary of what he found, when it started, why he was suspicious, and who, he felt, was responsible. It's a bombshell of a find for sure. It should help Jasmine pinpoint what exactly happened and tell us where to look post intrusion."

"Can you send that to me?"

"Just did. Let me give everyone a quick synopsis of my findings. Dom was a shift supervisor at HyDek, responsible for everything that goes on at the data center during his shift. Dom was looking for a way to look good and started training to increase his awareness in cyber security. He even asked Abdi Ali for help. Remember, they've worked together for years – Abdi even got a hiring bonus when Dom was hired. Abdi gave him some pointers and URLs to learn from. Dom tried a bunch of things out, including building out a Linux-based Virtual Machine on one of his computers. He played around with penetration tests, doing both external as well as internal assessments. In doing so, he opened up the proverbial can of worms. The servers at HyDek were not just doing what the clients wanted them to do. Someone installed software that took up minute pieces of processor time, memory, and hard drive space. That in itself is not necessarily bad, other than the clients didn't ask for it. Thing is, all servers in the data center were affected. So you have thousands of servers each tasked with these minute requests of their services and shazam, you have one big ass SETI-like data processing juggernaut. Any customer complaints could be attributed to the monitoring software used at HyDek. That software requires installation of agents. These agents communicate from each server to a central monitoring server. Each item needing monitoring needs an agent. So the more things tracked mean the more agents installed. It's a rather cumbersome setup but its worked over the years. I guess, why fix something that works?"

"Nice way to cover up using someone else's servers," exclaimed Jasmine.

"My thoughts exactly. Unfortunately, or fortunately depending on who's side you are looking at, Dom identified non-agent-related activity and activity that breached the firewall allowing data to come in, be processed, and exit again. See it's one thing to use the servers internally, but the data you want processed needs to get in there somehow. And then, you want to use the results, so they need to be sent out again. The kicker is, this access in and out of the data center was done using random servers and random ports which seemingly, mysteriously opened and closed."

"That sounds familiar," expressed Gloria. Jasmine concurred.

"Where else has this guy worked? You said he and Dom have moved around a lot?"

"We looked into that. Let me share work histories of both of them. There. Did you receive?"

"Got it. Opening now."

"Gloria, scroll down several years back. Do you see what I see?" asked Reggie.

Gloria and Jasmine scrolled down per Reggie's instructions and quickly scanned through that section. "Jasmine, did we just uncover proof of Chinese involvement here? Holy shit, this was big but now…" Gloria let that thought trail off to sink in.

Reggie offered more to the conversation. "Dom figured out Abdi was the one installing the software. Actually, Abdi had the software team install it when they installed so-called security patches. Abdi either wrote the code or received it from someone and then embedded it into the security patches routinely installed on servers. He simply created a ticket, uploaded the security patch, and let the team do his dirty work. Ingenious really. Finally, Dom started tracking down where the data was going. He couldn't pinpoint it, but it was staying in Minneapolis. He figured it was south of downtown, north of the airport. That's as close as he got. This has to be what got Dom killed."

"MKL-U-MD is located exactly in the area you just described," Jasmine noted.

Reggie continued, "Speaking of MKL-U-MD, I asked Dr. Pillery for a live copy of her ID card. It has all her clearances on it. That's the data they were after. I bet once Abdi's code opened things up, MKL-U-MD used a clearance they skimmed in order to infect the manufacturing processes. What did you mean about Chinese involvement?"

"Remember the project that got me promoted and sent to D.C.?" replied Gloria.

"Yeah."

"Abdi worked at that data center also."

"Holy shit is right. You need anything else from me?"

"No, that's it for now. Fantastic work Reggie. I'll make sure someone here tells your boss. I hear you need some props."

"Thanks, Gloria. Not necessary, but thanks." Reggie disconnected.

Chapter 46

"Nancy, thanks for letting me come in. Hi Matt, glad you could join us. Nancy gave you some background on how we met right? Good. The reason I asked to talk with you today stems from an autopsy on a young lady I just completed. She died from a subdural hematoma caused by a 15-foot fall from her deck onto the driveway one story below. The reason she fell was due to dizziness, convulsions, and fainting brought on by an insulin overdose. She used your new glucose monitoring system."

Matt looked at Nancy. Numerous other reports had surfaced regarding diabetics mysteriously dying. MnMedDev's marketing arm worked closely with pharmacies around the country to gather as much information as possible about their patients. Online profiles of registered users of MnMedDev's website helped immensely with this data tracking. Nancy asked her longtime friend, Dr. Horatio Blevins, a coroner for Hennepin County, to continue.

"This young lady had adult onset Type 1 diabetes. Several years removed from being a top cross country star in college, she continued to keep track of her daily workout and diet routine in a logbook. Once an athlete, always an athlete I guess. In addition to her diet and exercise, this young lady kept copious notes of her diabetes treatment and many other things. My wife has diabetes and I thought she kept good notes. But this young lady. Wow. My young assistants could learn a thing or two from her. But I digress. We first thought the fall was from domestic violence but we moved to potential suicide once the diabetic aspect was revealed. Her boyfriend shared the logbook with us to dispute our conclusions. I'm grateful he did."

Neither Matt nor Nancy offered anything.

"I think the blood glucose meter in your device doesn't work."

More silence.

"I've been a coroner for many years Nancy. I've seen most things. I know sometimes devices don't work as advertised. From the look Matt gave you when I said this young lady was one of your clients…"

Nancy had leaned back in her chair and rotated it so she could look outside while the coroner spoke. She raised her hand and slowly turned back to the two men. "You are my friend Horatio. You also own a lot of our stock if I remember correctly. So what I am about to say will affect you in many ways. You are correct. We do have a problem. I've already called in the FBI."

"The FBI?" intoned Horatio. "Why not the FDA?"

"We've been hacked. Somehow, somebody got into our system. Matt already identified a problem with the devices and we shut down the manufacturing lines. I think the hack was, one, intentional and, two, the cause of the device failures. That makes it espionage in the least and most likely criminal malfeasance of the highest degree. I know some people at the FBI who in turn know people at the Cyber Crimes department or whatever it's called."

Gloria Ransik and Dr. Jasmine Gomez at NCIJTF, in Washington D.C., and MnMedDev's Chief Engineer, Dr. Ranju Chatray continued working on both how and what had been done via what they were calling the HyDek intrusion. They had been at it for hours, each with their own team's full support. Gloria worked with Ranju on how the malware affected the blood glucose monitor while Jasmine tackled the intrusion itself. Gloria and Jasmine were engaged in a discussion which wasn't meant for anyone else to hear. They were tired from all the work and had neglected to mute themselves. It was a working conference call after all.

"Gloria, what are you talking about the Chinese for?" queried Ranju.

"Ranju, sorry. You weren't supposed to hear that. Oh well, let me read you in, at least a little. We've seen an uptick in state-sponsored corporate espionage with the Chinese Security Services spearheading the workload. We feel they are attempting to disrupt our economy by taking down high-stakes companies. This fits right in."

"I've heard of state-sponsored cyber-espionage before. Isn't that what the U.S. government did to Iran with their nuclear program. Something about centrifuges during the manufacturing process, correct? What did they call it – a malware?"

"You got it," responded Gloria. Jasmine chimed in, "It was called STUXNET. So let's assume the type of attack against a foreign government has been turned into an attack by a foreign government against one of our corporations. With me so far?"

"Yes."

"Dr. Chatray, how would you go about messing with manufacturing of blood glucose meters for your diabetes testing system?"

Ranju paced around his workbench. He took off his glasses to rub his eyes. The stress was getting to him. Ranju stopped his pacing. "Here is what I would do if I were trying to make MnMedDev look bad."

"It would have to be a two pronged approach. You would have to go after the manufacturing process and the quality control also." Ranju began discussing how he would go about making MnMedDev look bad. "One without the other would be a problem but we could overcome it without telling anyone. Mess up both and we wouldn't know, at least until it was way too late. With the new computerized design-to-build software we installed at the new plant, the type of intrusion we are discussing could do it I suppose. Look, everything is controlled by computers after all. Matt, our VP of Quality Control, first noticed a problem with the blood glucose monitors during a routine inspection. He is old school and doesn't trust the software. He felt the checks and balances were off. I fought him tooth and nail though. We are saving an incredible amount of money this way. In hindsight, given the circumstance we find ourselves in, I think he was right after all."

After a moment, he continued voicing his thoughts, "Malware could do a couple of different things. It could cause machinery to build things out of tolerances or it could mess with the software that drives many of our products."

"What type of software Ranju?"

"Mostly for the chipsets. We use a VHDL or Very high speed integrated circuit Hardware Description Language to program the SoC. That is the System on a Chip. The SoC basically tells the chip how to interpret inputs like blood testing and, in turn, provide an output."

"Like what gets displayed on the LCD screen of the blood glucose monitor?" asked Reggie.

"Yes, exactly. There are many more inputs and outputs but when it gets right down to it, if you can corrupt what gets displayed, then you've made the blood glucose monitor useless. In fact, the monitor could, I suppose, in theory, become deadly."

"I think we are on the right track, team. If that's the output portion, how could the input be corrupted? No software I know of can do anything to blood," said Gloria.

"You are right about software and blood, but we also make the test strips the blood in placed on. The test strip is inserted into the monitor thus becoming the input."

"Can the test strips be corrupted?"

"Each test strip itself has multiple layers which are compressed to make the whole. If any one layer is corrupt, the entire strip is corrupt. Measurement errors can be caused by small imperfections in the strip circuit. That's the layer that looks like a circuit board," intoned Ranju.

"Say an imperfection like having the metal in the circuit be too thick or too thin?" asked Reggie.

"Yes. That would alter blood glucose results. But I would simply change the test-strip code. That would be simpler."

"What's that?" Gloria inquired.

"Some manufacturers, like us, recognize the test strip manufacturing process is difficult. Making everything with a zero variance would be too costly. But we can identify variations within each batch. These variations can be digitized and embedded on the test-strip code. The variation becomes one of the inputs the monitor receives so it can adjust for different strips. This keeps the cost down for the user since one monitor can work with different test strips. It just has to use the code to allow for the variances. You could also simply not put in one of the layers of the test strip. The electrochemistry would be all messed up. Changing the code embedded on the test strip itself or telling the machinery how to build the test strip is a software process.

"You said the quality control process is also software driven. The malware could also be affecting QC and effectively cover up the corruption taking place in the manufacturing process."

"Yes, Jasmine. I can follow that hypothesis," stated Ranju. "What I don't understand though is how did they get past all our security once they broke in? You still have to log into the system and have clearances to do what they did."

Jasmine replied. "Ranju, MPD arrested a guy downtown who was electronically skimming what we first thought was only credit card data. He was caught in the skyways next to the building where your downtown offices are located. Reggie found some other data that had been skimmed. Your corporate identification cards hold a lot of data. We think this was the data the skimmer was after. Dr. Pillery sent us a live copy of her ID card. Turns out we guessed correctly. They were able to grab clearances that way. Unfortunately, the data this guy had did not have anyone who had the access you said is needed. That means, there was more skimming going on. We haven't crossed all our t's on that yet but are working on it."

"Understood. Gloria, is there anything else? I need to test what we've discussed. It shouldn't take too long now that we've focused in on two areas on my end."

"No, I think you are good. I'll check back in with you after I close out this conference."

Jon always felt this way at this point in investigations. Queasy, excited, filled with wonder that it was all coming together, and yet fully on edge. It could still all blow up in his face after all. It had before.

In 2003, Jon was embedded with a team of Army Rangers in the Taliban controlled Kunar Province. Jon spent months tracking insurgents, talking with contacts, locals, farmers, and other military leaders. Everything pointed in one direction. Jon and his team had double and triple checked their sources, even going to the extreme of checking with other NATO intelligence services.

Everyone was on the same page.

Based on Jon's intel, the general sent the Rangers to bring back the local Taliban leaders identified.

"Bring back – alive. From the moment we hit boots on the ground things went backwards. Yeah, we found them. They were there. So were one hundred others who weren't supposed to be. We'd been sucked in to one more ambush. We survived, mostly, only two dead. But the carnage left behind was something we could not explain. They blew themselves up, right as we surrounded them. We knew we didn't do it but that's not the word that was spread throughout the countryside."

SNAFU – situation normal, all fucked up – the military grunt's term for most activities dreamed up by officers – did not come close to describing the mess.

Nonetheless it looked like things were coming together. There were multiple teams working together not separately. Jon learned his lesson in the Kunar. To hell with Tony if he didn't like it. Tony was a numbers geek, if the indicator on his cost benefit analysis report was not green, then it didn't happen. That way he could always justify any action. The multiple team, coordinated approach was working. Gloria's team, in conjunction with the Minneapolis Joint Terrorism Task Force, pieced together the money trail. At the center of all of this was a local business called MKL-U-MD.

MKL-U-MD employed many Riverside Thugs. Paychecks found at the gang house provided evidence. After seeing some of the paystubs, one of the task force members asked if they could work there, just for a month. She noted if she did, she could pay off her mortgage. *"Who paid people, with a history of jail time, $200,000 per month? And for what?"*

The gang house offered up many other interesting pieces of evidence. The clothes for instance. When they searched the house the closets were not full of your basic gang clothing. First off, there were a lot of clothes, numerous styles even. The sheer number and sizes found indicated a lot of people used these clothes. Anything from hospital garb, to business suits, to casual outerwear to evening dresses. Really, it appeared as if they had raided a costume shop or movie set. Then there were the computers, mobile devices, fake driver's licenses, credit cards, and the money service business receipts for wiring money.

Jon knew MKL-U-MD received money from one and only one client. That client was a shell company out of China that, on paper, was paying for services rendered. Whatever that was. In fact, the FBI figured out MKL-U-MD was the clearinghouse for the corruption of manufacturing and quality control at MnMedDev and also for the laundering of money. But to whom and for what reason? The Chinese had paid a gang in Minneapolis to gain access to MnMedDev for some reason and paid them an incredible amount of money. *"Was that money making its way to ISIS? We just shut down a group doing that. If so, how?"*

Questions remained. Who owned MKL-U-MD when you removed the layers? Who or what was the Chinese company?

Dom identified the breach and paid for it with his life. *"Shit, I missed his funeral. I need to get out to check up on Donna, Mike, and the rest of the kids."*

Chapter 47

Jasmine ran into Gloria's cubicle. "Gloria, I figured out the second half of the money trail. This time after the gang got the money."

"Years ago the Arab community used a system called Hawala. It's an informal system of money transfer whereby you give money to service providers called a hawaladar who contacts another hawaladar they trust in the country where the recipient lives. This service provider then gives the money to the recipient when they provide an agreed upon authentication code. The money itself never moves. The hawaladars take a commission so they each make money. Since they do so much business together they rarely need to actually move physical money since their books eventually balance with one another. This system is built completely on trust."

"Well, seems like that system doesn't work so well when trying to get money to bad guys. It's still one of the ways money still flows but anymore it's a small portion. Wire transfers then became the main way. It's interesting to see how that manifests itself. The Money Service Business, also known as a MSB, allows anyone to deposit money at one location and have someone else receive that money anywhere in the world. The money is tied to a person's name and a transaction number. All you need on the opposite end to get the money is an ID and the transaction number, especially if the amount is small, say $1,000 USD or less."

"In the olden days you'd just transfer the money to the ultimate recipient. But not anymore. Now, the money gets transferred multiple times in an attempt to hide who ultimately receives the funds. For instance, let's go with our culprits in Minneapolis. Nine hundred dollars deposited with a MSB on, say, Franklin St in Minneapolis with a recipient in Hamburg, Germany. Once the recipient in Hamburg receives the money they go to another MSB and do the same thing. Only this time to someone in Sarajevo, Bosnia. This process repeats itself several more times until it reaches someone in Turkey or Saudi Arabia. Those two countries are referred to as conduit states. In the case of Turkey, the money is cashed out and taken across the Syrian border to ISIS. Alternatively, in the case of Saudi Arabia, the cash is taken into Iraq. Either way, the cash is now in the possession of ISIS."

"Now that was all well and fine until the U.S. and U.K. governments figured this out and pressured the MSBs to have better control over who passes what to whom."

"So now here comes plan C which is where it gets really interesting. ISIS is a master of the internet, social media, and the ilk. Would you agree?" asked Jasmine.

"Sure. Go on," urged Gloria.

"They set up false store fronts online. Purchases are made using PayPal, Bitcoin, or even, in some cases, from the credit cards they've skimmed off people. Nothing is actually purchased. It's just a way to pass huge sums of money."

"Aren't the banks suspicious?" asked Gloria.

"Well if they are, they must either be bought off or pressured in other ways to turn a blind eye to it. The money doesn't stay long in these middle-man banks anyway. Sooner or later it ends up in ISIS-controlled banks within Syria. Sometimes, those banks handle the transactions straight away."

"My guess then is all of the transactions are small so as not to raise suspicion in the first place," Gloria said.

"There are some big transactions, but for the most part you are correct. Postage and handling fees and other types of service fees actually make up the largest part of those smaller transactions. I guess people are just so used to seeing exorbitant fees it doesn't look wrong. The real key is the tremendous number of transactions across an ever-changing landscape of these false storefronts. That way, no one company looks like the next Amazon or Alibaba."

"Interesting. If they are always changing storefronts, how is the information getting out there? Oh, I see where you are going. Of course, social media!"

"Now you are catching on. They use Facebook, Instagram, Twitter, even SMS apps like WhatsApp to spread the word."

"Jasmine, that tracks OK, but even if all the employees spent all day making purchases, they couldn't go through the $200,000 per month they were getting paid."

"I thought maybe they were sharing the money with friends and family but that would encompass too many people. Like you said, it's the volume of transactions. Computers are doing it for them. The programmers they have at MKL-U-MD or the Chinese connection have done a bang-up job. I found a program they wrote that scrubs a list of social media outlets for the storefronts. Once identified the program logs into a site and goes on a shopping spree. It's all automated. The employee only needs to tell the computer program where to get the money from. This has been thought through extremely well."

"Finally," Jasmine continued, "MKL-U-MD has been paying for services it never receives. There are a host of payments to consultants, vendors, and employees that don't exist. The company itself plays the same shell game. Money comes in from its client and out, ostensibly, for basic business expenses. Makes the bottom line look like they are hemorrhaging money, but that makes sense for a newer company. They have venture capital to cover that so, as far as their bank is concerned, all is good. The money itself goes, guess where? You got it, the same money transaction routes right to ISIS."

"How much money per year?"

"Near as I can figure out, there are fifty actual employees, so using that number as a basis, that is $10 million per month in total salary, add in fifty percent of that for the business expenses I've seen so far. That makes upwards of $180 million annually."

Chapter 48

Jon stewed the entire drive to the Seragosa house. He had missed Dom's funeral. Technically, he didn't have to go. He was an FBI Special Agent who tracked down his killer – or at least the man responsible for Dom's death. But he knew better. Would telling Donna that Abdi died at the same time Dom's body was lowered into the ground make up for his absence? Probably not. Moving forward, Jon wanted to make sure the cycle of hate and retribution did not enter this household. You fought that one family at a time. The fact is that Abdi was a radical Muslim, involved in a fundamentalism action that took their husband and father away. There was too much animosity being directed in the media against Muslims in general right now – and that could only lead to more problems.

Jon called ahead so Donna was expecting him and had the kids ready.

"Donna, can I come in?" Jon asked from behind the screen door. Donna didn't look ready for this but she relented and let him in. Jon scanned the living room to see the kids sitting on the couch. No one had their shoes on, including Donna, so Jon obligingly took his shoes off, placing them by the front door. That made things less formal. Jon's preparation, as always, was thorough. He wanted a relaxed environment, hence his request the children be present.

What he heard next made his heart leap. A cute little snicker from the youngest when she finally noticed his multi-colored socks.

A friend of his who was an administrator in the children's ward of a local hospital wore the most colorful and obnoxious socks he had ever seen. When asked why he wore them he would only smile and say "watch this," walk into a room full of children, find a chair or other object to place his shoe so his pants would rise up and reveal his socks. Snickers, huge smiles, and even outright laughs emanated from each child – even the ones who were the sickest. So he copied the concept and put it to use whenever children were involved. This little icebreaker worked the world over. It didn't matter if the children were poor, rich, sick, Protestant, Muslim, Buddhist, or what color their skin. The goofier the socks were, the bigger the smiles, and the easier it was to communicate. Jon's Army buddies had chided him until they witnessed the results.

Jon smiled. Kylie was eleven, the youngest of the three. Mike, the oldest, and the middle child, Laura, entering 8th grade this fall, now smiled back at Jon. He could tell the two oldest didn't want to, but he did look a bit silly. The same went for Donna. She tried the hardest not to let herself grin.

"Damn you, Jon," she couldn't hold back anymore, goofy socks or not. She hit Jon on the shoulder. Not hard, but hard enough to get his attention. Her anger just starting, she hurriedly turned away from everyone, looking out the window. The smiles vanished from the children. Jon would earn his keep today.

"Sorry I missed your dad's funeral. Mike, it's just not right that I couldn't make it. I know it upset you and I apologize. I make no excuse for my lack of, well, you know." All of a sudden he was tongue tied. This didn't happen often. He walked from the entryway to Mike offering his hand. "We have some things to discuss. You are the oldest so I need to explain some things." Mike looked directly in Jon's eyes to gauge the man. A trust had developed over the years on the lacrosse field. Jon had never let him down before. Maybe he still hadn't. It was hard to tell. Mike took Jon's hand and shook it half-heartedly. Jon was willing to accept that.

Jon then turned to Donna. "Donna, I am so very sorry for missing the funeral. May I explain? I would like everyone to hear and then I can answer any questions that you have." Donna had watched Jon with Mike. She slowly walked to him, softly placing a hand on his face in a small act of forgiveness. "Yes, please sit down." Jon grabbed a chair from the kitchen, brought it out, and placed it in front of the couch.

"Last time I came out and spoke with Mike, we found something your dad left for me," Jon explained to the kids on the couch. "Your dad was a very smart man. I don't know how much you know about your dad's job and responsibilities. He made sure the computers running many of the largest companies in the Twin Cities worked – and that nothing bad would happen to them. Well, someone decided to do some bad things to those computers. If no one found out, lots of people would be hurt. Some would even lose their jobs or maybe even die. Your dad, smart man that he was, found out. You may remember he was a bit stressed out the past month. The bad people were smart but your dad was smarter. It took him a long time to piece everything together. He knew what he found was important so he called me. I work at the FBI. I'm a Special Agent and I mostly work with anti-terrorism and corporate espionage."

"Do you understand what I am saying so far?" Each of the kids nodded their heads in agreement, as did Donna.

"Your dad was killed by the bad people when he tried to give me the information to put these bad people in jail. The bad people stole that information before it got to me. But your dad hid a copy of that information in a USB drive that he hid in the lacrosse stick he made for your older brother. Mike, that USB drive blew the case wide open. The information your dad provided is the key to everything we are doing."

"But why did you miss my dad's funeral?" demanded the middle girl.

Jon looked at Donna. She nodded for him to respond. Jon had told her about Abdi. They agreed he needed to tell them.

"A man at your dad's work was responsible for your dad's death. His name was Abdi Ali."

"Abdi? I know him. Dad introduced me to him. They worked at a bunch of places together!" Mike's eyes nearly popped out of his head as he jumped off the couch. Tears began to flow. He looked pleadingly to his mother. "Mom, he was Dad's friend. How can that be?"

"Mike, sit down. It gets worse. You need to hear the rest." Jon's tone was firm but fair. "Abdi was the leader of a fundamentalist

Islamic gang. You will ultimately hear about this and more in the news. So we need to talk through this here, now. All of us. You need to be prepared to talk about it with your friends at school." None of the kids expected this and all looked unsteadily at Jon.

"What do you mean, we need to be able to talk to people at school? Why do they know about my dad?" the youngest daughter, bravely fighting tears, squeaked out. She hid her face in her older sister's arms.

"You are aware of all the news about Muslim fundamentalists and terror groups right?" The two older kids acknowledged the question. "This Abdi character was the leader of an offshoot of a Somali gang in Minneapolis who had set up a complex scam to get access to a major medical device company called MnMedDev in St. Paul. They did this to get money from another group. They used the money they made to send to ISIS in the Middle East."

"Those are the terrorists that are always in the news, right?" asked Mike.

"Yes, Mike, that is correct."

"What did they want with that company?" the older girl asked. She was still comforting her sister but was fully engaged in the conversation.

"Good question, Laura. Donna, did you want to say anything before I answer that question?"

"No, keep going. I'm too upset to answer without getting mad. Kids, that's why Jon is here. We can't let this get the better of us so Jon will help us understand what happened and how to work through it."

"Thanks, Donna. Your mom is right. I'm going to be here to help you all through this. Laura, the answer to your question is that they wanted to make the company look bad. One of the things they make is a monitor for diabetics. Do you know anyone with diabetes?"

Kylie, the youngest, raised her hand. "You do?" asked Jon. "Do they have to stick themselves with a needle a lot to check their blood?"

She nodded her head in agreement. "She says it hurts but she has to do it or she could get sick and even die," Kylie added. "Sometimes, she even has to give herself a shot. Mostly her parents do that but she is learning how to do it herself. She has to be real

GREG GARDNER

careful though because she doesn't need the shot all the time and if she gives herself a shot and doesn't need it she has to go to the hospital."

"Wow. You know a lot of about that."

"She's my best friend," responded Kylie who was no longer buried in her sister's arms but on the edge of the seat cushion.

"It's nice to have best friends. Well, MnMedDev makes those things like what your friend..."

"BEST FRIEND!" Kylie crossed her arms over her chest and glared at Jon for making that mistake.

"Right. Like what your best friend uses." Kylie uncrossed her arms and let him continue. "The organization the gang worked for wanted to hurt people by making those devices give people like your best friend the wrong information, which, like you said, would make them go to the hospital."

"But that doesn't make any sense," said Mike.

"We think the organization wants not only MnMedDev to fail because of the problems, but also other companies like it all over the U.S. See, when people find out, they will be afraid. That is what terrorism is all about – making people afraid. If enough people are afraid, they won't buy those devices anymore and the companies will have problems. It could even be a big problem for the entire country."

"Would that be like when the automobile companies and banks were in big trouble?" Mike asked.

"Donna, your children are smart. You should be proud of them." Jon turned his attention back to the couch. "Mike, you are absolutely correct."

"And my dad stopped all that?" This time the question was from Laura.

"He got the ball rolling. Without him we would be in a lot of trouble right now."

"Did you get that Abdi guy and the rest of those Muslims?" Laura was the most visibly upset one now.

Jon lowered his head a bit. He had hoped the last part of that question would never come. Nonetheless, it was exactly why he was here. "Laura, we got Abdi. We also got the gang. But, and this is very important, don't lump all Muslims together as bad. Please. Your dad wouldn't want that. Your mom doesn't want that. Doing that is the easy way. It's also the way we keep getting into the same problem all over the world. I've spent the past twenty some years working to stop terrorism. But I'm not out to stop Muslims. There is a huge difference. Does that make sense?"

"I suppose, but all you hear on TV is about the Muslim terrorists," Laura responded.

Jon stood up allowing Donna to sit on the chair. He took position directly behind her so the children could see them both - united. Donna had remained quiet for long enough. She cleared the tears that welled up in her eyes and spoke. "That is part of the problem my love. I need you to be the leader you are and make a change in people's attitudes about that. Your dad would be so proud of you if you could make something good come out of his death." Donna looked into Laura's eyes and then at each of her other children. She then looked at her slightly swelling belly. "This child growing inside me, your little brother or sister, needs to enter a better world than the one that took their father from them. Can you help with that?"

The children each looked at each other. As they did, sounds of laughter from outside filled the air. The neighborhood had already moved on, life continued. The difficult choice they had to make now, was how to continue. The three walked to the other side of the room, gathered, and discussed the question. After several minutes, it looked like no agreement would be made. Donna started rising out of her chair, but Jon held her back. "They need to make this decision. Give them a moment," he whispered in her ear. Finally, Mike, the eldest, having received approving nods from his sisters, spoke for all of them. "Mom, we won't always want to. You'll have to help us. You too, Jon. But, I think…" Mike looked at his sisters and choked back a sob. His sisters held him tighter. "If we all work together…just maybe, we can do it."

Kylie, the youngest, left her spot and took several steps towards Jon. She stopped in front of him, raised her hand indicating with her finger that Jon should bend down to get to her level. She wanted to tell him something. Jon moved from behind the chair, bent forward enough to face the 11-year old at eye level. Kylie reached down and hugged Jon. She whispered into his ear, "Thanks for being my daddy's friend."

A tear flowed down Jon's cheek as he returned her gesture.

Chapter 49

Nancy called a meeting with the CEO, the COO, and the Chairman of the Board. During the meeting she laid out what happened with MnMedDev's new Blood Glucose Monitoring system. It was the most uncomfortable meeting of her career. She took full responsibility for the problem and proposed solutions. The solutions came straight out of the playbook Johnson & Johnson used during the Tylenol tampering case in 1981. Go public, take everything off the shelves, put consumer safety before profits, and tell the public not to use any of our diabetes products until we fixed things. Doing so, she professed, would be a potential long-term win for the company. Not doing so would surely bring the wrath of the American, if not world-wide, consumer down upon them.

The Board did not agree. She was directed only to shut down the lines, fix the problem, and have vendors remove remaining stock from shelves. The public was to remain in the dark. Nancy argued the last point in a heated debate with the COO. Nancy relented, but only as a tactical retreat. If she pushed any harder now she would be fired and have no further say in the matter. That wasn't an option.

The morning's stock report showed a significant decrease. Analysts on the 24-hour business and finance programs began asking probing questions. MnMedDev's PR department was in full battle mode. Business is fine. Every company sees dips and swings in stock prices. Our stock continually outperforms our competitors. All the while it kept dropping. The old guard couldn't figure it out.

Nancy implemented the limited recall. Ranju identified and corrected the manufacturing problems for both the test strips and the devices themselves. The entire software process was cleaned with the assistance of the NCIJTF. Gloria and Jasmine provided the fixes. NCIJTF's library of malware and other corporate hacks was massive, extensive, and essential to the expeditious corrections. Armed with that and after seeing Abdi's code, the fixes were actually quite simple. The access points to the corporate network were now plugged. MnMedDev had control once again.

And still the stock went down.

New devices and test strips rolled off the lines.

And still the stock went down.

Why?

Zhang Xe's vast network stepped up their social media campaign. They had been foiled in the extent of damage desired for the initial round of this conflict. So be it. The enemy was hurt but Zhang always felt round two was the actual knockout. Perception ruled in the capitalist world. Flood social media with the information the public needs to ruin themselves. Orders were given. It wouldn't be long before the prey was cornered and killed.

> *The device chirped. The Twitter notification flashed across her screen* – #MNMEDEV *kills* #diabetics. The woman in the coffee shop felt she had to retweet.

"Gloria, do you see the activity on social media sites with respect to MnMedDev?" queried Jasmine.

> *A Facebook post appeared on the man's page. His child had diabetes. Glucose monitors from MnMedDev kill people. NO RESPONSE from this company. Can you believe it? Those blood suckers only want your money.* "Those assholes," the man in the backseat of the taxi said aloud as he shared it with everyone he could.

MnMedDev was getting hammered.

A short six second video showed a number of deaths attributed to the MnMedDev blood Glucose Monitoring system over the past two weeks appeared on Vine. It too spread with the rapidity known throughout the social media world.

"Reports of 100 deaths of diabetics are being tied to MnMedDev. It's going viral," said Jasmine as she and Gloria stood watching the monitors in "The Pen" display social media activity from around the globe.

A chart showing the yearly bonuses of MnMedDev CEO and COO titled 'Killers of diabetics' flashed across 100,000 devices in just the first ten minutes of posting on Instagram.

"Who is behind this? I know MnMedDev didn't leak anything," responded Gloria.

"#MnMedDev to clients — we don't care; we have your money."

The stock continued its journey south.

About the only entities not participating were the other medical device companies, they knew what would happen in a panic.

The phone rang in Zhang's office. His assistant answered. Upon hearing the voice calling he quickly gave the phone to his boss. "This is General Xe. Yes, sir. Thank you for your kindness, the plan is moving forward. Using an enemy's strength against them is rewarding. Yes, sir. They will continue to slide, several more days and the entire economy will begin its descent. No. It may be a bit premature to start your phase. I know you have more ships now. But I caution you that the economy needs to be shaken to its core before you can begin to flood the South China Sea with the Navy. To move too soon is to lose sight of the plan."

The stock dropped a whopping 85% from its position just one week ago. The Board was a mess. Investigations by the FDA and DOJ loomed on the horizon. Nancy knew how to fix it all. It would take courage. Her career was at stake. Yes, she had that Golden Parachute written into her contract but a Golden Parachute made up of stock was only as valuable as that stock. Not that she needed the money. She'd been frugal, never married, no children to look after. She had nice clothes, a nice car, and a condominium in and up and coming part of town. Other than that, nothing to spend her money on. The money in her account was not tied into MnMedDev stock anymore due to her financial planner's foresight. She diversified Nancy's investments years ago. Anyone could live on the ten million she had in liquid assets. The stock and options were just a way to evaluate herself against other businessmen and women. Who had the most? That was the goal. To have the most. Well, not anymore. How you got there, after all, should be meaningful. What actions you took and the morality behind them while working towards your goals defined a person. How did she want to be defined?

She lined up support from the majority of the Board members during the previous week. They knew she proposed a different route and agreed with her. She was named the Interim CEO and immediately fired the COO. Both he and the recently removed CEO had been adamant about maintaining secrecy. The DOJ would have fun with both of them. She already informed Jon of their negligence. Her task was to take over the reins of the CEO until the ship was righted. Afterwards, if there was an afterwards, the Board would reevaluate. Nancy knew what that meant and she was fine with it.

Priority number one was the immediate press release stating all Blood Glucose Monitoring systems and test strips manufactured by MnMedDev over the previous six months should not be used. Furthermore, a recall of those devices was also implemented. MnMedDev knew that its newest system was flawed. To be safe, it also recalled not only the four Blood Glucose Monitoring systems and test strips it developed but also all other diabetics related products. Overboard maybe, but she knew it would work.

MnMedDev's marketing department gleaned such a tremendous amount of data with respect to its clientele they even knew what TV stations, websites, and social media outlets were used on a regular basis by 90% of the users of these systems. Armed with this knowledge, the PR department went on a full ad campaign buying commercials on every major channel and all the shopping, and DIY channels. Social media was ablaze with information about the dangers of continued use, directions for the recall, and which competing systems were most compatible.

Nancy's network within the industry was invaluable in coordinating a synchronized ramp up of device manufacturing by her competitors to reach her clients. She knew she would immediately lose money with every decision she made. She trusted her judgement that by doing so and being as transparent as possible, she would gain back the consumer's trust over the next several years.

Nancy had never made a commercial or been on television before. Several of her sorority sisters were media majors. They routinely asked, even begged, her to let them interview her for campus television news. She always declined. The camera scared her. Not much scared Nancy Pillery but those that did created a fear deep in the pit of her soul. Now, however, everything changed. She needed to be the new face of the company. The studies she was counting on to guide her felt that only when the CEO came out strongly affirming the problem and providing a solution that did nothing for the company bottom line would success be achieved.

"@MnMedDev fires CEO, COO initiates recall #BloodGlucoseMonitors & #teststrips"

"We know about the problems and are addressing it. We take responsibility for our products." The company Facebook page stated.

"Use our competitors' products for now. Once we fix ours we'll prove why you should come back," states new MnMedDev CEO.

MnMedDev Sales Department quickly flew in all its sales representatives for training on how to make presentations to retailers and members of the medical community. These presentations showed, in detail, what parts of the manufacturing process were tampered with, when the tampering started, and the safeguards now in place. Furthermore, MnMedDev promoted making available test centers at retailers and medical offices in which the Blood Glucose monitors and test strips could be examined against baselines for consumer safety. New, even more tamper-resistant packaging would be introduced within the next few weeks to coincide with MnMedDev's planned re-introduction of their devices.

A YouTube video was uploaded to the web showing consumers which of MnMedDev systems were affected, how to return recalled merchandise, and where to buy devices manufactured by competitors. It went viral within hours.

CNN, Fox News, CNBC all had Dr. Nancy Pillery on their broadcasts. Nancy almost ran out of the first interview when she first looked into the camera and saw a reflection of herself. It was as if the camera knew all her deepest secrets as it searched her soul. Her abdominal muscles contracted so much she almost collapsed. A quick detour to the ladies' room for a cold glass of water and a short set of power posing and back out she came. More determined than ever. She took a heavy beating, but the message was consistent. "Former Chairman of the Board of Johnson & Johnson, James E. Burke, told everyone during the Tylenol Crisis in 1982 that 'it will take time, it will take money, and it will be very difficult, but we consider it a moral imperative, as well as good business.' We are taking the same approach. We are willing to take a financial hit to fix this. It is our product that went out and caused problems. Yes, MnMedDev experienced a high-level and complex hack into our systems which led to the failure of our devices, but those were our devices nonetheless."

That last bit, which went out over every news station, including the BBC, TASS, and Al-Jazeera, ended up being the salvation bit. Until then, word of the hacking was not made public. The public, finding out MnMedDev was the target of hackers which caused the problem slowed the slide of the stock. It even inched north, ever so slowly, the next morning.

"Shannyn, Jessica tells me you found some interesting information regarding a Chinese businessman conducting business in Minnesota, most specifically Minneapolis? Please explain to everyone on the call. We have the Minneapolis team on the line." Gloria looked at the up-and-coming analyst Jessica spoke of so highly.

"Yes, Ma'am. Let me explain. After working through MKL-U-MD's networks I continued to dig through the business documents themselves. I know I went down a rabbit hole, but Jessica always says that we should never take things at face value." Shannyn looked as if she was in trouble.

"That's right. I taught her that. Please continue," responded Gloria. She then stole a glance at Jessica who was trying to smother a large smile.

"We always suspected Abdi was not the number one. He was really the scapegoat, he and his gang. The Chinese connection bothered me. Where did the venture capital actually come from? Turns out a businessman from China who has been doing business in Minnesota for years is. He's even gone to dinner with one of the governors of Minnesota."

"Are you telling me the guy behind all of this is someone that the State of Minnesota does business with?" Gloria took a step back, removed her glasses, and sat down. "Fuck. A. Duck. A fucking Peking duck."

Shannyn had never heard the boss talk like that before. She looked for guidance from her direct supervisor. Jessica, knowing Gloria better, let her smile burst through now and encouraged Shannyn to continue.

"Chen Li came from China to study at Stanford and MIT in the 90's. He spent several years in D.C. at a dot com and then up and went back to China. There, he all of a sudden created and owned an internet security company. That single company grew to an empire of companies spanning different industries worth several billion dollars. There is an interesting connection to automobile manufacturing in China – he was at the Sino-Germanic economic talks in 2005 and then was given a monopolistic share of the IT security contracts for those joint ventures. We also connected some industrial accidents with economic hiccups on the Chinese stock exchange. I had help from Jessica and others doing this, ma'am." Jessica added that last bit in after she noticed Gloria look at Jessica.

"That's fine Shannyn. Keep telling me what you found. So far everything is tracking and making sense."

Shannyn breathed a sigh of relief. She was excited now and stood up. She found it easier to talk when she walked around. It gave her something to do other than shake her legs up and down. That bothered people and made the table rattle.

"We called some people at the NSA and ran this by them. They now believe those were not accidents but cyber-attacks – from inside China itself. We only know one group capable of that. Hard to believe they would do that to themselves but…"

Jessica took over, "Gloria, Chen Li is not who he says he is. The man travels all over the world, has contacts at companies and governments everywhere. The CIA has a photo from one of their operatives in the Chinese government." Jessica pulled up two photos and put them side by side on a large wall monitor. "Say hi to the head of Chinese Cyber Security, General Zhang Xe."

"We need to go after Chen Li or Zhang Xe – whoever the hell he is. I want his ass hung up and dried. Not only is he responsible for my friend Dom's death, how many diabetics died because of what he put in place? Then we have to look at what he did to our economy." Jon slammed his hands down on the conference table in the Minneapolis FBI office complex. The others at the table looked at him as if he were an alien.

"We can't do that Jon," Tony Suarez said flatly.

"Why not?" demanded Jon.

Tony suppressed a laugh. "Why am I not surprised this is your reaction? You really are a gung-ho grunt after all. The FBI does not kill people. We're the good guys Jon. Don't you get it? Of course you don't. I don't know why we even let you into the FBI."

"Are you telling me this guy gets a pass? It's as if he were a diplomat who got drunk, drove, and then hit and killed someone. They just get shipped home with a do not enter stamped all over their passport. That's it?" Jon's eyes were filled with hate. His body tensed like it did when he had his nightmares. He slowly looked at the remaining people seated around the table.

"No one wants to start a war over this. You are ordered to stand down Special Agent Wells," the voice came from the video conference unit on the wall of the conference room.

"Start a war? One already got started. What do you call this? This is cyber warfare, economic warfare. No matter the name it's the same game – war." Jon threw his folder at the monitor and left. He slammed the door with such force the glass shattered.

Chapter 50

Ahmed looked at the report on his iPad. Ninety million dollars from the MKL-U-MD project deposited in various ISIS controlled accounts worldwide. It was less than he wanted, but more than he expected to be honest. His investment was minimal. One man. One very important man, but still only one man. Years of planning, several million dollars in seed money. He wanted the money transfers to last longer than they did, but what he got was far more than the expected during the short time span the operation was up and running. *"If I had not acquiesced on the gang issue. I knew better. Those people always make bad decisions. Those bad decisions led to the demise of this scheme."* he thought. *"Oh well, just a minor setback."* This was not his only source of funding. He had other operations.

He fired off messages to his assistants to shut the American end down. Additionally, any accounts that were closer than two transactions from an American account also needed to be closed. Opening more accounts was easy. Closing them made the trail go cold.

He closed the portfolio cover of his iPad and basked in the sunshine streaming down on his yacht anchored off the Dalmatian Coast of Croatia. A servant brought him the noon meal. He would eat, get changed, and go about his business in Dubrovnik. Yes, Allahu Akbar, God is Good.

Chapter 51

FBI Headquarters, Minneapolis

"Jon, can you come into my office?"

"Yes, sir." Jon put down his phone, looked at his partner Rick and got up from his desk to head into the office of the Chief of the Minneapolis office of the FBI. Jon rarely, if ever, interacted with the guy. *"This can't be good,"* he thought. Oh well. He had his own reservations about the job anyway.

"Sir. What can I do for you?" Jon asked when he entered the office.

"Close the door, Jon. When you're done with that, see that chair? Sit down. I'll be right over." The chief continued his phone conversation for the next few minutes. Short grunts, a few "Yes, sirs," and an "I understand" later, the chief slowly put the phone back in its cradle. He got up from behind his desk, looked out the window and strolled over and into the chair facing Jon.

"Congratulations on a job well done. Too bad you aren't getting any of the credit for it." The chief let that last comment sink in before continuing. "I gather you saw Tony is no longer with us? He was promoted, Special Assistant to the President. Tony has connections in the political arena Jon. Do you see what I'm getting at?"

"Good for Tony, sir. This office will be better off without him." Jon's response came with a blank non-committal facial expression.

"I didn't think you would. The President of the United States of America, Jon. Shit boy, when will you learn this job has more politics involved than anything else? You were a career officer in the Army for Christ's sake, and you still don't get it do you? You can't go shit all over someone, especially when those people are A) senior to you, B) your boss and, C) most importantly, done in front of other people. Jesus, Jon. You embarrassed Tony in front of a Minneapolis Police Detective. How did you think that was going to end up?"

"Nothing I said was out of line. Tony was out of line. Tony was always out of line. He cared only for Tony." Jon was not going to back down from his beliefs. Mostly for the same reasons the boss laid out against him. You always stood up for your people, you never let an external department see a loose cannon in your own shop but if it did happen, you cleaned it up, firmly and promptly. Finally, Tony was a problem and would ultimately get people killed.

"Not coordinating with the St. Paul Police Department when MnMedDev is clearly in St. Paul, not Minneapolis, caused a lot of problems that Tony and I had to smooth over. And then there is your little outburst about offing one Chen Li. You were taken seriously, Jon."

"I was and still am serious, sir."

"Jon, in case you haven't noticed we are a nation of laws and rules. We don't just kill off bad guys because its expedient. You might get away with that shit in the Army but not here. We're the FBI Jon, Department of Justice, not retribution."

"Was that call about me?" asked Jon.

"What do you think?"

"I think Tony took all the accolades for the case we just finished, got promoted, and used my suggestion as cannon fodder for a final parting shot. He talked to someone and now I'm in their crosshairs."

"You can say that again. You see it so clearly most of the time, Jon. Do you know who Tony worked for when he was in law school? He was an intern for a certain politician when she was running for her first term in the U.S. House of Representatives out of the great state of Texas twenty years ago. Now she is, you got it, Tony's boss again, the friggin' President of the United States of America. I can't tell you how gloriously screwed you are."

233

"So how does this work? I'm sure I could find some hot shot lawyer to make a big stink about this. It doesn't look like you actually agree with it so that is an option."

"Jon, you have every right to do that and I will not stand in your way. But, I will also not help you in any way shape or form if that's the direction you take. There are other alternatives. If I were in your shoes, I would wait a couple of weeks, make them sweat just a bit to let them know you aren't backing down easily, and then resign. Something will present itself. The people in the business who should know who actually did the work do know, and not just in the FBI. I took care of that when I saw Tony making his move."

"Thank you, sir."

"You deserve better than this Jon. Go on and take some vacation. You have a lot of that coming anyway."

Jon stood up from the chair, straightened his trousers and shirt, stood at attention, and saluted his superior officer. "Looks like I'll be taking some vacation then. Give me a few hours to clean things up."

"Fair enough." Jon then shook hands with the man who could no longer protect him, said thank you one more time, pivoted, and exited the office.

Rick was watching the chief's door the entire time and immediately turned to his monitor when the door finally opened. When Jon sat down, he looked up, leaned over his desk a bit and said, "What happened, I couldn't hear anything, so I guess it wasn't all that bad, right?"

"Not right, Rick. But that's OK. Time for me to move on anyway." He returned his attention to his computer blanking out everything else. Four hours later he said his goodbyes, gave Rick his keys and access card, and left.

"A flotilla of forty ships left their homeport of Zhanjiang, Guangdong Province headed for the Nansha islands and reefs three days ago, according to a new release by the Chinese Minister of Defense. Nansha being the Chinese preferred name for the Spratly islands and area. The size of the flotilla is the largest in modern Chinese naval history. The makeup of the vessels indicated a long-term blue-water exercise. If it isn't an exercise, this marks a certain escalation in…" the reporter's voice was cut off when the bartender changed the channel of the television directly in front of Jon.

"Hey. Turn that back please. There are enough other televisions on the game. Besides it's just a replay of last night's game anyway." Jon fidgeted with the plate of food in front of himself and nursed the beer he was drinking. The beer was warm, with no hint of hops, and dark. His Guinness was perfect for the day. A front moved in last night bringing rain down in torrents. No job. Nothing to do. No sunshine. He couldn't bring himself to order a bourbon at noon on a Wednesday.

"China also could be seeking to emulate the U.S. ability to project naval power and build influence. The size of the exercise in larger than when, in May 2013, the Chinese Navy's three operational fleets deployed together. Those combined naval maneuvers in the South China Sea coincided with the ongoing Spratly Islands dispute between China and the Philippines as well as deployment of the U.S. Navy's Carrier Strike Group Eleven to the U.S. Seventh Fleet. So far, no word from The Pentagon or The White House."

"Exercise my ass," Jon muttered. He served two years at The Pentagon, assigned to the Chief of Naval Operations for his joint duty assignment. All military officers needed at least one tour with a sister service, called joint duty, in order to be considered for promotion past field grade. He knew the 7th Fleet was on high alert and had submarines tailing the Chinese. Probably two attack submarines. Those were stealthy and would not cause tensions to rise like a carrier and F-18 flybys. He leaned forward on his chair, grabbed his phone from the back pocket of his jeans, and placed it on the counter. His eyes continued to gaze at the screen but his mind was elsewhere. His fingers spun the phone in increasing speed until it semi-launched into his plate. Utensils flew off the counter and several chips ended up in his lap. He only snapped out of it when the bartender gave him a new knife and fork. "Thanks, appreciate you changing back to the news. I'm watching…really." The bartender nodded and let him be.

Jon picked up his phone and made a call. "Hey, it's me Jon Wells. Long time. I think I have some information for you that you are probably not aware of."

"Sorry Jon. Not a good time right now," the voice responded.

"Too bad. You need to hear this. This is an open line so I'll keep it vague but you'll know what I'm talking about. They aren't just having an exercise."

"I know that Jon. I read your report. It got sent to me the day you submitted it. You got screwed by the way. We have been communicating with our friends and they are splitting their forces as we speak. We are watching to make sure they head off in separate directions. Told them we could practice together but they declined. Got to go. Be in touch." The line went dead.

Chapter 52

China

The door of the limousine opened. The windows were darkly tinted. The only part of the interior Zhang could see was the entry to the spacious rear seating area. *"So this is how it ends,"* he thought. The security guard who collected him from his apartment deftly placed his strong hands on Zhang's elbow and moved forward. The door was opened by a second with the third bringing up the rear. Fellow occupants of the complex unfortunate enough to enter the lobby at this time either turned around or ensured they looked only at the floor tiles while making wide berth of the men. Similarly, pedestrians who had not noticed the limo, spread to the sides of the wide steps leading to the street like the wake of a passing ship as the entourage made its way to the waiting vehicle. There were no phones raised and pointed at the men, taking videos to be uploaded to one of numerous social media sites. This was just not done in China.

The limo meandered its way through the streets. Zhang wondered when the prick of a needle would put him under. At a minimum a dark hood should be placed over his head so he could not see where he was going. But no. This was worse – the unexpected. His heart rate increased with each landmark that he recognized. *"They don't care if I know where I am,"* he thought, *"that can't be good for me."*

The building looked like a hospital. In fact, people were coming and going freely. Men and women in the garb of nurses, doctors, lab technicians, and patients walked; some with a determined stride and others seemingly only passing time. *"Am I being committed? No. Anything but that."* Sweat began to drip down the sides of his temple even though the air conditioning was on and the vents all pointed directly at him. His shoulders involuntarily shuddered. He was losing control of his emotions and no one had yet to physically inflict any harm to him.

They led him from the limo through a set of doors and into an elevator. Still only the three guards who gathered him at his apartment. The carriage slowly descended to what had to be a sub-basement. Zhang's stomach did a small flip when the carriage slowed, it was not a smooth transition, and the doors opened revealing nothing but a large dimly lit hallway of concrete walls. The smell hit him first. It was a sweet, sickly odor that permeated the hairs in his nostrils, causing a quick short breath. This only forced the odor to be absorbed fully by more of the 40 million olfactory receptors in his nose. Electrical impulses raced to his brain in a vain attempt to correlate the odor into something he could understand.

Death. Long, drawn out death.

This was not a hospital, at least, not this part.

It was an interrogation center or more aptly put – a torture chamber.

His muscles tensed. The hands holding him gripped harder. He slowed his pace. They pushed him harder. He tried twisting. Why? He knew he could not physically overwhelm the beasts surrounding him. He just could not bring himself to simply continue walking forward. He refused to move his legs. They simply dragged him through an open door into a room containing only one metal chair that appeared to be fastened securely to the floor. He was forced into the chair. His forearms were extended and placed in clasps. Only his right leg was clasped leaving his left leg to swing freely if he so chose. Why? The men exited, quietly shutting the door behind them.

He was alone.

There was a drain on the floor in front of him. His head was not secured so he peered to his left. Just a concrete wall. Wait, something was on it. The room was dim and he could not focus. He shifted his attention to the right. Same vision, except the wall contained streaks instead of smears. He returned his eyes forward towards the door. It opened. A large man entered. Behind him several more with rolling trolleys followed. The trolleys were filled with equipment.

The man leaned forward and ripped Zhang's shirt from his navel to his throat with a large knife. Flicking the shredded shirt off to the side the man turned and grabbed items from the closest equipment trolley. Two large clips attached to wires appeared. The man grabbed each of Zhang's nipples, connected the alligator clips to them. A piercing volt of electricity quickly surged through Zhang's body forcing his head back and his body to arch forward and up out of the chair held in position only by the clasps. Zhang couldn't breathe. Each beat of his heart seemed to explode from his chest.

"What do you want to know. Just ask!" he screamed. But his mouth formed no words, his diaphragm forced no air through his vocal chords. No one heard what was not uttered.

This and other pain inducing measures continued for days. They provided water, in the form of water boarding, but no food. His clothes had all been ripped from his body. No orifice had been left un-violated. He would never father a child. The fingers of his right hand lay in ruins and they had re-broken his left leg with a machine that twisted and snapped both bones in the same place he had broken so many years ago in Vermont. He hadn't slept but had lost consciousness repeatedly. No questions were ever asked.

Zhang slumped in the chair, hand quivering; his left leg elevated on a stand offering full view of the damage inflicted. The door opened and a voice he thought he recognized spoke. Something about…he could not focus enough to comprehend what was being said. The voice trailed off and he was alone again.

Darkness.

Emptiness.

Pain? Maybe. Is that what he felt?

A vicious slap brought him out of his stupor. Cold water splashed onto his face. He moved. Pain shot up from his leg. Bright, all consuming lights appeared. He attempted to move his eyes to avoid them only to feel the brightness invade him from all sides.

"Zhang!" He heard his name.

"Zhang!" Again, he heard his name.

"What?" he managed to mumble through his cracked and blood encased lips.

"Good. You can talk. This can all end."

"Yes. Please. Kill me now," croaked Zhang.

"We should. But you convinced me not to," the voice continued from somewhere in the room. It came from a different direction every time. At least that is what Zhang thought.

"I did what?" Zhang was gaining a faint bit of clarity.

"Golden Peacock was not your only active operation was it?" the voice was soft, almost soothing. Something touched the muscles above his broken right collar bone. A chill swept over Zhang. Was this a wild ghost come to seek vengeance on me for my offenses? Zhang's mind was cluttered and spinning wildly between reality, nightmares, and remembrances of childhood stories of the underworld.

"Are you going to take my soul oh wandering ghost?" Zhang pleaded. His mind was not right.

The hand squeezed the broken collar bone. Zhang shrieked in pain.

"Zhang, shape up. Answer the question. We need to know."

"We? Who is we?" Zhang's mind snapped back to the present. It was not a ghost but someone representing the committee.

Zhang gathered his remaining strength, straightened up as much as he could and peered forward. "Yes. There are more and only I know of them all. I can fix everything." His head fell forward as he used all his energy replying.

"Well said. We are done."

Zhang heard more steps and felt someone releasing the clasps on his arms and leg. Another set of hands cleaned a spot on his inner forearm. A needle jabbed into his flesh. His vision collapsed. "I am now dead," he said aloud before he lost consciousness.

Zhang now used a cane to walk. Without it he could only move short distances. The damage inflicted during his torture would never allow him to be free of the cane. Three months had passed since he woke in the hospital room. He was seven floors above the room where his torture had occurred. A full service facility. *"Well at least my humor is starting to return,"* he thought as he gazed out the window. He turned towards the mirror. He attempted to adjust the medals on the blouse of his uniform but the fingers of his right hand no longer functioned well with small motor tasks. The adjutant assigned him took over.

"You look good sir," he said. "It's time to leave, you don't want to miss your own promotion ceremony, do you?"

Epilogue

Four months later

Jon looked at the woman sitting next to him in his condo. She was beautiful and smart and sexy…and here. With him. She must have felt his eyes on her because she put down the Wall Street Journal and gave him that look. Wow, he liked that look. It was the look of complete acceptance, of being comfortable enough with herself to be comfortable with him. "Looks like you saved the company Nanc. Everything appears to be normal in the markets too, right?" Jon knew she liked explaining business to him. Especially now that she was also out of work. She was released from her duties as CEO of MnMedDev shortly after bringing the company back from the brink of disaster. Nancy told him on several occasions she knew that was in the cards when she took the position. He loved her for doing the right thing for the right reasons.

"What can I say? Saved the company, saved the industry, saved the economy. All in a day's work. Damn, I'm good." She giggled and threw the paper at him. Her smile was all he needed. Well almost. He jumped from his chair, sidestepping the paper, and swiftly moved in behind her. She still had her robe on. He was in cargo shorts, a tee shirt, and flip flops. It was late morning but neither of them had anything planned for the day. He untied the robe's belt, nuzzled her neck, and let his hands slowly open the robe revealing her thin black satin nightgown. She arched her back ever so slightly and raised her arms to his face providing the opportunity she thought he was after. Instead, he tickled her sides until she almost fell off her chair. Her laughs echoed off the countertop and filled the loft with the sounds of life. Jon helped her back into the seat and softly caressed her shoulders. He leaned in to inhale her aroma.

"You better be good," she admonished with a smile.

The phone rang. Jon shut his eyes. Not now. Maybe if he kept his eyes closed the phone would disappear. Several rings later, Nancy, who had been enjoying the attention, pivoted in the chair. She slowly removed his hands from her body and whispered, "Go ahead. Answer the phone." She knew who was calling. He called her yesterday. Jon needed this more than he thought.

He didn't want to stop. She raised her eyebrows. Jon's left hand moved to the base of the phone and selected the speaker button. "Jon here."

"You still want to get that bastard?" the voice on the other end of the phone line was one of the only voices other than Nancy's he was remotely interested in hearing, especially right now. "Hell yes. When, where, and how?"

"Jon, I'm leading a new semi-autonomous division within Homeland Security. You're the perfect fit. Military background, law enforcement experience, intelligence within the terrorism field, and most of all, a strong moral foundation. We have too many 'patriots' with low morality quotients running around, losing sight of the big picture and ending up doing more harm than good. You interested?"

"Absolutely. Can I base myself out of Minneapolis?"

"Not a problem. In fact, we won't have a home base so to speak. I need more like you spread across the country who can be mobile and still maintain their built-in network. I want you to set up a security consulting firm with an office in downtown Minneapolis. It can be as low key as you want. We can talk about any support staff you may want later on, for now the legal structure and office space is the minimum. You don't even have to show up at the office unless you want to. I would, at least now and then, so people think it's real, which it is actually. The rest can be handled right from your place."

"What authority do we have backing us up?" asked Jon. General Carter Jensen was an old Army buddy, commissioned at the same time as Jon. He and Jon commiserated together during Ranger school and stayed in touch over the years, often meeting on the battlefield and other postings. Carter stayed in when Jon retired. His first star came one year later. He just accepted his second star when the Homeland Security position opened. "Great question Jon. We are a combined military and private organization much like the NSA. I'm the head and retained my military rank and associated privileges. I'm employing mostly retired or former military and FBI personnel like yourself. I don't need any CIA types. They tend to be more trouble than they are worth. You will mostly work by yourself and occasionally with one or two others. We have authority world-wide but, we do need to be gracious to any host country we operate in. That being said, you can take Mr. Chen Li/Zhang Xe anyhow and anywhere you can."

"Oversight?" asked Jon.

"Yes, I report to the Director who will be called upon from time to time to answer to the Senate Intelligence committee." Carter knew what Jon was getting at. This was not a death squad. He was leading a legal law enforcement division which was authorized to work inside the U.S. and external to U.S. borders to track down, and in limited cases, capture terrorists.

"Any issue with the President or how I left the FBI?" asked Jon.

"Glad you asked Jon because there are no problems. Let's just not send you into any situations where she is present, OK?"

The phone was on speakerphone. Nancy heard the entire conversation and gave him her nod of approval. She was looking into starting a non-profit and this new position was perfect for Jon who, after leaving the FBI, needed something to focus his energies on. He also needed to get out of the house and be part of the solution again.

"Carter, count me in. When do we start?"

###

Author's Notes

First and foremost, this is a book of fiction. I wrote it because I enjoy these type of novels and always had that aching thought in the back of my head that maybe I could do this someday. One of my favorite authors is Steve Berry. At the end of his novels he always has this wonderful section in which he identifies what is real and what he made up. I thought I'd emulate his technique. So here goes.

While many real events, places, and things inspired me during the writing of this novel, it is a novel born out of my imagination. The plot, storyline, and people depicted are all fictitious. In doing so, I created many things that are not real, so let me differentiate the real from the made up (fact from fiction with a nod to Steve Berry.)

I've visited all of the locations mentioned in the novel with the exception of those in China, including the Spratly Island chain, and the Dalmatian coast. Parts of this book contain descriptions of some of the places my wife and I have visited. On one trip, our youngest son sang with a choir in the courtyard outside the Palace of the Popes, in Avignon, France. We watched numerous locals and tourists walk up and listen to them sing. This provided the inspiration for the scene where Zhang Xe and Ahmed Al Khadi Nihal meet.

Das Rathaus is fictional. I created it based on years of sports bar-hopping through university and stadium districts. The craze to re-purpose old warehouse buildings into ritzy and expensive establishments provides great background into a bar like this. My hope is, that while you read those scenes, you envisioned a favorite hangout of your own. I tried to give a sporty, fun, and exciting feel to Das Rathaus. Last year, my wife and I were eating at one of our favorite sports bars, close to the university, waiting for a football game to start. We sat several booths down from a group of medical students who were eating, talking, drinking, and studying. Numerous laptops graced the tables next to beers, nachos, and other food. They were an animated group. Most had their hospital garb still on. Numerous people came and went during the two hours we were eating while waiting to head off to the stadium. This group was the inspiration for two scenes in the book when Abdi and Sam pass information. Many bars and gathering spots are now open along the newly running "Green Line", giving the terms "bar-hopping" and "riding the rails" a whole new meaning for many students.

The "Pig's Eye Grille" in St. Paul is fictional. Pig's Eye is one of the first names for the area now known as St. Paul. The area around the Excel Energy Center or "X" as I referenced it, has many wonderful eateries and bars. I took bits and pieces from many of these, infused with some of my own ideas, when I created the atmosphere of the "Pig's Eye Grille".

Data centers in Minnesota are real, including the reference to the city that provides electricity with good rates. The description of the interior of the HyDek data center, which is fictional, comes from my memories of working as a shift supervisor at one during the dot-com era. No, Dom is not me; neither is Jon.

The Ford Auto Assembly Plant in Highland Park neighborhood of St. Paul was real. It produced its last Ford Ranger on December 16, 2011, and is currently a large vacant lot waiting for re-development. I chose this for my fictional company since nothing is there. Hopefully, someday it will be developed again. I also wanted to highlight the beautiful Mississippi River gorge that runs from downtown Minneapolis to the confluence of the Minnesota River. I've cruised this part of the river on dinner paddleboats but did not know it is classified as the only true "gorge" along the 2,350 miles of the Mississippi River. This URL explains more of this beautiful part of the river.

http://www.fmr.org/participate/ongoing/gorge_stewards/history

Caves underneath Minneapolis are real. Although, I made up the connection to the Cedar-Riverside Complex. I can't say for sure that the water run-off system ever connects with the caves, especially as I described. This website is full of interesting facts about many of these caves:

http://www.actionsquad.org/underground.html

University of Minnesota Library Archives is located underground. Andy Sturdevant, MinnPost, explains this in the following URL.

https://www.minnpost.com/stroll/2015/10/subterranean-caverns-protect-us-andersen-library-collections

The FBI has an office in the Twin Cities metro area, but it is not downtown. Both Minneapolis and St. Paul have fantastic neighborhoods, especially in the downtown areas. I placed the fictional headquarters downtown simply to tell a better story. Who wants to read about driving off to work? Walking through the North Loop, stopping by a coffee shop, and being able to describe the area seemed more interesting. I also made up the ranks of the two people in charge of the FBI Minneapolis office. It made sense to me to label them Assistant Chief and Chief in the context of the story.

The FBI has violent gang task forces in many metro areas. Minneapolis and St. Paul are no different. This URL on the FBI website describes the function and history:

https://www.fbi.gov/about-us/investigate/vc_majorthefts/gangs/violent-gangs-task-forces

The Metro Gang Strike Force was real. It was shut down in 2009 as a result of investigations revealing extortion, financial, and other misconduct. Mara Gottfried wrote this article in St. Paul's Pioneer-Press newspaper.

http://www.twincities.com/ci_13180727

Little Somalia is real. I hope I captured the feel of the description of the Cedar-Riverside Complex. This history of the complex is very interesting. I took great liberty, however, when Jon, Rick, and Tyler chase Abdi into the Steam and Maintenance Facility and then into the cave system. More information on Cedar-Riverside can be found at:

https://en.m.wikipedia.org/wiki/Cedar_Square_West

I attended a gathering at our church in which a gentleman from the Somali community came to talk about his community and the struggles they have. I was relieved to hear I captured the spirit of the environment. I did, however, change the scene where Jamal was tutoring the young man and the mother appears loudly admonishing the teen. Prior to this, I focused on "not learning English." I found out this was not an accurate reflection of the community. The loud style of conversation and fear of authority figures are real. So I changed that scene to focus on that.

The terrorism links to the Somali refugee community I referenced in the novel are unfortunately real. The FBI did have an ongoing case where several young men in the community were jailed for going to Syria to fight with the jihadists. This novel is not an indictment of this community, nor their religion. I took bits of this information and built a fictional story around it that I thought people would enjoy. The Minneapolis Star-Tribune has great coverage of the events referenced. You can find some stories at the following locations:

http://www.startribune.com/from-the-heartland-to-jihad-heeding-isil-s-call-to-terror/324121191/

http://www.startribune.com/2-minneapolis-men-charged-with-attempting-to-aid-terrorists/283857371/

http://www.startribune.com/convictions-upheld-for-women-who-raised-funds-for-al-shabab/322827861/

Somali gangs in Minneapolis are real. There are gangs from all races and creeds in all metro areas so once again this is not an indictment of the Somali community. The Riverside Thugs, however, are fictional, as is the company MKL-U-MD I created for them. My imagination created all aspects of this gang and the activity in the novel. For further reading, check out this article from Matt McKinney of the Minneapolis Star Tribune.

http://www.startribune.com/shootings-targeting-somalis-raise-worries-of-gang-war/221883721/

Chinese State Sponsored Cyber activity is real. A good starting point for more information is this article by John Chin of the Wall Street Journal.

http://www.wsj.com/articles/cyber-sleuths-track-hacker-to-chinas-military-1443042030

MnMedDev is not real. Minnesota has a large medical device high tech presence. However, I did not focus on any one company rather the entire medical device industry. With the plethora of these types of companies in the metro area, this industry made sense to focus on in the book. The economic numbers I used are from the medical device industry reports. My made up company, what they made, and the cyber intrusion are all artifacts of my imagination. They were only created for the purposes of the story.

http://www.chi.org/uploadedFiles/Industry_at_a_glance/BattelleFinalAdvaMedEconomicImpactReportMarch2012.pdf

The Tylenol Crisis of 1982 was real. I felt in juxtaposing how Johnson & Johnson handled the situation versus how the fictional MnMedDev initially handled the crisis I created for them was interesting. Tamara Kaplan, from Pennsylvania State University, has an article that I used to capture the essence of how they handled it.

http://www.aerobiologicalengineering.com/wxk116/Tylenol Murders/crisis.html

Skimming is real. The way I wrote about it with phones and earbuds acting as antennae is something I made up. The same goes for skimming data from corporate id cards. Hopefully, it made the story interesting and encourages people to review their own cyber security measures. You can find more information about electronic skimming here:

http://komonews.com/news/local/digital-pickpockets-using-smartphones-to-steal-credit-cards-11-21-2015

The quote Dom uses about based on a quote from Op-Center Sea of Fire, created by Tom Clancy and Steve Pieczenik and written by Jeff Rovin. That full quote is, *"A sailor who could not sniff a change in the wind, feel a shift in the rolling deck, did not survive for long."*

My brother designed the book cover. He listened for months as I rattled on and on about the book. He provided, not only a soundboard to bounce ideas off, but also input on what he would like to read. He is a graphics artist and photographer who I have worked with before on other projects, so it only made sense to have him create the cover. Every aspect of the cover has meaning within the context of the novel. We wanted to share these with you.

The ones and zero spell out the name of the novel, "In Plain Sight" in binary code – the language of computers.

The stars in the top left and right corners represent China and Somalia.

The character in the middle is clothed in a hoodie styled after the U.S. flag. The character represents those who wish to harm the U.S. and hide amongst us, *In Plain Sight*. No face is shown meaning this could be anyone.

The smartphone and earbuds represent how the skimming took place.

The credit card is colored after the colors on the flags of Iraq and Syria, the two nations named in ISIS.

This is the first novel in the Jon Wells series. We wanted to make sure you knew more will be coming.

The first thirteen digits displayed on the credit card are the novel's ISBN.

Lastly, my name, as the author is on the credit card. We thought that would be an interesting way to place my name on the cover.

CPSIA information can be obtained
at www.ICGtesting.com
Printed in the USA
FFOW01n1756170816
26874FF